THE DAUGHTER OF FIRE AND FURY

OLIVIA M. GEIB

First edition, second print 2024

Unofficial Map by Griffin Geib

Official Map By Zs Graphics

Edited by Sierra Campbell - Editing By Sierra & Serena Braun

ISBN Hardcover (978-1-7380472-0-8)

ISBN Softcover (978-1-7380472-1-5)

ISBN Ebook (978-1-7380472-2-2)

Olivia M. Geib
AUTHOR

www.oliviamgeib.com

Please note this book is written in **<u>Canadian</u>** English.

Spellings may differ from both British and American English.

If you would like a high-quality PDF download of the map of Elphyne,

along with a bonus map, please go to www.oliviamgeib.com/maps.

To all of the angry girls: let your anger fuel you.
You are unstoppable and flamingly brilliant.
Show the world how you burn.

ELPHYNE
THE
The Spring Court
The Azalea Palace
The Fae of The Sea
The Bay of Renewal
The Land of The Wandering Fae
The Scarlet Palace
The Spring Sea
The Autumn Court
THE UNSEELIE CO

SEELIE COURT
The Ember Palace
The Summer Court
The Sunfire Isles
The Pool of Memory
Cyrissa Lake
The Land of The Wandering Fae
The Elphyne Sea
The Crystal Palace
The Winter Court
N
S
W
E

I was the only girl enlisted in The Queen's Royal Army. Thus, the men around me, young and old, made it their life's purpose to never let me forget it. Most outright refused to train me. They ignored me at best—taunting, harassing, and humiliating me at worst.

The abuse I endured only drove me to work harder. To be better and stronger than anyone who dared question whether I should be there. I ensured I never showed my full strength or range of abilities in practice. Not with prying eyes and loose rumour mill lips present. I needed them to believe what they assumed.

There was power in assumptions. Assumptions were a currency, and the world was a coin purse, overflowing. As soon as you took your first breath and the midwife declared, 'It's a girl,' assumptions were placed on your shoulders like a set of branded bricks. Those assumptions were dangerous for one to have in the presence of the wrong woman.

It wasn't forbidden for women to train in The Queen's Royal Army—simply rare and considered *unbecoming* of a young lady. I had a special distaste for the word as it seemed to apply solely to women. Nothing was ever *unbecoming* of a man.

The truth was, most young women had no need or desire to do such gruelling, unforgiving, deadly work. Families of means married their daughters off with a lump sum and a pat on the back.

My father taught me countless lessons before his abrupt disappearance when I was eleven. The day I stopped dreaming of anything beyond this life; the day I simply began trying to *survive*. He taught me to never show my full hand to anyone.

"To win any game, you must be a player, not a pawn," he said. *"You must transform the weight forced upon your shoulders from a hindrance into a tool."*

He was well aware of men's tendency to see what they wanted to see, teaching me that prejudice was a weapon I could forge into the sharpest of blades. Being underestimated could be a strength as powerful as any sword if you knew how to wield it.

Especially in a town full of rowdy drunks who took pleasure in corralling young ladies into dangerous games on moonlit cobblestone streets.

Cressa, the isolated capital city of Mayfair, is the kind of place where the rich get richer, and the rest of us scramble to make do with the scraps left in their wake. It is a lifeless place filled with once-promising young men turned unfulfilled drunken fools. Not that it was entirely their fault.

Opportunities in Cressa that weren't two steps from an early grave were hard to come by. Even being a young, able-bodied man meant your options were limited. Even fewer options existed for young women. Most men ended up signing their lives over to the crown to train for The Queen's Royal Army as a Knight. Everyone knew the signature was as good as a death sentence. I knew it when I signed my name, but I knew my other options were worse than death.

Too many of us—most still children—signed our lives away to be pawns in the Queen's war that started before we were born and would continue once we were cold in the ground. But unless you were one of the blessed souls born into a bountiful family by some unknown force—be it fate or the Gods or pure unadulterated luck—you weren't provided with the luxury of options.

Often, I wondered if it was none or all. A who or what that decided before there was even breath in your lungs if you would be born into easy luxury or desperate poverty.

I knew firsthand that it didn't come down to who deserved it. I knew kind, loving, giving souls who had earned much better than they were fated to receive. And handsome, deceitful, monstrous people who had more than they could ever spend, yet took from others anyway. Stomping on whoever and whatever to climb to the top. Using the decaying rib bones of those who had fallen victim to an avoidable early ending by the hands of poverty as rungs in their ladders.

Greed and power seemed to be the only consistent in it all. Those who had too much still thirsted for more, drinking down diamonds and power as if dehydration plagued their very bones.

Therefore, my father was adamant that Fabelle and I be well-educated and self-defence trained. He ensured that, as soon as our little feet could carry us, we learned the basics of hand-to-hand combat, how to wield a dagger with proficiency and master the art of archery.

Father wanted to ensure that we were ready for anything that life decided to throw at us. And I believed I was.

Until the day I woke up and, without a trace, he was gone. Nothing could've prepared me for the hollowness that swallowed me up in his absence. For the piece of myself that disappeared when he did.

Grief had my soul hostage with unrelenting cruelty, sinking its dagger-sharp, midnight claws into my childhood light. Shredding it into ribbons of ever-dimming gold and shattering any sense of what I knew. At that moment, I knew that no skill he had taught me or trick he had shown me could've prepared me for a life without him.

I am ripped from the deadly spiral of my thoughts by an approaching blade. The sword slams into my shoulder, my armour clanging as a yelp slips my lips. The blow tosses me onto my rear, plastering me with mud. My hands are slick as I scramble to retrieve my sword, pushing to my feet with a curse.

"You are more distracted today than normal, Willa. Shake it off, or you will find yourself running until your head is as clear as your lungs. Your opponents will not halt their assault until it becomes convenient for you. They will simply attack," Toryn lectures, lifting an arm to block the mid-afternoon sun.

Toryn is the first man who stepped up to train me. A new recruit who had transferred from another area. Even though he is young, Toryn is one of the most skilled warriors in his grouping. For that fact alone, his fellow brethren laid off me when he was around.

"I know, I know," I mutter, wiping my muddied hands on my pants.

"Then prove it," he challenges.

A feral smile parts my lips. "Gladly."

I watch my handsome, albeit annoying, opponent, anticipating his movements. I block his strike with a well-practised guard. He grunts at the impact, and I grin a little wider.

An opening presents itself, and I swing in an arc, only to be met by his guard. Toryn winks, taunting me, and the urge to land the winning blow grows. He does not know how badly I need this fight. This *win*. He does not know how much I need to work off the emotions haunting me from last night.

I push those unwelcome feelings away until only the swing of my sword and the certainty of my steps remain.

Toryn circles me, and I study him. Half a foot taller than me and all broad muscle—his natural strength outweighs my own. But my smaller stature allows me to move quickly and parry faster.

I deflect another blow and his breathing speeds. I fight a smirk as I force him in tireless circles. Ducking and dodging his blows, I find myself blinded as my hair worms free of its braid, bronze-red curls falling forward. I curse, shoving my hair back with my hand.

"What a foul mouth you have today," Toryn remarks, using my distraction to his advantage, landing a ringing blow to my side.

It stings. I recover, tracking his next approach, sliding down to the ground. I sweep his foot out from under him, catching the back of his knee, and he topples to the ground with a satisfying, hammering *thud*.

Mud splatters my pant leg and his silver armour. I plant my booted foot on his broad, heaving chest, sword pointed directly at his throat, and flash him my most obnoxious grin.

"Surrender?" I coo.

"Never," Toryn counters, grabbing my ankle and yanking it towards his face.

My feet vanish from beneath me as my centre of gravity plummets towards the Earth, an embarrassing squeak flying from my lips. My back smacks into the ground as the air rushes out of my lungs. I grit my teeth, my body aching, and jack-knife onto my feet.

By the time I've righted myself, Toryn is back and coming in strong with sweeping, precise blows that vibrate down my sword. My muscles scream in protest, beckoning louder with each forceful blow. I continue to counter, losing my stamina, no thanks to having the wind knocked out of me. I misstep and take another blow to my left shoulder.

"Ouch! Foul play! I had you down! Couldn't let me have this one, could you?" I spit with a halfhearted growl.

"I never claimed to fight *fair.*" He smirks. "I will not allow you to until you learn to prop—"

"Properly defend my left shoulder. I know. You keep telling me," I interrupt, running a hand through my wild hair.

Toryn notes my frustration and rushes my guard, slamming the hilt of his sword against my wrist. My fingers open on reflex. Gripping my shoulders, he spins my back into his chest, sword inches from my throat. I swallow, glancing down at my weapon lying uselessly in the mud then back to the sword at my throat.

Resistantly, I yield. Toryn holds me flush against him longer than necessary, our chests rising and falling in sync. I feel a little dizzy, resisting the urge to lean further into his touch.

"I would not have to keep telling you, Willa, if you would simply defend your shoulders. You know better than to let your guard down before an official yield," Toryn whispers in my ear, his warm breath tickling the hair on my neck.

"I know," I try to spit, but it comes out breathless, heat rising in my cheeks.

He clears his throat and releases me. I stumble forward, knocked off balance by his proximity. I cross my arms, avoiding his gaze. I am suddenly interested in the dark grey stone walls of the Kingdom's rise.

I wait for my breathing to even and the flush in my cheeks to die. I shake out my limbs and attempt to shed my frustration that doesn't feel *entirely* caused by this loss.

My eyes trail across the underwhelming stone. Everything in Cressa is grey. Especially if you live within the slate-coloured walls of the Palace's rise. I always felt as if some force had wrung the colour from worn cloth until nothing but washed-out dye remained. Or an angry God had cursed the lands to never know true colour, painting everything in a shade of their misery and displeasure.

Something was always missing here. But I could never put my finger on what.

In the moments I allow myself to indulge in daydreams, I envision escaping this place to lands of sprawling deep green trees, moss-carpeted forest floors, lakes and rivers and oceans with surfaces that dazzle like diamonds in shades of teal, turquoise, and midnight blue. A world of colour, magicks, and wonder.

I breathe deeply, letting the scent of spring flowers and dewy rain wash over me. The air thick with the promise of summer heat. I wipe the sweat from my brow and let myself linger, absorbing the rare pop of beauty and colour in an otherwise black-and-white world.

I pretend not to notice the small grouping of Knights gathering near the stables to sneer at me. Or the pointed laughter, darting eyes, and whispers of the ladies roaming the gardens. They do me no such kindness.

Toryn clears his throat, pulling me out of my daydreaming and immediately shattering my peace with a lecture. He pulls off his helmet, shaking the sweat from his curly golden locks.

"One day, it will matter. It will be life or death. You have gotten too comfortable fighting me, Willa." Toryn props his helmet under his arm.

I glare at him, crossing my arms over my chest. "I cannot help that you are the only one who will fight me," I challenge.

"It matters not. You cannot treat our practice fights as anything less than real ones. One day, your weak side could mean an opponent landing a deadly blow. I refuse to be held responsible for your death over a *fixable* habit!"

I sigh, nodding as he scans my face. A hint of worry slipping past his unnervingly neutral mask.

"Your head seems elsewhere today, more so than usual if such a thing is possible. Is everything alright at home?"

I try not to visibly cringe. A flash of the events of the previous evening racing through my mind. I shift, remembering the deep purple bruises on my sides, carefully hidden beneath my tunic and armour. The only remaining evidence of exactly how *not* okay things at home are. I assess Toryn closely to decide how much to share.

My eyes wander over his body. His golden blonde curls glow in the sunlight, forcing me to resist the urge to run my fingers through them. My fingers twitch at my side. He's always been extraordinarily handsome, but something about the way his sun-kissed skin and golden hazel eyes glint in the daylight makes him irresistible like the Gods reached up and stole a piece of the sun to craft him.

"Everything is fine. As fine as it always is. Mother is… well," I shrug, "you know, you have met her," I finish, waving my hand through the air dismissively as if I can ward off his concern.

I try to refocus my mind on anything but the gorgeous man behind me and the wrath my mother will likely unleash as soon as I get home. I fail, mostly at the former.

"Let us try again. We are not leaving until I see an improvement," Toryn insists, plopping his helmet back on with a metallic clang.

My lips thin. It is not that I do not *want* to stay. I do need to improve on this drill. But panic is building in my chest as the sun starts to make its slow descent into the horizon.

"I cannot. I must get Elle from school—class is out soon. I don't have time to run it again," I mutter, holding his eyes.

"You will make time. Again, Willa," he commands in an authoritative tone I have faced many times.

We go through the motions, focusing on what he has taught me. *Focus on the enemy, clear your mind of everything but your survival. Lock down your emotions.*

I allow my mind to empty of everything but the sword in my grasp. Toryn stalks to my left, swinging hard. I counter the blow with greater success, and we repeat until my lungs burn.

I am panting, and my muscles are burning by the time he dismisses me.

Finally.

The stable hand lazily leads my chestnut mare, Cinder, to me. I impatiently shift from foot to foot, trying to ignore the growing panic in the back of my mind.

Could he move any slower?

The mare reaches me, huffing a giddy breath. I run my fingers through her mane, stopping to pat her neck. Cinder is one of the last pieces of my father I have. He purchased the mare for my sister and me when we started school. His reasoning was that the school was too far to walk on foot in the harsh Mayfair winters. Winters that froze your breath into icy white lace as it left your lungs.

Many children would simply stay home, but Father put too much value on our education to permit us the same luxury.

Fabelle had been overjoyed to get a horse, proclaiming that she would be the one to name her. Of course, my Faerietale-obsessed little sister named her Cinder after Cinderella, a princess whom her teacher had read about days prior. I nearly lost my head for pointing out that Cinderella was *blonde* and our mare's hair was a deep reddish brown—not unlike my own. The glare Fabelle shot me promised undue violence. So I let it go.

I grab the reins and aim for the gates, lost to my reminiscing. We trained on Palace grounds but were rarely permitted inside the Palace itself. However, last winter, when the air had chilled to a bitter cold, Queen Giana held a Winter Ball. All Knights and Knights-in-training were permitted to attend.

I was awestruck and slightly disgusted at the pure, arrogant luxury of the Palace. I couldn't understand how the Queen could afford to have detailed stonework veined in gold, carved golden lions, and crown-moulded walls when she claimed she couldn't afford to ensure all her people were fed. The event was grander than anything I had experienced in my seventeen years of life.

I am jolted from my thoughts as I almost collide with Toryn.

"What do you want? I'm late and—"

My protest is cut off abruptly by the warmth of his lips against mine.

The instant fluttering in my stomach is as dizzying as the intense heat filling my cheeks.

"My *sincerest* apologies," he teases, not sounding sincere in the least, "for making you late, my darling. It's my job to make sure my girl can protect herself. A job I take very, *very* seriously," he says, nipping at my bottom lip and pulling me flush against his warm sculpted chest.

I melt into him, rolling my eyes. The blush in my cheeks deepens as he runs his calloused fingers gently up my arm and across my collarbones.

I hum a happy noise, forgetting for a moment about my lateness and worries.

"You're forgiven. If, and only if, you come by later." I smirk, meeting his sunlight eyes.

"Very well. I am grateful for your mercy," Toryn says, eyes swimming with amusement. "I feared you would make me fall to my knees and beg for your forgiveness."

"That can be arranged," I tease, poking at his chest.

I first saw Toryn in the Palace training yard a week after I had begun basic training. I was instantly drawn to him, awed by the effortless way he carried himself with confidence and grace. He reminded me of the royals who often roamed the nearby gardens in luxurious clothes. The same royals who took the time to linger shamelessly whenever Toryn trained in the yard.

I was certain I had absolutely no chance with him. And yet, after my second week of training, he caught me in the stables.

My heart leapt into my throat when he said, "You must be the famous Willa. I have heard an abundance of rumours about you. I must say, I am intrigued."

"All dreadful things, I am certain. I am not well liked."

He grinned, wide and warm and a little terrifyingly. "That only adds to the mystery." He paused, studying me. "Are you aware that I can see you staring and drooling when I train?" he asked, eyes trailing from the tips of my toes to the top of my head. "Or do you simply not care to hide your lustful looks?"

My entire body turned beet red in embarrassment, and I contemplated running as I tried to mutter out a reply but only came up with vowel sounds.

He put me out of my misery and said with a devious wink, "Worry not, Willa. I did not say it was a bad thing."

At the start of the next week, he offered to train me, and we had fallen into an easy routine of combat training and spitting playful jabs at one another since.

His warm fingers press into my hips as he lifts me effortlessly onto my horse, and I feel weightless. I am not particularly tiny. My build is not akin to the delicate royal ladies who wander the court. My body had been sculpted by combat training and heavy meals. Built to be a warrior, fed like a Knight. All soft, full curves honed to protect strong muscles. Yet, he makes me feel featherlight.

"You are aware that I am perfectly capable of mounting my own horse, right?"

"I know you are perfectly capable of *a lot* of things, Willa," Toryn counters, gazing at my mouth, slowly tracking his eyes back to mine.

I shoot him a glare as my cheeks burn like a wildfire, kicking Cinder into a gallop.

I crest the hilled street as Cressa's School for Girls comes into view. A sad grey rectangle building with a droopy straw roof that reminds me of melted candle wax.

An easy grin appears on my lips when my sights land on my little sister reading under her favourite oak tree. Head buried in the text, her kind, pale face twisted in concentration, school dress stained with mud, long legs crossed at the ankles as she leaned back on the tree trunk.

Even though I was older, she was taller. A fact I found rather unfair. Her strawberry blonde waves gently framed her face and shoulders, reflecting the last of the long day's dying sunlight. Freckles dotted her doll-like nose, bright hazel-green eyes intense as they scanned the text on the page.

I always envied her, even if I would never admit it out loud. She had an ease with people that never came naturally to me. Always overflowing with carefree grace and confident charismatic charm. Even seated under a tree, splattered in mud, she held an air of importance.

Fabelle could easily slide into any role. Kind, cunning, mischievous, and far too good for the life she had been dealt. The sole reason I didn't hesitate to sign my own death certificate. I planned to save up enough money and start over somewhere new with her. Somewhere we wouldn't have to fear returning home.

Once Father disappeared, our mother's cruelty became her crutch. She shamelessly replaced her husband with bottles of liquor. Drinking away every coin he had left behind.

Mother had outright refused to work, and when the food ran out as I neared thirteen, I became the sole provider of our household. I took odd jobs, some I never cared to look back on and others I couldn't bear to.

It still wasn't enough. I wasn't enough. And I couldn't bear to watch my sister waste away. Her cheeks hollower with every passing day. So, I signed up for The Queen's Royal Army at fifteen. That day, I made a vow to myself that I would find a way to free us from my mother's cruelty.

I call to my sister, and her head bobs up from her book. A glint of mischief in her eyes as she smiles wildly. *What did she get up to this time?* Hurriedly, she gathers her things and races towards me.

"Willa!" she calls, grinning like mad.

"Care to explain the mud?" I question.

Her cheeks flush. "The girls were picking on me." She flashes me a too-innocent smile. "I may have lost my temper. And maybe, may have, sprung up a trap that sent mud pouring all over them." She giggles, eyes churning with chaos and joy.

"May have?" I question, fighting a smile, eyes narrowed.

"A brilliant prankster never tells," she remarks, crossing her arms defiantly.

I cross mine back.

"I don't like that they pick on you, Elle. Makes me want to show them what I learned in training."

Her grin falters. "I can take care of myself."

"I don't doubt that." I smile, gesturing to the mud. "But I can't pretend that I don't wish I could protect you."

She shakes her head and slips onto Cinder in front of me. I roll my eyes as she clutches her book bag as if it contains diamonds, kicking the horse towards home.

Elle had an insatiable fascination with literature. Devouring any book she could get her hands on. Fingertips always stained with ink like a permanent pair of gloves from the hours she spent writing. Filled with dreams of being an author or a Princess on an epic adventure. Preferably the latter. At fifteen, she had filled countless journals with tales of her own creation.

"Jenny didn't show up for class today. Second girl in a fortnight," Elle mutters.

"Another one?"

Elle hums with a nod as the hair on the back of my neck prickles.

"How many does that make now?"

"Nine." I blink. "The girls are saying that she's been kidnapped by giant green Trolls or stolen away by an evil Knight riding a Dragon or a Faerie with purple skin and needle teeth. Alexandra said she saw a Dragon flying in the sky yesterday," Fabelle rambles.

"Is that so?" I feel a smile creep onto my cheeks. "She has quite the imagination. If only life was that exciting. Is this the same girl who said her mother had wings made of spider silk and a father who was part ogre? Foolish, childish, make-believe," I tease, tickling her side.

She squeals, swatting my hand away. "I do not care. Let me be foolish if I wish. Let me dream! I wish to live in a world of wonder! Don't be so boring, Willa."

I chuckle, but unease swirls in my chest. There was nothing magickal or wonderful about little girls disappearing. But Fabelle was not discouraged by my silence, diving headfirst into talking about all the Faerietale stories she read and wrote that day. I half listen.

Young women have been disappearing at a concerning rate over the last few years, not only in Cressa but across all of Mayfair. The same story every time—everyone in the household goes to bed, only to wake up and find their daughter gone.

A scrap of paper with their daughter's name signed in their own scrawl lying in the empty bed. The Royal Guard investigates, but it's as if the girls simply cease to exist.

I attempt to push aside the unease and pain that bubbles up in my chest at the thought of girls vanishing. But all I can think about is their poor families. Never knowing what happened to their children.

We arrive on our congested cobblestone street, my unease reducing on the ride. Pushed to the back of my mind by Fabelle's incessant rambling. We leap from Cinder beside the rows of worn, thatch-roofed, two-story twin homes tightly lining the street.

I am lucky, most families could not afford even this. Opting to squeeze into one-bedroom lodges with shared accommodations. Father had purchased and paid off this home, the only remaining piece of his assets. Without him here, it felt less like a home and more like a gravestone.

I hand the reins to Fabelle, and she skips off towards the local stable, humming a tune. Sucking in a deep breath, I prepare to enter the lion's den.

I step inside and am engulfed in a smog of heavy smoke. My arm flies in front of my face as I squint, eyes watering.

"Mother, did you forget the bread in the oven?" I call, shuffling through the smog to the cast-iron oven.

I brand my hand on the side of the charred loaf, cursing. I toss it onto the counter and kick the oven door shut. The clang of the oven door seems to mockingly sing, *'welcome home.'*

"Willa!" Mother shrieks as I rush to open the front door, waving a small towel in the air to clear it. "Willa, you useless, insipid fool, did you burn the bread?! I cannot trust you to do anything. Utterly incompetent just like your father!" she screams, swaying on drunken limbs from her room by the stairs, glassy eyes filled with fury.

"Mother, I only got home, training ran late. My apologies," I say, biting down my anger and dousing my panic. "It will not happen again, I assure you."

"It is your job to cook dinner, Willa. I am starved! I only put the loaf on because you are late. *Again*. Stupid girl! Good for nothing! You can go to bed without dinner. Wasting a whole loaf of bread, do you think this family is made of coin?" she screeches inches from my face.

I flinch, feeling her vile spit spray on my cheek. Her stale, liquored breath assaults my nose, and I stifle a gag, my composure cracking.

"I know exactly how much coin this family makes because I make all of it!" I snap.

Mother rears back as if slapped, pressing her frail hands to her chest, wide eyes sparking with tears. I immediately regret the words, squeezing my eyes shut.

I have a hard time holding my tongue. Father used to joke that I was born with a venomous viper where my tongue should be.

Even though I know it is coming, the slap is a shock. I feel my teeth scrape against the inside of my cheek. The strength of the blow vibrates through my jaw until stars dance in my vision, lip splitting on my teeth as blood trickles down my chin. My eyes well with tears I refuse to let fall.

I learned a long time ago that any reaction made it worse. She feeds on my fear, urges on my defiance, and takes pleasure in my pain.

"You never learn, do you? You have a roof over your head because of *me*. Without me, you would be nothing," Mother hisses. "You will live by my rules, under my roof, or you will find somewhere else to go," she spits with a sickening smirk.

Hopelessness gobbles up my anger. She knows I do not earn enough to rent elsewhere, buy food, and support Elle's schooling costs. She wields this knowledge like a sharp blade, a sword with the longest reach.

My stomach plummets to my toes as Elle skips in from dropping off our mare. She halts, her eyes shifting from Mother to me. Her eyes widen with panic when she notes my swelling cheek. But her panic morphs into a heated emotion I cannot identify, causing my stomach to knot.

I quickly swipe my arm across my chin, smearing the blood onto the fabric of my tunic, staining me with shame. I open my mouth to explain, to say something, *anything* to make this better, but I am interrupted.

"What is all over your school uniform, Fabelle?" Mother demands, sneering at the mud-stained dress.

Elle opens her mouth to explain, but I hold up a hand, and she snaps her mouth shut. Her gaze is pleading, but I slowly shake my head.

I spin a lie about accidentally splashing mud on her when dismounting Cinder. Mother hungrily accepts it as the truth, happy for any excuse to prove I am unworthy. Tension melts from my shoulders as her fury shifts away from Elle and back to me.

"Wretched girl. You really are good for nothing. Not a damn thing. You are *nothing*," she snarks, disappearing into her room.

I step outside to get some much-needed air as the world is cast in the grey haze of dusk. I feed the burnt pieces of bread to a flock of curious ravens.

Heading back inside to finish my chores, my stomach protests its emptiness. My hands crack and bleed in dry, angry lines by the time I've managed to scrub the mud from Elle's school uniform. Stopping to change the water twice, painting it red.

Exhaustion plagues my body as the long day catches up to me. I bathe in cold water, too tired to heat and haul pails.

By the time I've made it to my squeaky bed, my leaded eyelids pull me to sleep as soon as I settle onto the mattress.

The forest around me is bright with roaring, angry flames. I can hear Father begging for me to run as he bellows in pain.

"Willa, run! Take Elle—you have to run. Do not look back. Run!"

I do, my little bare feet going as quickly as I can manage over the mossy forest floor. Flames lick up both sides of the woods, corralling me, and I struggle to pull little Fabelle along with all my strength.

My lungs burn as smoke fills the forest. I wanted to turn and wait for Father, but he made me promise not to stop running until I found somewhere to hide.

I am so afraid. It is so dark. The flames are my only guiding light. I can hear Father screaming but cannot make out what he is saying. My feet are bloodied, and I know I cannot run much further. Fabelle is too heavy. I am too tired.

Father's screams echo through the trees as I stumble across a cave. My little body collapses inside its open mouth as Fabelle cries. I beg her to stop crying as a haunting scream rips through the air.

I wake with a start, my heart battering my chest. I gasp in rough breaths, surrounded by darkness. My head is in Toryn's lap, and he strokes soothing lines through my hair.

"Hush, it's alright," he coos.

Trembling, I look up at him. He reaches to light a small candle, setting it on the milk crate that functions as my side table. Toryn gives me a reassuring smile, and my breaths start to slow. I let myself sink into him. The one place in this world that still feels like home.

"How did you get past Mother?" I ask, my voice rough. I must have been screaming.

"She passed out in her room. Whisky bottle in hand," he replies, tracing the line of my spine over my nightgown, sending flutters across my skin.

"Oh, goody," I murmur.

"Was it the same dream? The nightmare of the flaming forest?" he whispers, pushing a strand of my untamed hair behind my ear.

I nod, wringing my hands together. "Yes. It comes in bits and pieces. But I was so young. I do not know how much of it is real." I sigh, rubbing my eyes to clear the sleep and wipe the memories away. "I do not remember a great deal of my childhood."

Toryn lifts me into his strong arms, cradling me to his chest. I lean my sore cheek against his chest with a content sigh. *How did I get so lucky?* He could have anyone—one of the gorgeous, rich ladies of the court. And yet he is here, he is *mine*.

Mother would kill me if she knew I had a boy in my bedchamber. She says, *Young men can never be trusted, they always want something.* When it comes to Toryn, I doubt that is true. Out of all the people who could offer him something, I have nothing.

"Are you alright?" he asks gently.

I twist out of his arms, sitting cross-legged in front of him. Toryn stills, his eyes igniting with rage as he surveys the damage on my face.

"Who did this?" he growls, his eyes intently searching the marks as if they alone could tell him the answer.

I hesitate to answer, shame sitting heavy in my stomach like an anchor.

"Mother." I sigh, shaking my head. "I was late. But it matters not—if it was not that, it would have been something else." I bury my head in my hands.

Toryn gently grasps my wrists, tugging my hands from my face, taking my chin in his fingers, directing my eyes to his. "You do not have to hide this. Not from me. *Never* from me. I shall be more mindful of the time moving forward," he swears. "I brought you something."

He pulls a marigold flower out from his bag and gently places the flower behind my ear.

"Stealing from The Royal Gardens, are we?"

"Oh, how dare I. Are we above stealing?" He nips at my nose, and I chuckle. "Shall I return it to its rightful place?" he teases, reaching for it as I bat his hand away playfully, laughing.

"Your laugh is beautiful," he mutters. He catches my wrists, lowering me back on my bed. My body burns as his chest meets mine. Toryn dips down, dragging dangerously intoxicating kisses across my neck.

"It's stunning," I murmur breathlessly.

"Splendid. It would be a shame to return it when it looks ever so lovely in your hair," he drawls between kisses.

His thumb slowly traces my hurt bottom lip, trailing the damage left on my cheek. I squeeze my eyes shut and wish that we could always be like this.

When he leans in to kiss me, it's gentle as he avoids the broken skin on my lip. My cheeks flush crimson, and my stomach twirls. He kisses the line of my hurt cheek and jaw, worshipping the skin as a small, knowing chuckle leaves his lips, tickling the underside of my jaw. My breath catches in my throat, a small gasp escaping parted lips.

"I love how easy it is to make you blush," he murmurs against my neck. "Your entire neck is flushed."

"Oh, hush," I whisper.

"If I do that, you will truly be blushing," he counters and pulls away, meeting my eyes and studying my face. "So beautiful. Those gorgeous green eyes remind me of the forest after a summer rain," he whispers, lowering his mouth to my ear. He sighs. "I should go. Training starts early tomorrow, and you must rest."

"I wish you could stay."

"One day."

"One day," I whisper to myself as he vanishes out the door.

I am jolted awake by a piercing wail. Adrenaline chases away my lingering sleep, and my heart slams against my chest. I fling myself out of bed, shove my feet into slippers, and swipe my dagger off the milk carton beside my bed.

I crack my bed chamber door open and creep towards the source of the commotion. My lungs squeeze with panic, icy claws shredding my stomach as my grip on the dagger turns punishing.

The sobs grow as I turn to Fabelle's open bed chamber door and find Mother kneeling beside her bed. *Her empty bed.* I gaze out the window and find the darkness of the night has not yet given way to the morning sun.

"Mother, whatever is wrong? Where is Elle?"

I sink to my knees, rubbing my hand down the back of my inconsolable mother. Something is clutched in her palm too tightly for me to identify. Between sobs, she explains that she woke in the night and came to check on us. Finding Elle's bed empty, she searched the house but could not locate her.

Elle never goes out alone at night—she knows how dangerous it is. I survey the room, trying to come up with a logical reason for her absence. Piles of Faerietales, novels, and worn journals sit in leaning heaps around the room. The smell of book pages and fresh ink lingers in the night air.

My heart beats so rapidly I start to fear it will leap out of my chest. My eyes lock on her favourite journal seated beside her bed as dread pools in the pit of my stomach. She never goes *anywhere* without that journal. It is as vital to her as her limbs.

I flashback to the night my father disappeared. An empty bed, mother's sobs, his missing boots. *She cannot be gone. She cannot be gone.* I repeat it like an oath in my mind, willing it to be true.

My mother shifts, her palm falling open to reveal a small piece of rough paper with only two words scrolled across it. *Fabelle Capri.* The world stops, restarts, and burns to the ground. Fear digs its way into my chest, clutching my flesh with needle-point claws. The roaring of rushing blood is deafening in my ears. I feel sick.

I haul myself from the floor, rushing to the bathing chamber as my stomach empties in the sink. I lift my head and catch sight of myself in the mirror. I am ghostly pale, the life drained from my already alabaster skin. Even the freckles that line my nose and cheeks seem to have paled.

I suck in desperate breaths trying to force myself to calm down. To think. The countless names of missing girls battering my brain. My mind transforms into a raging waterfall of a million thoughts, rushing too quickly to grasp.

Desperately, I force my trembling legs into action. Ripping through the house in a tornado of panic, checking all the rooms, and sending clothing flying from the closets. But I find nothing.

I stand, turning in slow circles in the centre of the kitchen. Trying to slow the pace of my thoughts so I can strategize, but all I can think is that Father would be so disappointed. If she is gone, I failed. I failed to protect her. I failed my father.

All I've endured—the pain, the blood, the gut-wrenching exhaustion. The hard shell I curated, the hollowness I live with, so she could remain a child... If she is gone, it was all for nothing.

I search the house again and again. Hoping I missed something, but still I find nothing.

I make my way back to Elle's room as something integral in me shatters. I collapse to the floor, sending a wobbly pile of books scattering. The storybooks seem to laugh at me as they fall, taunting me with worlds of happily ever afters.

The hollowness that has taken up residence in my chest aches and expands swallowing me, feeding off my agony. Sobs fill my body, and grief floods my veins, choking the air from my lungs.

I don't know how much time passes. But light begins to pour in through the window as I lay with my knees pulled into my chest on Elle's floor, frozen by grief. Shaking and exhausted. My sobs reduced to silent, defeated, hopeless tears.

"Willa, where are you?!" Toryn shakes me from my thoughts. "Willa, look at me. Darling, what happened?" Toryn asks, the panic in his eyes echoing my own.

"She's gone," I choke.

"What do you mean she's *gone*, Willa?"

I hand him the scrap of paper and watch as his face pales. His arms wrap around me, and tears rush forward without warning. I fall into his chest, retelling the events of the night.

"How did you find me here?" I whisper.

"You did not show up at the mess hall for breakfast. You *never* miss breakfast. I started to worry that something had happened to you," he replies gently. "I should have stayed. I should have been here. I know how much Elle means to you.

"We have to find her, Toryn. I will find her."

Toryn and I spent the morning canvassing the entire block, going door to door, speaking with the neighbours and the local guard. We check the stables and find Cinder happily chewing on hay in her stall.

As noon rolls around, a sense of failure settles upon me. None of my neighbours saw or heard anything out of the ordinary. Other than my mother's broken wails. And anyone who heard those assumed it was simply a regular night at the Capri household. We have no more answers than when we began.

I sink down on the front steps of my house, burying my head in my hands. I give myself a moment to drown in the grief, and then I shut it down. Fabelle needs me.

Pushing back to my feet, I begin to pace the street, Toryn watches me with weary eyes for a few moments. I wish I knew what he was thinking.

I pace and pace until Toryn blocks my route, attempting to pull me into a hug, but I shove him off. His tenderness threatens to crack the lock on my walled-off emotions. His lips thin and he steps back when I refuse the touch, a sliver of guilt beads in my chest.

I think of my father's words. "*Be a player, not a pawn.*" But I do not know where to start. *How do you be a player if you do not know the game, the board, the pawns, or the players?*

"Willa?" Toryn says gently, interrupting my thoughts. "It has been hours, darling. The guards said they will begin a search. Let us go for a stroll in the forest, clear our minds, and come up with a new plan."

I nod, gazing up at the overcast sky. A walk sounds better than returning home with nothing. Being anywhere but my sister's empty bedchamber sounds like sweet relief. Those four walls are now a ghoulish reminder of what I am set to lose if I cannot find her.

As we walk across uneven cobblestone, a gentle spring rain falls from the sky, and I take in the scent. Something about it feels grounding and refreshing.

Toryn takes my hand and leads, heading towards the Palace where we crawl through a crack in the stone rise. Instantly, we are greeted by heavy woods and tall green trees. Moss coats the forest floor and hemlock trees dance in the wind as the light of day breaks the canopy, glittering on the damp ground.

I cherish it all. I've always been drawn to the connected choreography of all the living things in the forest. How it all seems to dance as one, breathe as one, grow as one. For a heavenly moment, I am free of my racing thoughts, one with the forest, simply a part of its dance.

We wander in companionable silence for a while. I am careful, watching my steps over the slick gnarled roots. Toryn hefts me over a fallen log that is blocking our path.

A high haunting howl of wind shatters my peace, the rain picking up in heavy sheets, pounding down on us. A shiver runs up my spine. Water drenches my cloak, leaving the fabric weighted and flush against chilled skin. I am about to suggest we head back, but Toryn pulls me further into the forest.

I let him lead, dreading the return to the city. I peek back to find I can no longer see the city's rise. As we wander, I lift the bottom of my cloak, wringing out the water, droplets splatter the forest floor in a patter.

The wind picks up further, howling like a furious beast. I wrap my wet cloak tightly around myself as a creeping feeling stirs in my gut. I open my mouth to say we should turn back, but Toryn abruptly halts, his body stiffening.

"What is wrong?" I ask, hand instinctively drifting to my dagger.

Toryn turns to face me, and I am struck to the spot by the look on his face, the *wrongness* of his expression. I step back, almost losing my footing on the slick ground. The smirk that paints his lips is a cold, hollow thing of nightmares. I blink, confused, my eyebrows knitting together as my heart begins to pound.

"Toryn?" I say hesitantly.

He says nothing, looking at me with a sense of victory that consumes me with dread.

Something is wrong. Something is wrong with *him*. My breath catches as I study his face, his posture. The warmth has bled out of his eyes, but it is not the coolness in his expression that stuns me. It is the *transformation*. Toryn's ears are now pointed at the tips, his irises slightly *aglow*.

"Toryn?" I demand.

He *grins*, leaning forward, and I flinch, stumbling back a step. The warning in my gut intensifies. And I step back again, resisting the urge to flee, feeling like prey being sized up by a predator.

"Toryn? What is wrong?" I whisper, pleading. "Are you alright? What is happening?"

Toryn's shoulders rise and fall with a long sigh. "I am disappointed... but not surprised. You and your sister made this almost *too* easy." I blink. The mocking in his tone is unmistakable.

"I truly believed you would make this more difficult, Willa, darling." He *tsks*. "So very trusting. You have so much to learn."

"W-what are you talking about? This is not a game, Toryn. What do you know about my sister?" I snap, fury rising with my fear as I scan the forest for the fastest route back to the rise.

The heavy rain makes visibility poor as a thick, claustrophobic fog descends on the trees. It swirls around the trees, like eerie fingers wrapping around the trunks.

Toryn takes a step forward, and I retreat one step back. My heart squeezes in an iron fist of panic. I feel as though I am looking at a stranger, a *monster* who wears the face of my best friend.

"It is unfortunate, really. I imagined the pair of you would pose more of a challenge," Toryn says thoughtfully. "I believed such a stubborn, clever girl would be harder to lure. But no, you were won with sweet words and soft-spoken promises..." Toryn studies me with blatant disdain. "Kisses and kindness. I should not be all that surprised—you were so very *desperate* to be loved." He chuckles darkly. "That little sister of yours is even more naive. I did not think such a thing possible..."

My stomach knots and unknots and tumbles. Heart racing in my chest as if it alone can outrun this horrifying being. An undercurrent of rage rises in me, fed and flamed by my pain and confusion.

You were so very desperate to be loved.

"What are you talking about? Where is my *sister*?" I snarl. "I swear to the Gods, if you hurt her, I will make you pay." I fist my hands at my sides to cease their trembling and straighten my spine.

Toryn simply smiles, all teeth. I reach into the slit of my cloak, hovering my hand over my dagger.

"It is a sweet irony, my darling girl. You loathe weakness, and yet you lead me right to yours." He cocks his head. "I do so love the taste of victory." Toryn licks his lips. "Now, let me be clear. If you want to see that slip of a sister of yours again, you will do exactly as I say. It is time to abandon this fragile little mortal world. A shame, really. I have grown almost fond of it." Toryn sighs, surveying the trees. "Though I do miss the luxury of home."

"It is far past the time I've returned. We will travel to Elphyne this eve without you so much as making a peep. From this moment until your last, you will do as I please. And only as I please. If you fail to please me... I am certain you are wise enough to understand what will happen to poor little Elle."

"To *where*? Have you entirely lost your senses? I am not going *any-where* with you! Where is my sister? What do you want from us?" I shout. "What have you done, Toryn?"

I turn to flee but hesitate—*what if he is telling the truth?* If he has Fabelle, my best option is to go with him. I cannot risk her being harmed. I shut my eyes and take a breath, sorting through the hailstorm of my emotions.

"There is so much you fail to understand. Mortal minds are feeble, brittle things. It is almost endearing. It is a true wonder you have yet to drive your pathetic species to extinction," Toryn sneers, tapping the side of his temple. "Come now, dear."

Toryn reaches for me, prepared to tug me along. But I step back.

My hand closes around the hilt of my dagger, and I begin to pull it free, but a hand closes around my wrist with staggering strength. I step forward, slamming my shoulder into his stomach but he does not stagger. It is like trying to move a boulder.

My eyes find his, which flood with sick amusement. Toryn's lips twitch into a smirk as his grip tightens painfully. I bite down on my tongue to keep from crying out, narrowing my eyes at him.

"I should have known you would not make this easy." He laughs without humour. "Very well, I will indulge you. Do show me if anything I taught you stuck. I certainly hope my time was not wasted," Toryn drawls, stepping back and gesturing to my dagger.

"When do I make anything easy?" I snarl, closing the distance between us in a flash.

I whip a leg around to catch the back of his knees, knocking him to the ground. A groan leaves his lips as his back slams into the forest floor. I shift, preparing to lunge—

He is up and racing towards me with alarming speed. To my horror, I realize I was not the only one holding out at training.

I slide under his approaching arm and past his guard. Slamming my elbow into his ribs, bone meeting bone with a startling crack.

I pivot, ready to strike the dagger into his heart, but he follows my turn with graceful ease, like a dancer performing their best waltz. In a heartbeat, he dips beneath my guard, spins me, and pins both my arms to my side.

I fight wildly as he tugs me into his body. But he blocks every blow, I grit my teeth, chest heaving while he remains completely unaffected.

I force my hips into him, hoping to throw off his balance. A trick I've used once or twice in practice successfully. Toryn anticipates the movement and steps to the side with a small *tsk*. I lift my leg and slam my heel into the top of his foot, and his grip loosens with a hiss.

I turn, driving my knee into his groin, and he doubles over, groaning. I bring my knee up again, connecting with a crack to his jaw. He stumbles back, cupping his hands to his face.

I do not hesitate, racing into the forest, dagger in hand. My lungs burn, and I curse myself for not taking sprints more seriously in training. My legs pump furiously as I fling myself over fallen logs and across slick moss.

My feet slide as I take a corner too quickly, my hands finding a tree trunk to steady me. I fling myself around the trunk, making for the rise. I do not glance back, unwilling to lose my momentum.

A slight change in the breeze is my only warning as my feet are lifted from the forest floor. Strong arms wrap around my body, pinning me.

I curse, fighting the hold, but Toryn is undeterred.

"Is that all you got?" Toryn growls in my ear.

Yes. "No," I spit.

I grit my teeth so hard my jaw aches, biting into the flesh of my cheek. I attempt another few sequences of movements to break his hold, but he does not falter. I am about to attempt another when his grip abruptly tightens to the point of pain, and I yelp.

"*Enough.* I have places to be. I do not have time to play with you all day. Drop the dagger," he commands. I struggle, and he lets out a hiss of frustration. "Now! I am getting impatient, Willa. You will not like what happens when I get impatient."

"Oh, I'm sorry. Am I not taking the kidnapping of my sister how you would like, you arrogant asshat?" I growl.

Fingers wrap around my throat, cutting off my air supply and forcing me onto my tiptoes. I wobble, fighting for air.

"Speak one more word of disrespect, and it will not be you who pays the price," he hisses, nails piercing my skin.

He keeps his hold on my throat until my lungs begin to burn and my body thrashes. Only then does he release me, causing me to stumble, but he keeps me upright.

"Who are you? *What* are you?" I demand, heaving in gasping breaths. "What do you want?"

"What part of doing as I please was not clear?" Toryn growls. "Drop it, or I kill her," he vows.

The threat is sobering. I force myself to relax. I need him to take me to my sister. I cannot run from this. I cannot fight my way out. I must change tactics. I must play along.

I let my dagger fall to the ground, and his grip loosens. Toryn steers me by my arms, forcing me to face him—a stranger wearing the face of my lover.

I stare into his eyes. Heartbreak shattering my grief as the full scale of Toryn's betrayal grips me. I shake my head over and over again as if I can deny this reality. Deny that the person who has become my lifeline has been *using* me. The words slip before I can stop them.

"Was any of it real? Did you even like me? I loved you," I choke, the words tasting like ash on my tongue. This is not the way I imagined I would first say it. Despite my best efforts to keep my voice from wavering, it cracks. "Was it *all* a lie?"

As soon as the words leave my lips, I wish to pull them back. They drip with raw vulnerability. *I feel so stupid*. For trusting him, for *loving* him.

"Darling girl, *Faeries cannot lie*," Toryn remarks. "I liked you for what you were," he eyes my body, "something I needed. A means to an end, if you will. The Fae do not love as humans do... human love makes one weak."

"*Faeries?* Like the mythical creatures in Fabelle's book? The Fae? Do you hear yourself?" I scoff. "Faeries aren't real, Toryn. You've been reading too many of Elle's stories."

He smiles too sweetly down at me. "You know nothing."

A broken laugh erupts from me. I've gone crazy. Or he's gone crazy. This cannot be happening. This has to be some kind of elaborate prank that Elle is in on. I am going to kill her.

"I would not be laughing if I were you. Not with what you stand to lose. I do not expect you to understand." He waves my words off like a pesky bug. "You are only an insignificant, ignorant *mortal* girl."

My laughter dies.

"This is not funny," I snap. "You are lying! This is one of Elle's stupid pranks, isn't it? Elle! You can come out now!" I yell into the trees, but nothing but the howl of the wind answers.

"I am no jester!" Toryn growls, grip tightening to the point of pain as he shakes me. "Nor is this a prank. I have had enough of your foolishness. We do not have time for your feeble little mind to wrap itself around simple concepts. Let me simplify this for you—behave, or I will harm your sister. And I will enjoy it. Let's go, darling," he commands, hauling me along.

"Don't you dare call me that," I snap, tugging on his grip.

His eyes meet mine, blazing with a fire I never knew that my soft, sweet best friend could ever possess.

"You always were too stubborn for your own good. That smart mouth is going to get you into real trouble. You are lucky I find it amusing." He clicks his tongue, scanning me with scrutiny. "You will find the other Fae are not so forgiving," he remarks. "Now move." He shoves me forward.

"Fight me once more, and Fabelle will find herself on the sharp side of my blade. Do I make myself clear?"

"*Crystal.*"

Toryn drags me along, nails digging into my forearm. I take a few centring breaths, searching my brain for anything to give me a leg up. I think back to all of Fabelle's endless stories about Faeries. Now I wish I had thought to pay more attention. There has to be something...

An idea strikes me. Elle once mentioned that Fairies operate on bargains, vows, and swears. They have trouble resisting them, especially if they believe they can manipulate the outcome in their favour. Once set, they cannot break a promise, bargain, vow, or swear, the words are magickally binding. Internally, I laugh at the insanity of even considering a magickal promise with a mystical being.

"Wait, please. Please just listen. I promise I will go with you. But only if you make a bargain with me," I say, digging my feet into the ground.

"You are not really in the position to be negotiating." He sighs, over-dramatically. But despite himself, curiosity shimmers in his eyes. He is silent for a moment, and I worry he will deny me. "Fine. Humour me, dear girl. What do you propose?"

"If I go with you to Elphyne without further argument or fight. You will swear that no harm will come to Fabelle by you or *any* other Faeries hand while we travel or while she resides in your capture," I propose, straightening my spine and holding his gaze.

"Hmm." He rubs a hand over his chin. "I see you did learn a thing or two from your sister's silly little tales. Intriguing. But I digress. I swear no harm will come to Fabelle in Elphyne by my hand or any hand I command while she resides in my capture. If and only if you come with me to Elphyne without a fight or argument. I cannot and will not promise to control the actions of those outside my rule," he surmises. "If you break your vow, the bargain is broken."

"Your rule?" I question as he tugs me forward again. I stumble.

"Yes. *My* rule." He smirks a mask of casual arrogance. "Does this please you, little mortal?"

I nod.

"Then let it be. It is a bargain."

"It is a bargain," I confirm.

I suddenly feel dizzy as I am hauled through the forest, the air taking on a metallic buzz. I dare a glance at Toryn, my mind at war with itself.

I recall my mother's words about young men. *Young men can never be trusted; they always want something.* My chest aches, and I squeeze my eyes shut.

"You are not going to enjoy this part," Toryn remarks.

"Pardon?"

He slows, and I search the forest, seeing nothing of note except for a circle of plump red amanita mushrooms on the forest floor.

Toryn leans in close, too close. The kind of close that used to mean late nights of lazy kisses. My breath stalls. I attempt to pull away, banishing the memories, but he holds me firmly. His eyes abruptly warm, welcoming, and glazed. He almost looks like the man I know, his voice sweet, echoing, and heavy as he commands, *"You will sleep."*

When I wake, my head pounds like the time Elle and I snuck some of Mother's whiskey. I press the heel of my hands to my eyes, groaning as the ache slowly lessens.

I find myself lying in a ginormous carved sandstone canopy bed decorated by inlaid sea shells, with gauzy white curtains tied to each corner by golden ribbons embroidered with suns. The cloud-like mattress beneath me is so soft I almost moan with delight.

Pushing myself to sit, I assess my surroundings. I am in what appears to be a lavish bed chamber, better than a dungeon. The smell of sea salt and citrus lightly scents the air and silky sheets.

The walls are constructed of a golden brick, and the floor is carved of white marble with gold veins. The air feels thick with a smothering humidity that hangs onto my clothes and skin.

The room contains a small table and chairs, a large wardrobe, and tapestries depicting scenes of tragedy and triumph, along with a few mostly empty bookshelves.

My daggers are missing from my sheath and boots. A string of foul whispered curses slip from my lips.

I check the walls, table, wardrobe, and shelves, searching for any possible passageways or passable weapons. I hunt through the vanity drawers of the adjoining bathing chamber—a bathing chamber without a door, just an arched marble entryway, which I find a bit odd. My search comes up empty, revealing nothing more than lint, hair pins, fraying romance novels with questionable covers, and a tray of food.

I stand in the centre of the room in a mixture of awe and disbelief. The sheer size of the room baffles me—my own bedchamber could fit inside tenfold.

My mouth waters at the delicious, still steaming food in front of me. I shove my rising panic to the back of my mind as my stomach gurgles with hunger. Before I can start to worry that it may be poisoned, I have already scarfed down three perfectly cooked bacon strips, a hard-boiled egg, and half of a scrumptious bread roll without taking a breath. I never could resist a good breakfast.

My mind clears with the ache in my stomach, allowing me to sort through the facts. I know I am no longer in Mayfair, so I am assuming I am somewhere in Elphyne—where or what that is, I am unsure. I do know, based on Toryn's wording, that the plan to kidnap my sister and lure me here has been in motion for a long time. I am assuming since he met me. That thought alone is enough to send a wave of pain through me.

I feel foolish. I was stupid and naive, all for a boy I am now realizing I know *very* little about. Toryn never talked about his family or his life before he became a Knight at Cressa Palace.

As my search of the bedchamber and bathing room comes up utterly useless, I decide to reassess. Reaching for the pins holding my braided bun to my head, I pull them free, shaking my hair down around my shoulders. Crossing the room, I break a leg off one of the wooden chairs, holding it up like a dagger.

I eye it wearily and sigh. "It will have to do."

After Father vanished, Mother would go through rages where she would lock me in my room for days. I would beg and cry for her to open the door, pounding until my knuckles bled and wooden splinters embedded themselves in my skin to no avail.

I never understood why she blamed me. What I had done to make her hate me so viciously. There had been so many times I'd gone hungry, but this was one of the first times I truly learned what it felt like to *starve*. To have your insides be so hollowed with ravenous hunger that you feel them start to gnaw at *you*. Ever since, the feeling of being trapped or restrained has set me on edge.

One night, when I could not stand to listen to the sound of my own aching hunger anymore, my anger ignited into determination. I waited until the whiskey pulled Mother into a deep sleep. Then, I spent the evening trying to pick the lock with hairpins as I had seen the older boys do when they stole from the stable's shed.

It was harder than I expected, but after an hour, I heard a satisfying click, and the door opened. It was the first time in a year I had felt proud of myself. And the first time in two that I had felt *free*.

Fascinated by the craft, I spent the summer practising on every lock I could get my hands on around Cressa. The art of it slowly clicking into place. I earned a good beating from Mother when she caught me one night, but I did not stop. The rush of satisfaction and joy every time I would master a new lock was addictive, *thrilling*.

I snatch my worn leather shoulder bag from the side table, shoving the splintered wooden table leg inside. Happy to have something familiar in a place of unknowns. Whoever searched it must have decided the contents were harmless. Relief floods my chest as I feel Fabelle's journal inside.

I cross the room, pausing in front of the wooden door. I lean down, pressing my cheek to the cool marble floor to peer under the threshold. I squint against the light, waiting for my eyes to adjust. When they do, I find nothing—no shadows, no boots, no chatter.

Rising, I slide two pins into the lock until they meet resistance. I fiddle with the mechanisms inside, and after a small click, the handle is freed.

After one final check, I venture into a long golden hallway, shutting the door quietly behind me. The hall is built with shimmering bricks that sparkle in the sunlight from the large windows framed by marble columns.

The knowledge that Toryn did not regard me as enough of a threat to place guards outside my door is slightly insulting. Though, I am grateful for it now. I smile to myself, wiping my hands on my pants.

I keep to the shadows, making my way further into the hall. The smell of sea salt intensifies as I walk and the sound of waves crashing can be heard in the distance. I make a note of all the windows, doors, and halls. The large circular windows are as tall as I am, shaped into giant suns with wavy rays lining the hall every few feet.

I creep forward, taking extra care to tread lightly in the echoing space. Cautiously peering out a window, I see the ground not far below. I shove at the window pane, but it does not budge. *That would be too easy, wouldn't it?*

Ducked down, I survey the grounds and the striking, golden-armoured Knights doing rounds in the gardens below. Tall, golden-leafed trees stretch for the sky, greedily reaching for the sun, a hard-shelled yellow fruit hanging high at the base of their trunk. Sunflowers line a golden stone path and extravagant multi-tiered fountains of water and what appears to be a purple *wine* dot the gardens.

Creeping away from the window, I turn back to the hall. The space opens into two hallways shaped like a U. Unsure which way to venture, I head to the right. There are countless doors situated along the hallway, I check a few as I go—locked. I stop in the arched alcoves, checking for passages, but find none.

I startle as, down the hall, voices sound. Panic swells in my chest as I swerve, scanning for a hiding spot only to be faced with more locked doors.

I take off in a run, head on a swivel. At the very end of the hallway, I spot a stone arch leading to a spiral staircase. I race down the harrowingly narrow steps, dizzy as I turn in loops.

Down and down I go. My lungs burn in protest, and I am worried these stairs never end when my feet finally slam into the landing. The stairs spit me out into a large underground cellar that smells of mildew and grapes. My arms brace on my knees as I fight to regain my breath.

My breathing slows, and I study my surroundings. The cellar is the opposite of the opulent, warm, and shimmering stones above. And though I know there are no windows this far down, I peer around for some anyway as my claustrophobia threatens to choke the remaining air from my lungs. To my relief, the voices have not followed my descent.

Four narrow pathways branch from the main circular cellar lit only by wall sconces, shadows dancing on the walls. I pick a pathway based solely on a gut feeling that tugs me to the far left.

Summoning every trembling ounce of my bravery, I force my wavering feet forward deeper into the Earth. With every step, the air around me chills further. A shiver creeps up my spine and across my skin as goose-bumps rise along my limbs.

"Next time you get kidnapped, pack an extra cloak," I whisper, my teeth starting to chatter.

The end of the pathway nears, and I arrive in a small wine cellar. Hundreds of bottles of fragrant floral and fruity wines line the walls from floor to ceiling. I pick up a bottle, studying it before setting it back on the shelf.

My mother would love it here, I think as a cynical smirk playfully pulls at my features.

I survey the rows of shelves and the walls but find nothing of use. Slowly, I back out of the wine cellar, taking a final look to ensure I haven't missed anything. But I am halted as my back collides with a cloaked figure.

I freeze, swallowing the scream that rises in my throat with a painful gulp. I pivot to face the hooded figure concealed in a heavy midnight cloak, whipping my table leg dagger out of my bag. But, an almost boyish chuckle of surprise causes me to hesitate.

I make a split-second decision to pretend I belong here as my heart pounds relentlessly. I drop the table leg to the ground, kicking it under a wine shelf behind me. It clangs on the ground. The figure laughs once more.

I straighten my spine and mask my expression. The figure cocks its hooded head to the side and, to my pleasant surprise, makes no move to restrain me. I let out a deep breath as I stare into the shadows of their hood, trying to make out any features. But it seems as if the shadows cling to the figure.

"I thought I was the only one who likes to steal Summer Court wine," the tall figure teases.

"I am not stealing," I counter coolly.

"What a shame," he shrugs, "for I am," he replies, with a mischievous chuckle, moving around me at an alarming speed. He kicks my table leg playfully out of the way. "Say what you will about The Summer Court, but they do make *delectable* wine."

He glides across the floor with a confident grace, striding through the cellar as if he owns it. He takes his time, causally studying labels and shoving bottles into his cloak.

He seems to exist within a bubble of power, a being with its own gravitational pull. As if everything he could ever want would throw itself at his feet for the honour of serving him. It's obnoxious and intoxicating. I can't peel my eyes away.

"Oh goody, I sincerely hope the thievery works out for you," I drawl. "Do you happen to know the way out of here? I seem to have gotten turned around," I say, feigning boredom and gesturing to the space.

"Of course..." He pauses as he nears me. "You have something on your face."

My eyes flare, and I slap a hand to my cheek. Mortified that I attempted a master escape plan with leftovers as war paint. Hastily, I wipe my hand over my chin. His head tilts to the side, and my heart kicks wildly against my chest.

It takes all my self-control not to fidget under the intensity of his gaze. Even without being able to see his eyes, the look feels cutting. He pauses his assessment on what I can only assume, without seeing his face, is my shoulder bag.

"A mortal... how *curious*." He hums, smoothing his cloak. "Whatever is a mortal girl doing sneaking around The Ember Palace's liquor supply?" he asks. "Also, my dear little creature, you missed."

He reaches up to brush my cheek, gentle fingers wiping away the remnants of my breakfast. The motion causes his hood to tip back far enough that I can see his eyes. Mischievous, stunning eyes.

I blush, deeply unprepared for the sudden contact, as a gasp slips from my lips. His touch is cool, almost *icy*. He pulls away, and I study his hand, countless silver rings lining his slender fingers, nails painted as black as coal.

I can see the hint of a crooked smirk under his hood. He's *enjoying* this. And I find myself wanting to punch the look right off his face.

My eyebrows shoot skyward as he places his finger into his mouth, licking it clean all while humming in approval. I step back, blinking. He watches me with twinkling eyes as he drops the hood of his cloak, smirk deepening as he winks.

I swallow.

"Bacon. My *favourite*. Well, one of my favourites," he concludes.

It's hard to tell with the cloak, but he seems leaner than Toryn yet still muscular, definitely taller. He has more than a foot of height on me and appears to not be much older than I am, maybe even younger.

I manage a scoff at his arrogance, crossing my arms over my chest, but the flush on my cheeks isn't fooling anyone.

"Alright, thief. Make yourself useful, will you? I would hate to call the guards on you," I threaten. He grins, calling my bluff without muttering a word. I do not let it deter me, rolling my eyes. "Can you show me how to get out of here or not, *wine-stealing, cloak-wearing mystery man?*"

The grin on his face is undeniable, little dimples rippling his cheeks. His notably handsome face. Somehow, that only makes all of this worse.

"What an interesting title. A new favourite." He lifts his fingers to his chin, tapping in exaggerated thought. "Funny, I do not think I have ever taken an *order* from a mortal."

"This *mortal* is losing her patience," I hiss.

His eyes dart over me as if I am a puzzle he is determined to solve. Like I am a complex equation, and he cannot resist the challenge. I run my eyes up and down his body in return. Dark blue-black curls spill from the top of his head and in front of his storm cloud-coloured eyes.

"I can and will show you to the exit." He pauses. Like he is purposely trying to draw out this interaction. It's infinitely annoying. "*If.*"

"*If* what," I challenge.

He playfully fiddles with his fingers, considering his options. Impatience swells under my skin, itching. I do not have time for this. I should walk away. And yet, despite my better judgement, I let him continue. Entirely too engrossed in whatever this is.

"If, and only *if*, you promise to sit down and share this wine with me."

His hands reach into his cloak, and he presents a bottle of wine like an offering, dipping into an overly elaborate bow. My stomach flips. And I know I should turn away from the trouble brewing in his expression but...

His sharp bone structure and angular jawline are undeniably striking. Paired with high cheekbones, it gives him a sharp, elegant, almost feminine beauty. I am too curious to turn away.

"Oh, how you flatter me," I smile too-sweetly. "Does that whole drawling dimpled act have all the ladies fawning over you?" I ask, gesturing to him.

"Not only the ladies." He winks and considers me. "You are an oddity. I am accustomed to much more swooning."

"I do not *swoon*. Ask one of your many admirers to join you."

"I am."

My mouth pops open. "What arrogance. You are not."

"Aren't I?" He brushes his fingers over the heated swell of my cheek. "I have been told by many that my arrogance is one of my finer qualities."

"You must have few fine qualities. I do not have time to sit around being courted by Faerie thieves." I wave him off, tone level, even as the butterflies in my stomach multiply and turn ravenous.

"You believe me to be courting? Oh, sweet thing, if I was courting, you would be pleading for me to whisk you away to my bedchambers." He runs his thumb across his bottom lip. "Alas, I would be *delighted* to oblige. Who am I to turn down such a beauty," he says, pressing a hand to his heart, brow raised. "Say the word, and I will have you swooning."

"I will have to decline. The last Faerie I trusted got me in all kinds of trouble. I will not be making *that* mistake again."

He looks genuinely taken aback. And I wonder if he's ever been rejected before, let alone by a mortal. The hand he placed over his heart turns to a fist, and he groans as if mortally wounded. I roll my eyes, remaining unmoved by his theatrics, and his eyes darken in calculation.

Some sort of understanding brews on his face. And before I can even process what is happening, the thief kisses my cheek, winks, and then raises his cloak.

"Your *first* mistake was trusting the Fae. Your second mistake was trusting The *Summer* Court Fae. I look forward to seeing what your third mistake will be, sweet creature. Until we meet again."

As quickly as he appears, he is gone, vanishing into the wine cellar behind me so fast I wonder if he was some kind of beautiful ghost or a figment of my imagination.

"Wait! You were supposed to show me how to get out of here!" I whisper-shout, flooded by frustration.

I rub a hand over my forehead. A string of curses fowl enough to curdle milk slip from my lips in an exasperated whisper. Following his path into the wine cellar, scanning the rows of wine for any sign of the mysterious thief or his escape route, I find the room completely empty.

I stand there dumbfounded, running a hand through my hair. He was *just* here. I blink at the walls.

"Am I hallucinating?"

Shaking my head to clear it, I search the perimeter of the walls, running my hand along the cool stone. I feel for any cracks or indents in the stone. There has to be a passageway. People don't just vanish through walls. At least not in Mayward.

But still, I find nothing. It's as if he sunk into solid stone and disappeared. At least the chill in the air has lessened. I sigh, deciding it's best to backtrack my steps to the main cellar and try another hallway.

Halfway back to the main cellar, I hear voices descending the stairs.

"No one in or out until we apprehend the girl!" a male voice orders.

Panic builds in my chest, and I pivot, sprinting back into the wine cellar. But I trip over something in the doorway. *A dagger.*

Snatching the dagger from the ground, relief floods my body, only to be swallowed up by the realization that I cannot fight my way through a group of armed Fae Knights with a single dagger and no plan. Especially if those Knights fight anything like Toryn.

Desperately, I survey the walls, praying to every God or Goddess I can think of that the passage the thief used to escape will magickally show itself. That somehow, I missed something... *anything.* My heart rattles wildly in my chest, icy panic rains down on me in cool, unforgiving sheets.

Still nothing. No exit. No escape.

I stop my frantic search near the back of the cellar, sticking to the thickest shadows.

The Knights' footfalls near, and I spot two shadows in the arched entryway of the wine cellar, backlit by the sconces in the hall. Two, I can handle. It's what happens once I pass the two that I am worried about.

I have no real way of knowing how many are out there. I can only pray that Toryn has once again underestimated my abilities.

I hold my breath, worried even a single exhale will give me away. Wedging my body between a wine rack and the far left corner wall. The shelf wobbles, causing a soft symphony of clanging bottles. The Knights murmur something to each other, moving into view and pointing vaguely in my direction.

I shut my eyes, cursing the person who bought these flimsy shelves under my breath. This building is full of excessive luxury, and yet whoever designed it chose useless, wobbly shelving that is going to get me beheaded.

I breathe, unable to hold my breath any longer. The smell of grapes, flowers, and apples mixed with the inescapable scent of damp, earthy soil rushes my lungs. The dark stone is icy on my back as I press into the wall, desperately wishing I could sink into it and disappear. I try to force my heart rate to calm, but being crammed into a small space only heightens my panic.

The Knights pass the threshold of the cellar, weapons at the ready. One holds a sword, the other double axes. They search each dimly lit row diligently. Too diligently for me to go unseen when they inevitably pass. They split up, searching opposite sides of the chamber. I like what that does for my odds.

Running my fingers along the hilt of my new dagger, I try to get a feel for the weapon's balance, weight, and size. My fingers brush over small lines of indented circular carvings on the side of the hilt. With my fingers alone, I can't tell what they are.

Axe in hand, a Knight begins to search the opposite end of my row, less than a few feet separating us. The air seems to thicken with my fear and anticipation.

I adjust the grip on the dagger one final time, and as he approaches, I jet out from the shelf. It wobbles, clanging. He begins to turn, raising his axe, but I grit my teeth and launch forward, thrusting the dagger into the soft, vulnerable spot between his helmet and chest piece.

Warm blood sprays from the wound with a sickening squelch, splattering my face and neck. The Knight crumples to the ground, and I wince. The crash of gold armour on the stone reminds me of the church bells in Cressa's cathedral.

So much for a stealthy escape.

"Sir Caleb? Is everything alright?" his partner calls.

An unwelcome wave of guilt assaults my senses. *Caleb.* His name was Caleb. He had a family. He was someone's son. He woke up this morning like me and said goodbye to someone he loved, who loved him. Someone who will never see him again. Today will be the last day he laughs, cries, or makes someone smile. Because of *me.*

The blood on my face burns my skin like a brand. *Murderer.* Dizziness slams into my skull, and my stomach threatens to empty as I place the back of my sweat-slicked palm over my mouth.

I am ripped from my guilt-ridden spiral by the other approaching Knight. I decide that if I can avoid ending another life, I will.

I throw my weight into the shelf beside me hard enough that my shoulder aches. It groans, wobbling. I slam myself into it once more. And it plummets to the floor with a deafening crash of wood, shattering glass, and rushing purple liquid. The Knight groans as it pins him to the stone floor.

I find myself reconsidering my earlier thought about wobbly shelves—they were a great choice.

Multiple pairs of footsteps sound from down the hall, and I curse. If the rest didn't know where I was, they do now. My body swims with adrenaline pumping my veins full of urgent fire. My eyes feel wider, more alert, my skin buzzing with a hundred frantic bees.

The pinned Knight calls out for assistance, moaning in pain. I can hear him shuffling to try to escape the weight of the shelf.

I sprint towards the doorway but am manhandled to the ground by three armoured Knights.

My dagger drops as someone applies pressure to a point in my wrist that forces my fingers to open. Struggling like a rabbit caught in a snare, I fight to escape their grasp.

I kick, landing a blow to one of the Knight's faces with my boot. A satisfying crunch follows as his nose breaks against his helmet. Blood flows down his face like an angry red river. He coughs back the liquid, gripping me harder. Another Knight grips my rogue leg and slams it into the ground. I yelp.

My head is shoved into the cold stone by a booted foot, pain exploding as my skull ricochets against the hard floor. My arms are yanked behind my back, my forearms pinned by a knee to my back. The position rips relentlessly on my shoulder joints.

I try to kick, wiggle, and fight out their grip, but a Knight slams down his entire weight, causing something in my chest to crack. The added pain borders on unbearable as white stars dance across my vision.

My body goes limp, and the Knights pull back slightly. My right shoulder sings with pain even with the reduced weight, and I can't help but wonder if it's dislocated.

I bolster my strength, gritting my teeth. I have felt worse. Endured worse at the hands of my own mother. I can endure this. I have to. For Elle.

My treacherous mind spins with images of my sister, sending a wave of hurt piercing through my heart like a flaming arrow. I think of Caleb. If I don't save Elle, he died by my hands for nothing. I cannot let that happen. This cannot be how our story ends. I cannot let his death be meaningless.

The world has to be more than *this*. More than loss, suffering, pain, grief, and sorrow. And despite everything, a small bursting bead of pure golden light explodes deep inside my soul—*hope*.

The hall falls ghostly silent as taut tension consumes the air, but it does not last. A voice shatters the silence—an all too familiar voice.

His voice.

"Your Royal Highness," a Knight greets.

Someone anxiously clears their throat. The eerie sound of armour creaking in sync echoes the hall. They must be bowing. I can't see, my cheek pressed into the floor, facing the dark cellar and the damage I have done. I resist the urge to scoff at the title.

"Report," Toryn demands.

"A guard went to check her room and found it empty. We immediately informed the Palace Garrison and began a search. She was located in the eastern wine cellar. She managed to kill one of ours and injure another. We are unsure how she managed to secure a weapon. Please forgive us for the lack of oversight, Prince Viktoryn. She will not be left unsupervised again," the Knight relays matter-of-factly, but I do not miss the hint of fear and pleading in his tone.

Prince Viktoryn? My mind struggles to grapple with this new version of the male I knew. There is an awkwardly long silence. But it is shattered as Viktoryn's deep, dark laughter fills the hallway.

"I must say, I did not know she had it in her. She truly managed to bring down not one but *two* Faerie Knights? You do not jest?" he asks in awe. "If you had seen her swordsmanship, you would understand my shock."

I grit my teeth. Someone must nod because his laughter echoes throughout the halls, louder and more boisterous this time. I am flooded with disgust as he *laughs* in the midst of his Knights still warm body.

"Impressive. I will admit, I underestimated a mere mortal girl's ability to cause such a ruckus." Viktoryn *tsks*, amusement bubbling in his tone.

"Can we stop talking about me as if I'm not here?" I strain.

"She *speaks*," Viktoryn drawls.

"*She* has a name," I snap.

"What a mouth."

Viktoryn blows out a dramatic sigh as the amusement of my actions loses its novelty. Rage spills into my body, mixing with the pain into a deadly cocktail that begins to loosen my tongue.

"*She* was always a feisty one, boys. Though her bite is not nearly as bad as her bark. You would think by now *she* would know when to hold her tongue. Maybe I should free her of it to save us all the headache," he muses.

Viktoryn strolls into my eye-line, crouching in front of me. His slightly glowing eyes and pointed ears are somehow even more defined than they were in Cressa.

"You look different. I cannot say it's an improvement," I muse.

Viktoryn's eyes narrow, his jaw ticking. With a snap of his fingers, the pressure on my head and back increase, causing me to groan. He chuckles, his lips tipping into a smirk, eyes flooding with a sick amusement as he savours my misery like it is the finest of wines.

I master my pain, forcing my watery eyes to hold his, scoffing at his over-indulgent clothes. *Prince* Viktoryn sports a ruffled white silk tunic with a low V neckline and luxurious deep maroon slacks. So contrasting to the threadbare clothing, he dawned when pretending to be but a lowly mortal Knight.

His tunic is belted with a golden buckle adorned with rubies and sheathed with an expertly crafted sword, the pommel glittering and bejewelled. If I didn't personally know how talented he was with a blade, I would assume he was overcompensating for a lack of skill with *sparkle*.

"Very matchy-matchy. Did your mother pick out your clothing for you this morning?" I taunt, forcing a wicked smile to my lips.

Viktoryn eyes the ground, shifting his weight and bracing the stone floor. His deep blood-red cape drapes across the floor behind him, and I imagine the red of his cape is his blood. That I have somehow miraculously escaped the Knight's hold and thrust my dagger into his lying, hateful, evil heart.

He snaps his fingers again, and the pressure on my head and joints becomes immediately unbearable. I yelp, deciding for the good of my joints to shut my mouth as I narrow my eyes at him.

"I require no assistance dressing or *undressing* myself, as you are well aware," Viktoryn coos, leaning forward until we share breath.

My cheeks heat with embarrassment, my tongue sharpening. But I keep my lips planted firmly shut, gritting my teeth, ignoring the urge to lean away from him.

"Nothing to say now? Come on, *mutt*. Do not lose your bark," he challenges, twirling a lock of my hair around his finger. "It was just getting interesting."

Narrowing my eyes, I imagine forcing him to feel as helpless, betrayed, and scared as I do. But I say nothing. Refusing to rise to the bait. Refusing to give him and his Knights the satisfaction of a mortal puppet show. His eyes narrow back, expression turning cold and bored.

"What of the injured Knight?" he asks no one in particular, rising.

"He is still in there. Our goal was to apprehend the girl immediately."

"Who was responsible for guarding her door?" Prince Viktoryn demands.

"Sir Brandon, Your Highness."

Viktoryn considers this as he gazes into the cellar, expression turning cruel. A shiver runs up my spine.

"Correct me if I am wrong in my assumption. I do not see Sir Brandon before me. Do the pathetic little whimpers I hear coming from the cellar belong to him?" he asks, surveying the Knights' faces.

"You are correct, Your Highness."

The Prince nods, his eyes flicking from the cellar and then to me.

"Kill him," Viktoryn commands as if ordering a tea or commenting on the weather while studying the shelves of the cellar. "What a waste of *perfectly* good wine."

The Prince moves from the threshold, forcing my gaze back to Brandon. His helmet lies uselessly on the ground beside him, having rolled off his head with the fall. His face distorts with rage and pain. His misty eyes find mine, and my heart crumples like a piece of paper in an iron fist.

He murmurs, *please, please, please,* like a prayer under his breath, and with each repetition, I break.

"No! Toryn! Please, don't. I did this. Not him," I plead. "Punish me."

Viktoryn does not bother to acknowledge either of us, examining the hilt of his bejewelled sword—the picture of disinterest. I fight the grip of my captors, attempting to inch my way towards the fallen Knight.

"Toryn, please don't do this."

"It is already done."

My lungs burn with panic as I worm forward.

I could've killed him. I wanted to spare him. I made a choice, so no one else had to die today, only to watch as it is undone by two careless words. The hollow, endless grief that lives inside me howls and thrashes with fury.

A Knight steps into the cellar, and everything within me revolts, pleading with me to shut my eyes. But I force myself to watch. To see what happens when I fail. To know the cost of my mistakes.

I cannot afford to shy away from the truth. I need to know what Viktoryn is capable of. I need to see it, see *him*. I need to stop grasping onto my naive perspective of who he pretended to be.

Time seems to slow to a crawl as a Knight moves to complete the Prince's order with brutal efficiency. I cannot help but wonder if they were friends. If he will grieve this death. And yet, the Knight does not question or hesitate as he brings his broadsword down in an arc.

It happens so fast—one heartbeat Brandon is alive, and the next, his head is rolling away from his shoulders. The sick squelch of bone and sinew separating churns my stomach, and I fight to keep the contents of my breakfast from spewing onto the floor. The Knight steps back with vacant eyes, looking at Prince Viktoryn as a deafening silence fills the space.

I want to look away as Brandon's head—mouth twisted into a soundless scream—rolls to a stop mere inches from my face. But I can't.

My lungs seize.

No one dares to breathe as if they fear that, if they move, Prince Viktoryn's predatory stare will land on them. Demanding more bloodshed, a monster not yet sated. It makes me wonder what they've seen. What he has ordered them to do.

How many nightmares does Viktoryn star in? How many bodies has he ordered slain? Tortured?

Viktoryn, pleased with his show, steps back into my line of view. He claps slowly, the loud sound obliterating the silence and causing me to flinch. A manic grin glides onto his lips.

I stare at this monster—fueled by pain, triumphant in the presence of death—and I wonder how I ever loved him.

His gaze shifts to Brandon's decapitated head, and he chuckles, lightly tapping the gory head with the toe of his boot, rolling it closer. I swallow a scream as Brandon's nose settles an inch from mine, still leaking blood.

The pool grows, staining my cheek, so warm in contrast to the icy stones. I hold my breath, my body trembling violently.

Viktoryn frowns when I do not react, instead turning his attention to his Knights.

"Ensure that *this*," he gestures carelessly at the gruesome scene, "does not occur again. Unless you would all like to accompany dear Brandon to the afterlife." His narrowed eyes find mine. "Hopefully, our little guest has learned that her actions have consequences. Lead her back into her room. I have seen enough."

13

The trip back to my room is a blur. A world drained of colour. I've disconnected from my body. The hollow darkness of grief and guilt coating me in a thick blanket of heavy numbness.

Time passes. I do not know how much.

I find myself in my four-poster bed. Back where I started this morning as if nothing had happened at all. As if the events of this morning were all a horrific nightmare and I have only just woken up. I wish that were true, but my blood-stained skin tells a different tale.

I lay with Elle's journal pressed to my side, silent tears tracking down my cheeks as I ricochet between intense pain and bottomless emptiness.

My body aches relentlessly. My shoulder socket and broken rib scream. Each of my breaths is hard work, lungs wrestling for air.

I cannot decide which is better. The minutes of nothingness where I cease to exist at all or the hurricane of sharp emotions and pain that reminds me I am still real, still alive. That I still have a chance to rescue my sister.

Exhaustion slams my body like a landslide. My eyes droop and remain shut longer with each blink. I plead for sleep to pull me under, but every time my eyes close, I see myself thrusting a dagger into Caleb's neck, feel the wet spray of his blood, see Brandon's head rolling towards me.

My stomach turns and riots. I rush into the adjoining bathing chamber, each step agony. Emptying my stomach into the sink again and again. Until nothing but acidic bile burns my throat.

I do not dare peek at myself in the mirror. Unable to face myself. Unable to face what I have done.

I turn and find the tub is full—it must've been filled by whoever brought me breakfast earlier. I dip my hand in. The water is long since cold but I can't find the will to care. The need to scrub the blood from my body too much.

I plunge into the freezing tub, a sob ripping from my lips. Manically, I claw at my skin with my good arm, trying to erase all I've done and all I didn't do. I lean back, submerging my head, screaming into the water, bubbles racing to the surface.

When I can't hold my breath any longer, and my lungs ache for release, I surface, gasping. I scrub and scrub and scrub until my skin is raw, red, and bleeding. Feeling like no matter how much I scrub, my body still drips with the slain Knights blood. The water around me turns red.

My scrubbing slows and stops as fatigue wraps me in its arms. I try to pull myself from the water, but my knees buckle, pain wrapping around my bones.

I collapse, laying my head on the side of the porcelain tub, welcoming the cold, welcoming the nothingness. My eyes close as my lips chatter.

I fall asleep, unsure if I want to wake up. Wondering where the girl with all the fight in the world went.

I am vaguely aware of *light*. Everything is cold. My eyelids are glued to my bottom lashes. My mouth is numb and cottony. The space around me echoes and distorts.

"What is wrong with her?" someone demands.

I do not hear the response.

"She is practically blue! Do something! I do not know much about mortals, but I know they are not supposed to be blue. If she dies, I will kill you. Do you understand?"

I am gone again.

"A Knight heard a splash. By the time I got here, her head was underwater."

A pause. A muffled reply.

"I do not know! You are all incompetent fools. Wake her up! I am ready to mount your head to the gates! She has to wake up. You do not understand. She is *everything*."

I am gone again.

Warmth. Pain. Everything is tingling. A metallic taste floods my mouth. I am coughing and convulsing. Yet I feel somehow separate from it. A doll with her stuffing removed. A tree severed from its roots.

Then I am back. Water spills from my lips, and my lungs are burning. When the coughing subsides, I try to speak.

"Am I dead?" I whimper.

Someone grasps my hand in theirs, the touch warm, familiar.

"Not if I can help it," the familiar voice says.

Too familiar. But my senses are scrambled, and I cannot place their identity.

I pry my eyelids open. It takes concentration. Tiny weights dangling from each of my eyelashes. The aching in my shoulder and rib has miraculously lessened. Nothing compared to the unrelenting pain I remember. But *gods*, my head.

Stunning golden eyes lock on mine, and for a second, I am *home*. A rushing sense of warmth fills me. I grasp onto it with desperate hands.

The hand holding mine tightens, a thumb brushing the back of my hand in reassuring, gentle strokes. It feels nice.

The gears in my water-logged brain click into place. I recognize who holds my hand. Panic. The relief is chased away by frenzied claws.

"Get away from me," I hiss, ripping my hand from his.

I try to sit up, to flee, but someone has replaced my bones with stone and iron. My head plummets down, colliding into my pillow with an audible puff.

My ears are ringing and singing and rushing and screaming. My stomach tossing and turning and flipping inside out and upside down until it has tied itself in knots. A flock of birds are pecking their pointed beaks into my temples. And all I can think is that I wish I was unconscious again.

"Do not move, Miss," a female voice says gently. My eyes find her hovering at the end of my bed. A tiny little thing. Kind brown eyes. She shoots nervous glances at the Prince. Her mousey brown hair damp with sweat. "Please get her to stay still. I have done all I can. A mortal body is not equipped to handle our magicks. She must rest."

I feel the slightest bit better when I see the look painted all over Viktoryn's face. He is *vibrating* with rage.

"You are sorely mistaken if you think I can get her to do anything," Prince Viktoryn snaps, fists balled into knots. "If I could, we would not be in this situation."

He sucks in a ragged breath, running his hands through his dishevelled golden locks as he dismisses the healer. She scurries from the room like a frightened mouse.

I glance at my own body and startle. I am in a warm, pale pink, silky nightgown. The fabric feels like a gentle hug on my skin, but the sensation does not chase away the panic of realizing someone changed my clothing while I was unconscious.

"Did you, uh, did you?" I awkwardly gesture to the nightgown, wincing as my ribs twinge.

Viktoryn scans my body, confusion replacing his rage. What I am inferring clicks, and his cheeks glow crimson. Something about his reaction is wildly satisfying. I bite my lip to keep from smirking.

"No. Worry not, I only wish to take your clothes off when you are begging me for it." His eyes sparkle with mischief, and I narrow mine. "The healer assisted you. I left the room. Though I was hesitant to let you out of my sight in your condition. Knowing you, you would find a way to get into trouble, even unconscious. If it is of any comfort, Faeries are less concerned with modesty than mortals."

I nod, my eyes scanning the bedchamber. Viktoryn leans back into a velvety maroon wingback chair. A chair they must've brought in for him. It was not here before.

I study him, noticing for the first time the dark half-moons beneath his eyes.

"You have been out for two days," he murmurs, and if I wasn't likely severely concussed, I would think he sounded *worried*.

I am suddenly uncertain.

I've never seen him look so unsure of himself, not even as a lowly Knight. His usual mask of unbreakable arrogance is cracking in front of my eyes, and I do not know what to make of it. The worry is written all over his face, in the bloodshot veins brightly lining his eyes, the crinkle between his brow, and the way he is rubbing his forehead. It's echoed in the way he won't meet my eyes.

My hands ball into fists. I wish to throttle him. His worry is like an itchy shirt that does not fit. *How dare he?* I would not be lying broken in this bed if he did not enter and implode my life.

Viktoryn shifts under my gaze, scraping dried blood from his forearm with his fingernail. I do not wish to know where it came from as I recall the way he looked smiling as I lay on the ground, face to face with Brandon's decapitated head. He was so cold and cruel, completely opposite of the Viktoryn sitting before me now.

How do I know this isn't but another act?

An overwhelming hurt grips my heart as I realize I will never be able to tell what is real and what is pretend with him now. Which pieces of the Knight I fell in love with in Mayfair truly belong to the Prince in front of me?

He is a mosaic of two half-real beings slamming together and shattering. All sharp pieces—broken glass reflecting maybes, what ifs, and half-truths. A creature of fractured traits that do not quite fit together.

The unbearable grief takes me by surprise. I stare at him, this person I no longer know. A stranger in the skin of my lover. I can't help but feel like the Toryn I knew has died, and sitting in front of me is a ghost full of broken promises, a gravestone of a man created from make-believe. All at once, the silence of the room is too much, too heavy, too real, too intimate. I butcher it.

"Why could I not see your real ears and eyes in Cressa?" I question. "How did you hide your true self?"

His brows pinch, lips forming a tight line. "You almost died, and *this* is what you wish to know?" he asks incredulously. I nod. He shakes his head, running a hand over his chin. "You are...I used a glamour. A type of magick. It makes things appear differently, distorts reality."

"Like you," I whisper, mostly to myself.

Viktoryn's eyes find mine, almost pleadingly. Sitting straighter, he moves to brush a stray strand of hair out of my face. I flinch. His hand hovers, frozen, inches from my cheek. His outreached fingers slowly close into a fist. Before he snatches his hand back, averting his gaze, jaw tight.

"What were you thinking, Willa?" he growls, all the warmth drained from his expression.

"I wasn't."

"*Clearly.*"

"I was trying to save my sister!" I hiss.

"I see. And how did that turn out for you, *darling*?" he challenges.

"Oh! Am I Willa and darling again? *Huh?* Or just *her* and *she*," I snap, my eyes boring holes of fury in his head. "What even is your true name? Do I know you at all?"

He flinches. I wonder for a moment if I am seeing things. Viktoryn refuses to meet my eyes, gaze fixed on the wall across from him. His hands tense and relax around the arms of the chair repeatedly. I wonder if he is even aware of it.

"Are you certain you wish to hear it? It is rather a mouthful." I nod. "Very well. My true name is His Royal Highness, Prince Viktoryn Elio Cyrus Goldynlocke, Son of The Mighty High King Ambrose Leo Samson Goldylocke, Prince of The Twin Blessed Seelie Kingdom, Heir to The Radiant Summer Court Throne," Viktoryn declares.

I blink—maybe I didn't want to hear it. It is but a reminder of who he really is. What he has done.

Flashes of terror, blood, and golden eyes fill my mind.

"How could you order your Knights to kill your own Folk? How could you be so heartless?" I accuse.

This line of questioning stuns him. He blinks, adjusting in his chair. Viktoryn's eyes meet mine, churning with bitter, unbridled *hate*. Hate so potent it invades the room, snatching the air from my lungs.

Time passes. But he simply stares. Goosebumps rise on my skin. I begin to think he will not answer me, but I refuse to yield, staring back with equal fire.

"I am responsible for the safety of every being inside Ember Palace. I am the Goldynlocke Heir. It is my duty. I am responsible for *your* safety, the safety of my guards, and those who call the Palace home. Sir Brandon was supposed to be standing at your door. He left your room unguarded to flirt with a water nymph in the gardens. He knowingly chose to ignore a direct order. He abandoned his post. He failed to protect you from outside threats and from *yourself*. He failed me. I am not forgiving of those who fail me."

Viktoryn's gaze turns cruel. "He brought shame to my name and cast doubt into the minds of the Fae I rule about my abilities. He has handed them ammunition to question my competency as a ruler. That is unacceptable. *Treasonous*."

"I do not take kindly to those who disrespect me. And if that was not enough in itself, he underestimated you, but I do confess, so did I. You are always surprising me." Viktoryn chuckles bitterly. "So I ensured he paid for it. Not only with his life but his legacy. He serves as a message and warning."

He serves as a message and warning.

"To have you aimlessly wandering the halls is not only a safety risk to my guards, as you have so *generously* demonstrated." He shoots me a look but smirks. It falls. "I cannot guarantee your safety outside these four walls. I can barely guarantee your safety within them. What you did was *foolish*."

I watch him. Unsure of how to feel about how easily he has justified the murder of another, my hands knit together under the covers.

"Why would you need to protect me from anyone inside your *own* Palace? The only thing I need protection from is you," I spit.

Viktoryn heaves a sigh, rolling his eyes. He leans forward, settling his ankle over his knee. He opens his mouth as if to reply but shakes his head. But the thought of threats inside the Palace jogs a memory to the forefront of my mind. An axe dangling over my head, frozen mid-swing.

The mysterious thief! The wine cellar. Stormy blue-grey eyes. *Dimples.*

My mind floods with more unanswered questions. I almost forgot about him after the chaos of my capture. Though I cannot deny those eyes and damning dimples are hard to forget. I wonder if I should tell Viktoryn what I saw. I eye him wearily.

I find myself hesitant. If the thief wanted to harm me, he had ample time and opportunity. I would not categorise wine stealing and flirting as harmful to anything but Viktoryn's ego and precious liquor supply. And it is often said that the enemy of my enemy is my friend...

A small smile finds its way to my lips. I wonder how Viktoryn would feel to know I had garnered such attention. I wonder if he would be *jealous.* I wonder if I would like it. How absolutely, deliciously satisfying it would be to watch him squirm at the idea of another male taking interest in me.

He never had to worry about such a thing before, but here... Here, things might be different—here, I have some value, some hidden leverage, even if I do not know what it is yet.

I am snapped out of my scheming because the *Royal-Pain-in-My-Ass* has finally decided to grace me with an answer. Well, a half-truth, non-answer—his specialty.

"You are vastly important to the survival of The Summer Court and The Seelie Kingdom," he replies, expression betraying nothing.

I narrow my eyes on him. "It took you five minutes to answer, and *that* was the best you could come up with?" A disbelieving laugh slips through my lips, and I pay tenfold for it, clutching my ribs as they ache.

Viktoryn smirks even as his eyes narrow back.

The cryptic answer does little to sate my curiosity. But I do not know what I expected. The Prince hasn't exactly been exactly *forthcoming* since we arrived in Elphyne. Or previously, if I am being more honest with myself.

His answer doesn't explain why, if I am oh so important to his court's survival, someone within it would risk harming me. Or why I am important to the court's survival, period. Or what any of this has to do with the kidnapping of my sister. I find my patience slipping.

As for the thief... *If Viktoryn is not going to tell me anything, why should I tell him anything?* Stolen wine is the least of what the wicked Prince deserves. I should have helped the thief stuff more bottles in his cloak. Or smashed another few shelves full.

"Are you certain you stalked and kidnapped the right girl? What value could I have to some*thing* like you," I remark, "and furthermore, why, if I am *oh so important*, would someone wish to harm me, Your Highness?"

Viktoryn stiffens, but I am beyond caring. I glare at him with all the vicious rage I feel festering inside me. A coiled snake ready to strike.

"You do not know how badly I wish that were true." He smiles tightly. "Simply to free me from your wretched mouth and childish outbursts. If you think playing nursemaid to a whiney, entitled little *brat* is my idea of a pleasant pastime..." Viktoryn scoffs, "as if, as the *heir* to The Summer

Throne, I have nothing better to do. But alas, *you* have something we need." He laughs, throwing his hands in the air as if the idea is both irritating and ridiculous.

"What could I, a whiney, entitled, little brat, possibly possess that a Faerie Kingdom would need?" I push, tossing his words back at him.

Viktoryn's jaw tenses and ticks. He remains silent, and I have to reign in my desire to throttle him as a million more questions swirl around in my head.

"I have told you all I will."

I roll my eyes and pick a different subject.

"How did you get me to sleep in Cressa?" I whisper, a bit unsure I want to know the answer.

"Since when do you ask so many questions?" Viktoryn sighs, scrubbing his jaw with his hand. I continue to hold his glare, unwilling to back down.

"Fine. Faeries can use compulsion on mortals. Suggest or will them to do something, anything, really." He smirks at my expression and my stomach turns. "I could tell you to shove a knife through your eye, and you would do it with a smile. After today's little stunt, that sounds wonderful, actually."

"Since some entitled, lying, arrogant Faerie Prince uprooted and destroyed my life by kidnapping my sister," I shout, "I think that entitles me to ask a few questions. Don't you think so?" I don't let him answer. "When do I get to see my sister?"

A chuckle slips from his lips, his eyes wide and wild. "Do you think, after your little outburst today, you *deserve* to see her?"

Anger swells in my chest. If he wants to play games of intimidation and manipulation and half-truths, *fine.* Two can play this game, and one of us can *lie.*

Viktoryn, as unbreakable as he seems, has some sort of soft spot for me if his previous worry is to be believed. I force my breathing into uneven, sniffing breaths and flood my eyes with tears.

"I just need to know she's okay," I huff, my voice wavering and breaking. A single tear escapes my eyes and tracks down my cheek. Magnificent timing.

Viktoryn visibly tenses, his eyes following the tears' descent, softening slightly. So slightly that if I hadn't spent the last two years around him, it would be practically undetectable. The silence in the room grows charged, the air shifting like the moment before a lightning strike. Viktoryn grips the armrests of his chair.

"Your sister is fine," he begins dryly. "Unharmed as promised. She was alerted of your safe arrival to the Palace. You shall see her soon," he snaps.

"Safe arrival?" I gape at him. "Do I look unharmed to you?" I fume.

"You did *arrive* safely. I left you in this room, asleep. Any injuries you acquired after were your own doing," he counters.

"I would not hav—"

"I will leave you to rest," Viktoryn interrupts, holding up a palm. "You got quite banged up on your little adventures. Guards will be posted directly outside the door at all times in case you decide to go on another ill-advised grand quest... I have ordered them not to kill you." The '*for now*' goes unsaid.

"But to prevent you from exiting this room by any means necessary. So sit tight, darling. I hope to hear reports that you were a very good girl." He pats the top of my head, and I bat his hand away. He smiles and heads for the door.

The words are out of my mouth before I think better of them, slipping through my lips as he reaches for the door handle.

"Did you use compulsion to get me to fall for you?"

"No need," he coos. "You fell for my natural charm."

I nap, but nightmares chase me from sleep. My chest aches. I miss my sister. I miss her stories and her kindness, her cunning, and her laugh. I even miss her scheming and pranks.

I scold myself for every time I felt annoyed by her rattling on about stories. What I wouldn't give for her to be here, telling me stories from dusk till dawn.

I pull her journal from my shoulder bag, wanting to hold something Elle held, to read something she wrote, to feel close to her. But I freeze as my fingers brush something cool and metallic. My brows knit, and I scan my bed chamber for any prying eyes.

I pull the object from my bag and still when I find a dagger identical to the one from the cellar. *How did this get in here? Did they not search my bag?*

The hilt is carved from smooth, iridescent black stone, twisted with silver that wraps around the hilt to form shooting stars. Most remarkably, the phases of the moon are inlaid on the side. The blade itself has a slight curve. I hold it to the light, examining it with awe as the black blade shimmers iridescent.

A strange prickling sensation creeps across my neck. Once was *lucky*, twice is no coincidence. Someone left this for me. Someone who got close enough to place it inside my bag.

My brows crease as I glide the pads of my fingers across the carvings as if they will reveal some kind of secret to me.

They don't.

I spend the rest of the day reading Fabelle's journal. To my pleasant surprise, I find a lot of what's written immensely helpful. Along with short stories about Princesses, Dragons, Knights, and quests are pages overflowing with Fae mythology.

Sections on Faerie customs, rules for humans interacting with the Fae, facts on Elphyne, and more. How she managed to secure such information eludes me.

I startle when a knock sounds. A *human* servant enters with a tray of food, closing the door behind her before dipping into a bow. I startle then for an entirely different reason. No one has ever *bowed* to me. I am completely unsure of the proper etiquette.

My cheeks flame as I stare at her, clearing my throat. I settle on a reply that I can only assume is far from customary, but the awkward stretching silence causes me to panic.

"You're human."

Her full lips tip up, and amusement swims in her eyes. She moves her hand in front of her face, stifling a laugh. And I am glad, at the very least, that my confusion is amusing enough to warrant a laugh.

She is beautiful and middle-aged with chestnut brown hair pulled back into a tight bun set with a white ribbon. She has wondrous, kind, mahogany eyes and wears an almost motherly expression.

"Yes, dear child. I am," she replies gently.

I realize she is the first human I have seen in Elphyne. And I have to hold myself back from bombarding her with questions. I continue to gawk, and she is polite enough to ignore my utter lack of decorum.

"Would you like to take dinner in bed or at the table?" she asks, voice warm and welcoming like honey.

"Bed is fine. What is your name?"

"Beatrice," she replies, moving to set the tray on my lap. The food smells absolutely intoxicating. It takes everything in me not to begin to shove it all in my mouth right then. "Is there anything else I can do for you, Lady Willa?"

A chuckle slips out. If someone had told me a few weeks ago that any-one would refer to me as a '*Lady*,' I would have likely burst into crazed laughter in their face. Beatrice watches me with an amused expression.

"Please, just Willa. Thank you, Beatrice," I hesitate. "Before you go, have you seen my sister by chance? Her name is Elle, Fabelle Capri. She's a bit taller than me, reddish blonde hair."

"Oh, yes! Of course, I have. She has caused quite the frenzy at court. An absolutely lovely little thing. I hear Prince Archer is quite taken with her," Beatrice gushes, beaming.

Her smile vanishes as she scans my expression. I assume it's the combination of rage, confusion, and disbelief warring on my features. Her eyes glint with panic, widening.

"Prince who? *Taken* with what?" I mutter through gritted teeth.

I force myself to take deep, even breaths.

"I am sorry, my Lady," she winces. "Pardon, Willa, if I have offended you," she says, bowing and quickly excusing herself from the room.

I feel a pinch of guilt for startling her, but it is fleeting. The last thing Elle needs is to get entangled with a manipulative Faerie Prince—I would know. Fury heats the blood in my veins, and I resist the urge to hurl my dinner at the nearest wall.

My anger fizzles as a heavy realization settles deep within my bones. I am no help to Elle locked in my room. If my escape attempt from this morning proved anything, I can't fight or sneak my way out. Especially with the newly assembled boys' club directly outside my door.

I need a new game plan.

Elle's journal further confirms that the Fae can be cruel, cunning, strategic, and manipulative. Though they cannot lie directly, they are master deceivers.

If I cannot fight my way out, I must stay and destroy them from within.

Despite how it will pain me, I need to behave and play Viktoryn's game. I need to play by his rules, and I need to *win*. And I will win, or I will burn this Palace to the ground trying.

I wake up to knocking on my door. I do not remember falling asleep, but Elle's journal is clutched to my chest. Sleepily, I shove it under my excessive amount of pillows.

I pull a pillow over my head, wishing I could retreat back into the gentle embrace of precious, *precious* sleep.

"Come in," I call out, the sound muffled.

Footsteps approach, and the smell of food causes me to emerge from my hiding place. I squint as light assaults my eyes. Beatrice crosses the room carrying a steaming breakfast tray, and I am suddenly much more awake. Another servant trails, her arms overflowing with colourful fabric.

"Good morning! It is an absolute pleasure to mee—"

"Alice, *manners*," Beatrice snaps.

Alice sinks behind her mountain of fabrics, flushing. Beatrice places the tray of food on my lap with an apologetic smile.

But my eyes stay on the beaming blonde who reminds me a bit too much of my sister. My heart twists. The urge to demand to see her is almost unbearable. This whole behaving plan might be slightly more difficult than I expected.

"Pardon me, my Lady." Alice curtsies and I worry the army of fabric will pull her right to the ground, but she manages to right herself.

"Just Willa," I correct, grabbing a link of sausage and taking a big bite.

"Pardon me, just Willa." She curtsies once more, and I bite my lip to keep from chuckling. "Sometimes the excitement gets the better of me! It has been quite a while since I have spent time around a human my own age," Alice remarks, grinning like mad.

Beatrice blows out a long sigh, straightening her skirts. "This is Alice. And while she is young and prone to a bit of overenthusiasm, she is the Palace's most talented seamstress," she states.

I study Alice as she bounces on her heels. She cannot be any older than me, with too wide, deep blue eyes and an overeager demeanour.

"Prince Viktoryn requested we secure your measurements and begin construction of your Summer Solstice gown immediately," Beatrice relays.

"Wait, why would I require a gown? When do I get to see my sister?" I question. "And why can't the Prince be here to tell me himself?"

"He is otherwise occupied." Beatrice gives me a pitying smile. "And I am afraid that I am not at liberty to comment on the Prince's motives."

"If only he'd answer my questions," I grumble to myself. "I do not wish to attend anything. Thank you for your time, but I want to see my sister."

"Willa…" Beatrice takes a deep breath. "I know this must be confusing for you. But we have a job to do," she placates.

"I know, but I do not want a gown. I want to know why I am here. I want to know why the Prince has ordered you in here at the crack of dawn. I want to know why he cares if I have a fancy dress but not if I have my sister," I counter. "Must I nearly drown again for him to grace me with his time?"

"*Enough*," Beatrice hisses, stepping protectively in front of Alice. "I understand your frustration, but this is not Alice's fault. Nor mine. She is but a girl, not unlike yourself."

My cheeks flush, and I shut my eyes. "I-I know. I am sorry, Alice. I just don't understand what he wants," I mutter, pushing my tray aside, my appetite absent.

"I apologise, but you will have to take your concerns to the Prince…" Alice bites her bottom lip. "I only handle matters of fabrics and threads. It will be tight, but I am confident we can have your gown done for the ball at the end of this week."

"The Prince selected the fabrics himself," Beatrice says and gestures to Alice's arms. I note the fabrics are all in various shades of oranges, reds, and yellows, and cringe.

"Of course he did," I mumble, rolling my eyes. "In that case, none of them will do," I say gently. Alice deflates but nods. "Would you mind doing me a favour, Alice?" She nods eagerly. "Would you pick out other colour options? Maybe something green or blue."

"Oh! Of course." Alice beams, thrilled to be asked for her expertise. Even if it involves disobeying the Prince's direct order. I feel a wave of guilt for my outburst. I like Alice already. "It would be an honour," she squeals. "No one ever gives me any creative freedom around here."

Beatrice rubs her temples, and I can't help the laugh that slips my lips.

The Eve of The Summer Solstice arrives quickly. Elle's journal offers little insight into the holiday. Only stating it is a holy day of drinking and celebration.

My head struggles to make sense of how differently time moves in Elphyne. It was late spring in Cressa when the Prince took me from Mayfair. And though Elle's journal mentioned how time moves faster in Elphyne, experiencing it firsthand is a mind warp. Especially when the days *feel* no different.

Viktoryn does not visit again. He gives me no opportunity to question why he wishes for me to attend these festivities. He does not gift me an update on my sister. It drives me nearly mad.

I am pulled from my endless studying of Elle's journal by Alice. She enters the room alone, which I note as odd. She never comes here without Beatrice, who I have noticed behaves a bit like a mother to the young girl.

The hair on the back of my neck prickles, and I jolt as our eyes meet. A wild glimmer of manic joy gleams in her blue eyes. So eerily different from her usual pep. I am taken aback by the intensity.

She does not carry supplies or bow or address me. A sinking sensation fills my gut as warning bells ring in my mind.

"Alice, are you quite alright?" I question, standing from the bed, my hands held out in front of me.

She holds a single finger to her lips, making her way to me.

"I don't have very much time," Alice whispers, taking my hand in hers.

"Time for what?"

"Listen to me very carefully, Willa. You cannot trust them. Any of them. There are forces at play that outdate your existence. You were born to destroy The Summer Court. *You were born to burn.* You are The Princess of Secrets and Shadows. You are The Princess of Flesh and Flame, and you will end the reign of darkness," Alice mutters, her eyes wild with a burdening hope. Hope, I fear, is sadly misplaced.

"Alice, what are you talking about?" I mutter, shaking her hands like I can shake away her temporary fit of insanity.

"Do not tell anyone what I have told you. Do not show a soul this, and do not let it out of your sight. Keep it hidden—with you, it is the key," Alice mutters, undeterred. "The rains of May will be your guide."

She presses a cold metallic circle into my palm, closing my fingers around it. It sends a shock of warm electricity down my arm. I jump. She nods to me as if that is some kind of confirmation and flees the room on silent feet.

I open my palm and peer skeptically at the metal—a harmless-looking gold medallion on a chain. The size of a large coin, imprinted with a sun—half blazing flames, half eclipsed in shadows.

I turn it over in my palm, attempting to make any sense of the seemingly useless object.

With you, it is the key. The key to what? My eyebrows furrow as I look for any indication it could be manipulated into the shape of a key.

"The rains of May will be your guide," I mutter, shaking my head. "Nonsense... utter nonsense."

Another shock of warm energy kisses my flesh, travelling up my arm. My heart kicks into a gallop, and I resist the urge to chuck the medallion out the nearest window.

But I feel a preternatural pull to it as if somewhere deep in my gut, it is linked to me. A golden string wrapping around my core. As if it belongs to me and I belong to it. As if we were two pieces meant to meet.

I shake my head at myself. Maybe some of Alice's crazy was contagious.

"The Princess of Secrets and Shadows. The Princess of Flesh and Flame? What does that even mean?" I murmur, rubbing the metal between my thumb and finger.

The metal heats, pulsing in my palm at the words. I drop it to the ground, leaping away as if burned. *Am I hallucinating?*

The sound of armour clinking outside my door springs me to action. I snatch the medallion from the ground, shoving it under the mattress beside my hidden dagger.

No one enters. But I still do not dare reach for the object again. And yet... I cannot help but feel like it is reaching for *me*.

That night, it appeared in my dreams. When the nightmare of my father in the burning forest finds me, so does it. And to my horror, the medallion is now glinting around his neck. I wake, gasping, lifting my mattress to check that it hasn't grown legs and run away in the night.

For a moment, I wonder if I am still dreaming as I stare wide-eyed, heart galloping, at the sight before me. Around the medallion, the fabric of my mattress is *singed*. A wave of nausea slams into me.

I run to my bathing chamber, flesh on fire, and empty my stomach into the sink. Lifting my eyes to the mirror, I assess myself, my skin damp with a layer of sweat sheen. As if, in the night, a relentless fever has infected my bones, causing my blood to boil.

I meet my own wide eyes, and a gasp parts my lips. My green irises burn with a slight unnatural glow. My stomach churns and I retch into the sink.

When the retching subsides, I glance back at myself to find my eyes normal. No glow remains, and the sheen on my skin is beginning to dry.

I grip the sink so hard I worry my fingernails will shatter. Hesitantly, I reach up to pinch my forearm, but I do not wake.

Maybe this is it. Maybe I have finally lost my min—*no.* There must be a logical explanation. I must be ill. A fever can cause hallucinations. I need sleep. I need to rest. This must be some side effect from the Faerie using magick to heal my bones.

Back in my bed, I don't dare peek at the medallion. I force myself to calm down, but sleep does not find me. I spend the rest of the night staring at the ceiling. Unease sits heavy on my chest as Alice's words of warning crash around in my head like banging pots and pans.

As the glow of the morning sun peaks through the window, Beatrice and Alice enter to prepare me for The Summer Solstice festivities. Beatrice makes a comment about my tired eyes, and Alice pretends as if she never came to my room to wield crazed premonitions.

The solstice festivities are to begin at noon when the sun is highest in the sky and continue well past midnight. The halls of the Palace are filled with chattering voices and drunken laughter.

Alice explains the customs and traditions in a giddy rush as she pins my hair back into an elaborately braided bun. I pretend to listen, caught up in my nerves, nodding when she pauses.

The day is a religious holiday meant to honour The Goddess of The Sun, who wields something called The Kiss of Creation. First, there will be an outdoor party at Cyrissa Lake, followed by a formal ball of feasting and dancing.

Alice's words become a muffled blur as I recall my eerie evening. The medallion seems to whisper to me in moments of silence. I catch myself glancing at Beatrice and Alice's faces to see if they hear it, too. But if they do, they show no signs.

I ignore it, deciding to focus on the task at hand. As they work, I hound the girls with questions—questions mostly left unanswered.

The lack of transparency only pushes me to dig deeper for answers. If I am forced to attend, I might as well use it to my advantage.

I reckon the party will lend me an opportunity to gather more intel on the Palace and its residents. And the possible reason for the abduction of my sister and myself. As well as lending me the opportunity to study the terrain surrounding The Summer Court. The more I know about Elphyne and The Ember Palace, the better prepared I can be when the time comes to rescue my sister.

Alice presents me with a stunning blue dress that falls just above my knees. The fabric is light and flowy, meant to be wearable in the suffocating heat of The Summer Court. The colour reminds me of a clear sky, falling beautifully around my curves. Belted at my waist to give shape by a golden chain of small jewelled suns. But undeniably the best feature is the tieable pockets and built-in trousers.

"This is brilliant, Alice. I've never seen anything like it." I smile at her, searching her eyes for any sign of the mania they filled with last night. I find none.

"Of course, Miss. I overheard you mention to Beatrice that, though you like gowns, you prefer breeches. I worked tirelessly on a design that would incorporate both. It's one of a kind," Alice beams.

"When she says worked tirelessly, she means it. I nearly got my head bit off this morning because she was up all night finishing the details," Beatrice remarks, smoothing down her dress while giving Alice a look.

I fail to choke down my chuckle. "Alice! I never knew you had such a dark side."

"We all have our secrets." Alice smiles at me knowingly.

"Please, Alice, I've never met anyone who talks as much and as *openly* as you. You should hear the scandalous stories she tells me about all of her *conquests.*"

"Beatrice!" Alice squeals, nibbling her bottom lip nervously.

"Oh, you *so* have to tell me, " I tease.

"She prefers the Lords and Ladies. Not only for the gossip they wield," Beatrice teases.

Alice turns a horrified tomato red and lightly smacks Beatrice's arm. A wide grin stretches my lips.

We chatter on as Alice and Beatrice work. It feels nice, almost normal. Once they finish, I am led into the bathing chamber.

I turn to the full-length mirror and gasp. I look like me, but... *polished.* My hair is pulled back into a beautiful updo that makes the red in my hair shine bright against the pearl pins.

I smile at myself. Alice and Beatrice both beam at my reaction and nod to each other.

They exit to let the guards know I am ready, and I snatch the medallion from its hiding spot, securing it in the tied pocket of my dress. I can't help but wonder if that's the real reason Alice spent the entire night incorporating pockets into my gown.

I secure my dagger with a leather belt to my upper thigh, take one deep breath, and prepare to infiltrate a Fae Court.

The first indication of a party is the sounds of drunken revelry and music pouring through the trees as I am escorted to the shores of Cyrissa Lake by a group of armed and grumpy guards. I attempt to bait them into talking to me with limited… well, nonexistent success.

When we arrive, I spend the first few minutes gawking at the beauty of the landscape. Gorgeous teal blue waters sparkle, stretching for miles in the endless summer sun. White sand beaches line the calm waves, surrounded by stunning forests of whimsical golden, white, and pink blossomed trees.

I scan the crowd for Viktoryn but find him absent. *Good.* It shall be much easier to sneak about without him present.

On the shores stand elaborately decorated gold and white canopied tents filled with rows and rows of decadent foods. Huge golden statues of who I assume are The Goddess of the Sun line the waters.

Scattered across the beach are giant ceremonial bonfires that send smoke wafting into the sky. Some Fae take turns leaping over the flames, and I can't decide if they are incredibly brave, drunk, or stupid. But they seem to be having a grand time.

I know immediately what Vikotryn meant about the Fae being more open about their bodies, as I spot a few Fae who've decided to attend *naked*. I am not sure where to look... or where *not* to look.

Barefoot Faeries dance with wild abandon, kicking up heels of sand. All angelic and sculpted in a way mortals will never quite compare. They move with such an intoxicating wildness as if nothing but this moment matters. As if they are one with the free-flowing vibrant energy coursing through the air. The crowd is a living, breathing rainbow of madness and mayhem.

I am overwhelmed.

A striking male Faerie with deep brown skin, golden eyes, and close-cropped black hair swings a laughing female Faerie with light blue skin, like frost, into a choreographed dance.

Lively music swirls through the air in sweeping, celebratory notes, calling my body to dance. I resist the urge, remembering my true purpose here, surveying the crowd with strategic eyes. I note with no small amount of displeasure that I am the only human in attendance.

My gaze lands on two male Faeries. Decked in shimmering jewels and swaying on wobbly feet. *Perfect.* Drunk enough not to question my questioning and covered in enough riches that they must rank as Lords or higher.

Cutting my way through the crowd, the smell of heavily perfumed bodies and smoke fills my nose. Dancing bodies collide with mine from all sides, and I stumble. The guards who led me here do nothing to intervene as I am pushed around, milling around the edge of the chaos, drinking and flirting.

Some Faeries shout at me annoyed, tossing me aside, but I ignore them. Others attempt to pull me into their clutches to join the madness, but I decline.

Nearing my marks, I square my shoulders and paste on a too-sweet smile. But before I can make it, a body slams into mine, the crowd letting out an excited '*ooo*' as my path is blocked by a tall, thin frame.

Startled, I step back, cool liquid soaking the front of my blue gown, leaving a deep purple stain. I glance at the Faerie I collided with to find their gown in much better shape. If you can even call it a gown. It is little more than flowing scraps of near-sheer teal fabric and *carefully* placed diamonds. I frown down at myself and the dress Alice worked so hard on, now ruined.

"What is wrong with you, *mutt*? Why are they allowing the help at parties?" The Faerie shouts, disgust shrouding her words as she scans the crowd like she is looking for my keeper.

My eyes snap to hers, rivalling her deadly glare with one of my own. The female Faerie scoffs in my face, startling white eyes narrowed. She towers over me with long, thin limbs and an impossibly narrow waist. Her long, black hair flows freely in the soft summer breeze held in place by a tiara of sapphires and seashells.

A necklace dips between her full chest, skin tinted with iridescent blue scales that glimmer in the sun. I double-take at her teal-tipped webbed hands and feet as well as the gills flexing on her neck.

"I am not the help," I spit when my voice wades past my shock.

As if the sound of my voice summoned them, three Faeries fall into line behind her. One almost identical to her but male, followed by a pale female Faerie with cyan braided hair, and a tanned male with shoulder-length golden hair. Their glares as branding as their leaders.

"Do you know who she is?" the cyan-haired one chuckles in disbelief, eyes wide.

"No. And I find I am not particularly inclined to find out. If you'll excuse me," I reply, moving to sidestep them.

I am blocked as they form a wall of bodies.

"The mortal mutt has quite the mouth on it," the blonde male Faerie remarks, sneering at the others like I am not right in front of him.

"*It* has a *name*," I challenge.

"*It* has a death wish," the white-eyed leader says with a grin, and her minions nod eagerly.

The group exchanges a look, coming to some sort of silent agreement. Faster than I can react, the minions surround me, gripping my limbs tightly. I do not get the chance to reach for the dagger strapped to my thigh.

I think to call out but have the feeling no one would feel motivated to intervene on my behalf. Not even my assigned '*guards*' who have made themselves scarce. I cannot help but think of the last time one of my guards abandoned their duty. And the consequences that followed, ones still haunting my dreams. I swallow against a wave of nausea.

A knife appears at my throat, and I still. The leader smiles, tilting her head, not moving an inch.

"Can't fight your own battles? Can you? Need your little *minions* to do it for you? How very pathetic," I purr, my heart rattling in my chest.

The minion's grip on me tightens to the point of pain as sharp nails pierce my skin, but I keep an arrogant smile pasted on my lips, refusing to betray my fear.

"Watch how you speak to our Princess, *mortal* mutt," the blonde growls.

"Are you worried my mortality is contagious, Princess? Or are you really that intimidated by a mere human?" I challenge.

"Watch your mouth, human filth, or find yourself missing a tongue," the Princess states.

"Is that a threat or a promise?"

Her eyes flash with malice. And the small part of me with absolutely any survival instinct begs me to shut my mouth. But after being caged in my bedchamber for a week, I find the leash I keep on my tongue has snapped.

"Do you wish for us to kill her, Princess Naenia?" the cyan-haired Faerie asks, sounding delighted by the idea.

"What fun would that be, Leanna? If it wishes to be a spectacle, let it be so. Let it entertain us," Princess Naenia drawls, smiling with the promise of a fate worse than death.

She leans into me, lips by my ear, and whispers, "I am the future Queen of the Sea, a Siren, you worthless mutt. If you were wiser, the moment we collided, you would have sunk to your knees to kiss my feet and begun pleading for your inconsequential life. Ensure you say 'hello' to your traitor mother for me in the afterlife, will you?"

Chills snake up my spine, a spear of icy pain embedding into my heart. *Is my mother dead? Did someone go back to Cressa and kill her?*

Her minions pull me forward, taunting and mocking me with every step towards the water. The cool blade of the knife leaves my neck as I am shoved into the shallows, biting back my gasp at the shocking cold.

My head slips below the surface, cold water surrounding me. I push to my feet, water dripping from my pinned-up hair like a dead weight glued to my head. I stand in the waist-deep shallows, refusing to tremble.

I square my shoulders as the minions circle me, a predatory gleam in their eyes. They block my route back to shore.

I consider reaching for my dagger but am unwilling to give away my only advantage before I know what I am facing. I meet each of their eyes before turning back to the Princess.

"Is this it? Punishing me with a recreational swim? What torture indeed, Your Highness," I hiss.

The Princess laughs a cold, hollow noise that sends goosebumps down my back. As she stalks into the shallows with easy grace, a webbed hand shoots to my throat, gripping hard. My airflow vanishes as panic shoots lightning into my veins. I scratch wildly at her wrists, but her strength is staggering.

She watches me fight, a slow, serpentine smile stretching across her face. When I attempt a hold break, she clenches tighter.

Pain radiates from her grip as unbearable pressure builds in my chest. The need for air pushes all the thoughts from my mind as my body floods with adrenaline.

Someone *cheers.*

I glance over her shoulder to find a crowd gathering around the commotion. Princess Naenia lifts me out of the water by my neck, and my feet swing in the air, searching for purchase. Her smile grows sadistic when my eyes begin to bulge.

I claw at her hand until my nails crack. Her deadly white eyes lock on mine as she leans in, whispering in the same heady, luscious tone Viktoryn used to compulse me.

"Swim into the centre of the lake and wait for the Nixies. Only fight when they pull you under. Do not dare die without giving me a show, pet."

The panic vanishes. Her words are soft—a gentle, pleasing caress capturing my mind in a luscious melody. A song my heart yearns to answer.

She drops me unceremoniously, and I hack as air rushes back into my lungs. My limbs eagerly turn and begin swimming to the centre of the lake.

I reach the centre, still gasping, but my mind and body flood with rich, heady joy.

I am light. I am air. I am *floating.*

Treading water, I face the shore. The Princess watches with an expectant smile as cheers and taunts echo across the lake. I smile, pleased she is pleased with me. She lifts her shell necklace to her lips and whistles a two-note tune.

The water around me begins to ripple, three beings breaking the surface. Pale, green-skinned, decaying creatures with long dark hair, gaunt-hollowed cheeks, black void eyes, and pointed bone-white teeth grin at me. Animalistic hunger shimmers in their eyes as they surround me, the smell of rotting fish and flesh coating the air.

One reaches for me, placing a large, webbed, clawed-tipped hand on my cheek, caressing it gently. Slowly, it drags one of its sharp claws down my cheek and across my jaw, sinking into the flesh of my throat. Just deep enough to draw blood. It stings.

Warning flares in my gut, screaming for me to react, but my head continues pounding with joy. It wrestles down my fear and panic before it can fully form.

The creature leans in, licking the blood from my cheek, its black, snake-like tongue tickling my flesh. Its eyes flare with pleasure as all three disappear beneath the surface. Two webbed hands close around my ankles, and I suck in an expectant breath as my head is dragged below the surface.

Like a spell broken, the moment my head is submerged, my senses return. The leash of compulsion snaps, panic slamming into my chest like a landslide.

Instinctively, I glance upwards where the sun dances on the surface. I need to reach that light and leash my panic before it takes control. The second it does, I will drown.

Reaching for my dagger, my hand closes around the cool hilt, and I feel a bit of relief. I keep my eyes locked on the light of the surface for a second longer before accessing the nightmare creatures plotting my demise.

As I meet their eyes, the webbed hands vanish from my ankles a few feet below the surface. I kick, arms reaching for the surface desperately as my lungs scream for air.

Breaking the surface, I get a single gasping breath before I am pulled back under. My stomach knots in terror. They are toying with me, playing with their food, and putting on a good show for the rambunctious crowd.

I will not die today.

I think of Fabelle and how I need to survive until tonight to see her face. If I die now, she will be alone, trapped in this awful place surrounded by these dreadful creatures with no one watching her back. I refuse to allow that to happen.

I have never gone down without a fight, and I do not plan to start today. A calm settles over me—ruthless and cold and unending.

If they want a show, I'll give them one.

A razor-sharp claw slashes the skin at my hip as one of the beings anchors into my flesh. I bite down on my tongue to keep from crying out and filling my lungs with water. My mouth floods with blood.

The pressure in my chest grows, a steady, unwelcome reminder that I am a single breath away from my grave. I use my arms to steady my body in the water, trying to pull myself up while they drag me down. I whip my head around, searching for an advantage as my body goes numb from the cold.

I don't fight back, not yet, attempting to maintain my energy. Underwater, they have the advantage, and I have one chance to get this right. My body aches from the long swim, but I force the fatigue from my mind.

I gauge the distance to the surface as they surround me, taking turns ripping into my flesh. Every cut is agony, white-hot fire exploding through my body. I swallow scream after scream. The water around me paints itself red with my blood.

My legs are a shredded mess as the Nixies take swipe after swipe, teeth sinking into my thigh. I fight to keep conscious. As more of my blood spills, their attacks become less controlled, as they work themselves into a bloodlust. My lungs scream, and I fight the instinct to suck in a breath.

Just as I fear I will be unable to survive another moment, I am pulled to the surface. Desperately, I suck in air, and the pressure in my burning lungs eases. But I can feel the life draining from my body with each passing second. I grip my dagger like a lifeline as keeping my head above the water becomes more difficult.

The cheers from the shore become a roar of pleasure as the Fae watch the free party entertainment. The sound seems to push the beasts further into bloodlust. The Nixies' screech in pleasure—a sound I am certain will haunt my nightmares for years.

The chant of Fae cheering for my slow demise sends an unworldly fury through me, heating my blood. If I survive this, I will end each and every one of them. I will memorise their faces and hunt them down, one by one, when they least expect it.

What kind of sick, wicked creature cheers as they watch a girl fight to her death?

"That all you got, fish face?" I choke out, my fury pushing past the pain and terror.

They hiss—an inhuman sound.

I gather my fury, letting it forge into bravery, and swipe for the nearest creature, years of training take the lead. My dagger catches the Nixie in the chest. A deep slash that wells with deep blue blood. The creature shrieks.

I do not hesitate, using my legs to rotate as I take a swipe with my dagger at another. I slice its throat, blue blood splattering onto my cheeks. Webbed hands fly to the wound as it hemorrhages blood, sliding back beneath the surface as it wheezes.

A collective gasp rings from the crowd, and a long moment of silence follows before the cheers return. The remaining two Nixies pause. Something akin to shock registers on their nightmare faces.

Their hesitation gives me another opening. I turn, plunging my dagger into the heart of the first creature, its endless eyes blink in disbelief as life drains from its face.

The remaining Nixie shrieks—a shrill, keening noise booming across the lake.

I yank my dagger free, but the effort makes my head whirl. The world begins to blur, and my head bobs under the surface. I force my legs back into action, swiping at the last Nixie.

I land a shallow blow across its arm as it dodges late. The air fills with the sharp metallic smell of blood and the unmistakable scent of decay. My panic returns as stars begin to dance in my vision.

No.

I force my eyes to remain open as the creature lunges for me, plunging me below the surface. My strength fails me as I take panicked, uneven swipes at the watery shape. Some make contact, but the blows are weak, slowed by the water and my own blood loss. Panic pounds in my chest and rushes through my ears.

I am going to drown. I am going to die.

The light dims as I am pulled down, down, down. My lungs blazing with a relentless fire, begging me to breathe. My vision blurs, a night sky of stars appears, and I know the end is near. I make another series of desperate strikes, but the creature does not relent.

God, I hope Fabelle forgives me. I hope they tell her I fought until my final breath. I wonder if it will hurt to die. I squeeze my eyes shut, preparing to greet my fate with bravery and honour.

But scorching heat gathers at my side, followed by a flickering golden light that sends the Nixie scattering, teeth bared in a hiss. I use the distraction, attempting to kick to the surface, but my legs have become iron rods of unwilling weight. The light fades, and the Nixie re-grabs my ankles, anchoring into my flesh.

I slash at the hands, the dagger finding purchase as it releases me, only to return seconds later. My eyes fill with tears, but the water greets them, washing away my terror as if it means nothing.

I prepare to take my final breath, but the water around me whooshes, parting by an unseen force. My lungs plead for relief, and I will myself to hold on for just one second longer.

The Nixie's grip loosens as arms close around my shoulders, hauling me up, up, up. My vision speckles with black dots, and I ready myself for death.

For my true and final breath.

It doesn't come. My eyes open, and the relentless sun beats down on my face. A drenched, stunning blonde Faerie with sun-kissed skin wearing a dripping gown of pink flowers and a matching flower crown smiles down at me.

My eyes find hers, and relief floods her sapphire eyes. My own relief is short-lived as the pain of my wounds awakens within me. I groan, glancing at Siren Princess and her minions as they sneer from across the beach at the Faerie gently rubbing my cheek to keep me conscious.

The blonde hisses like a feral cat at them, teeth bared, and I decide right then that I like her. She pushes to her feet and fearlessly stomps towards them with battle-like command. They exchange heated words.

Naenia towers over the little Fae. But to my surprise, something akin to fear flickers in the Princess' eyes as the blonde leans in and whispers. She fixes the Faerie a killer glare, huffs, and then turns, gesturing to her minions. They stalk off into the forest. I blink.

I know the surprise shows on my face when the bouncing blonde turns back to me, shooting me a conspiratorial grin. I try to sit, but pain slams into me. I slump back into the gritty sand with an audible groan.

"Do not move," she says to me and then turns to the crowd. "Send for a healer and Prince Viktoryn now!"

Faeries part from the crowd on her orders. The rest of the lingering crowd watches me, some with disappointment and disgust, others with confusion. I give them a glare that promises vengeance, one that says I will not forget they watched and cheered as I fought for my life.

This sends more of the crowd scattering. The rest depart after the blonde shoots a hiss of threat in their direction. She meets my eyes with a warning as she slips my dagger back into my makeshift sheath.

I nod at her once, hoping my gratitude shows in my eyes.

"I am Princess Maylea Moonflower of The Spring Court. But you can call me May," she beams, adjusting her sopping-wet flower crown.

My eyes widen slightly.

The rains of May will be your guide.

May surveys my damaged limbs. "You lost a lot of blood. And I am not particularly skilled with healing magicks," she worries her bottom lip, "but I am going to attempt to patch the shallow cuts until the healer arrives. What is your name?"

"Willa."

Her eyes flare. "Pleasure to make your acquaintance, Willa. Regardless of the circumstances. You got yourself in an awful lot of trouble, even the most powerful Faeries here avoid the Siren Princess. You must be some special type of fearless or stupid. Either way," she shrugs with a breathtaking grin, "I respect it."

May runs her hands over the wounds, hot white light and warmth following her touch. I watch in fascination.

"To be fair, I didn't know who she was. Just that she was wretched company to chat with at a party. They must let anyone in these days."

May chokes on a laugh, mischievous eyes finding mine as she bites her lip harder.

A large figure steps over me, blocking out the glaring sun.

"Whatever happened this time?" Prince Viktoryn questions tightly, a healer trailing behind him.

"Your mortal picked a fight with the Siren Princess and, to her note, killed not one but two Nixies. The Princess decided Willa would be this evening's entertainment," May says, some of her natural confidence melting away as Viktoryn kneels at my side.

My eyes flick between them, and May covers a wince when Viktoryn's shoulder brushes hers. I note the change, meeting May's eyes, but she lightly shakes her head.

"I beg your pardon?" He narrows his eyes on May and then me. "I would ask what you were thinking, but it seems you never are," he growls. "I cannot leave you to your own devices for two minutes without you getting yourself killed."

"I believe it was closer to fifteen," I counter, a week's worth of pent-up rage thrashing in my chest at the sight of him.

"Beyond the point."

May continues as if he hasn't even spoken, "I pulled her from the water. To the Siren's credit, I do not believe she knew the girl belonged to you. And to Willa's credit, I have never seen a mortal take down a Nixie, let alone two."

"If we did not have a shaky alliance with the Sea, I would rip her and her little lackey's limb from limb for touching what is *mine*," Viktoryn hisses through clenched teeth, gently pushing a stray strand of my damp hair behind my ear.

I pull away from him, and his lips flatten.

"I am not *yours*. I do not belong to you. I am not a possession to be had. I can take care of myself," I spit at him.

"Most certainly not. Seeing as you almost drowned on your first outing," Viktoryn counters. "You have not the faintest idea what you are or who you belong to. There are worse fates in this world than being mine, my darling."

Maylea flinches, the warm healing light from her hands flickering out. She shakes her hands before lowering them to my skin. Light begins to glow once more.

"But I did not drown, Your Highness. Though each time you speak, I begin to wish I did." I narrow my eyes. "I would sooner belong to the Nixies at the bottom of the lake than be yours," I hiss, pushing myself to sit even as my head rebels.

"You are *impossible*," Viktoryn shouts, mask slipping as he pushes to his feet and runs his hands through his hair. "Do you not see? Are you so blind? You *need* me. You need my protection. Look at yourself." Viktoryn gestures to me.

I feel the gaze of the crowd shift. Eyes turning towards the outburst, Viktoryn slams his mask back into place, smiling politely at the guests.

"And you are arrogant, entitled, and spoiled. But who's keeping track?" I shrug with a too-sweet smile. "I need *nothing* from you."

"You need your sister," Viktoryn counters.

I slam my mouth shut.

"That is what I thought." Viktoryn leans in. "If you were not needed by my court, I would gladly drown you myself."

"I'd like to see you try, *Prince*."

Maylea tries and fails to conceal a smirk behind her hand. Viktoryn's eyes flit with rage, his hands forming white-knuckled fists at his sides.

"Your behaviour is ridiculous. What do you wish to accomplish here, Willa? Other than near death and the stoking of my temper?" Viktoryn demands.

"The stoking of your temper is enough."

"Then I congratulate you. Well done. You nearly died, and I am angry."

The next few hours are a blur. I am transported back to the Palace and looked after by not one, not two, but three healers who work in tandem to close all my wounds in time for the ball. A ball I was certain I would be barred from attending by Viktoryn after my behaviour.

But Viktoryn does not make an appearance at all. I am not sure what to make of his absence. I don't know If I should be worried or overjoyed that he isn't giving me a lecture long enough to make me wish the Nixies did drown me.

His comments about me needing his protection nag at me. *Did he put my life in danger to prove I require his protection?* I want to doubt he would go to such an extreme to prove a point but...

The healers assure me they can heal the wounds but that there will be some scarring. Once they are satisfied with their work, they nod to each other and leave.

I find myself alone for the first time since the attack. As the adrenaline leaves my body, the emotions I had shoved down climb back up my throat, raining down on me in a thunderous crash.

A knock sounds at my door, and Alice and Beatrice enter, faces grim. I wipe away my tears with the back of my hands, but from the look they share, I am not fooling anyone.

"We heard what happened, Miss," Beatrice says calmly, crossing the room to lay a supportive hand on my knee.

"Are you alright?" Alice asks.

"I am fine," I lie, forcing a small smile. "Are you here to prepare me for the ball?"

"Yes." Beatrice looks away, sighing. "But do you require anything first?"

I swallow, shaking my head, and Beatrice gives me a knowing look. Moving closer, the bed dips as she wiggles into the spot beside me, pulling me into her arms and murmuring comforting phrases. She smells of vanilla and lilies.

The comfort is foreign to me, almost motherly. I stiffen but then melt into her. The other side of the bed dips as Alice places a hand on my back, rubbing up and down in soothing lines.

I study Beatrice's calm face, grateful both she and Alice are here. But my gaze snags on Beatrice's eyes, they do not match her calm expression. I turn to face Alice, and she gulps down a nervous breath.

"What is it that you are not telling me? I narrow my eyes on Alice, and she averts her gaze. "I know there is more. Tell me."

They share a look, Beatrice clearing her throat to cut through the tension.

"The Prince... he does nothing without purpose. He is short-tempered but long-sighted. You must be careful. I am sure you have put together that no matter your behaviour at the party... you would not have been welcomed *kindly*," she winces, "by the Fae. I do not know his motivations, but I cannot help but wonder if he is trying to prove what his protection is worth... and perhaps what your world will look like without it," Beatrice whispers, eyes full of warning. "No matter, we will be here, dear. For you, not for him."

Beatrice attaches my sheath to my thigh, adding my dagger. Alice slips the medallion into my pocket, and I don't question how she got it from my soaked dress.

I feel a wave of guilt knowing how much trouble they would be in for helping me, even in this small way.

My hair is dried and styled into an elaborate braided crown with sparkly, diamond-tipped pins holding it in place. A deep forest green silk gown drapes alluringly across my body, settling by my heels. A white underbust corset rests atop the silk, detailed with golden vines that crawl across the bodice.

Alice and Beatrice leave me to prepare. I am so busy studying myself in the mirror that I do not notice the Prince strolling in. When my eyes find his, it takes everything in me not to curse his name and demand to know what game he is playing. Instead, I turn back to the mirror, placing an indifferent expression on my face as I adjust my already perfect hair.

Viktoryn clears his throat, eyes raking over me in a way both familiar and foreign.

I turn, studying him. A gold crown tipped with rubies sits atop his tamed curls, and he flaunts a deep maroon doublet detailed with golden thread. As much as I would like to deny it, he looks handsome. The colour compliments his sun-kissed skin and golden eyes.

"You look angelic. It is a pleasant surprise as when I left, you appeared half-dead," he confesses.

"Is this how you charm all the ladies?" I snip.

"What others do you speak of? There is but only you," he says.

I say nothing, cursing the wicked butterflies igniting in my stomach, forcing them to remember this is not the man we fell in love with. They are unconvinced.

Viktoryn rolls his shoulders. "Shall we?" He offers an arm.

I hesitate, wanting to reject the escort, but he does not know that Beatrice tipped me off to his games. Doing anything that would anger him further after the lake incident, especially when seeing my sister is dependent on his forgiveness, seems unwise. I link my arm with his.

After a short walk through opulent halls, we arrive outside two large wooden double doors carved with intricate images of Fae dancing with

Cyrissa, The Goddess of the Sun, shining down on them. A bright chorus of drinking and laughing echoes from within.

"It is imperative that you behave for me this evening. You must be my perfect pet. All of The Elemental Courts are in attendance. As well as some of The Sea and Wandering Folk. I cannot afford any of your *incidents*. Your sister will be arriving shortly," he whispers, trailing off as he tracks a finger down the bare skin of my arm. "Convince me you can play the part, and you will see her this eve."

I prickle. The hair on my arm raises as his finger drags across my skin. The mention of my sister has me pulling towards the doors, but his arm tightens around mine.

He *tsks*. "So eager," he coos. "We must wait until I am announced."

"After the dance, I will escort you back to your room. You are to remain within eyesight of me at all times. Not everyone here tonight will be thrilled that you are in attendance. But as long as you are on my arm, you will be protected. I swear it."

He snares me in his gaze, eyes overflowing with threat. "Do not be foolish. If you are, I will know. You will soon learn I *always* know."

I nod, swallowing hard, all the insults I want to throw burning on the way down. I take a deep breath and plaster on my most convincing smile. This seems to please him, and he returns to his full height, signalling the guards who flank the double doors.

I am not sure what I am expecting, but when horns sound, I jump. The guards open their respective doors, and the warmth of hundreds of bodies and the smell of divine food gush through. The room hushes, all eyes turning to lock on the Prince and then I.

The Folk rise from their seats and bow.

I bite my lip to keep from gaping. The ballroom is *massive*. Three long wooden tables with matching benches line the room, all packed full with Faeries and other Fae. A large table with blood-red upholstered chairs is placed on a raised dias containing the royal family.

The rectangular ballroom is lined with floor-to-ceiling windows on the far wall—gorgeous marble arches veined in gold line three of the walls. Above each arch is a sculpted burning sun emblem made of pure gold and crystal chandeliers depicting The Goddess of the Sun holding light in her palms.

The room is centred around a large circular skylight that allows the constant sunshine to stream through. I take it all in, too stunned to notice all the hate-filled eyes that have drifted to me.

After a winded introduction and a fairly ungraceful curtsy on my part, Viktoryn speaks the magick words *'you may rise'* to release the room from their bows. They return to their food and revelry. But stray eyes track my steps towards the table at the front of the room.

Slowly, the focus shifts away from me. Without the pressure of all the eyes, I scan the crowded space. Fae of all kinds line the tables—some with shimmering, gossamer wings of rich, iridescent colours waving idly from their backs.

Winged creatures the size of hummingbirds titter with laughter, buzzing across the room, one nearly colliding into the side of my head.

Another collides with a servant's tray, sending pastries and wine flying. The guests cheer on the chaos.

Everyone is dressed in extravagant clothing and jewels. All too fantastical to be real—what appear to be *live* blue-speckled butterflies sit atop a female Fae's head, creating a crown. Another wears live red snakes as armbands, tongues darting from their mouths. I feel as if I have slipped and fallen into the pages of a storybook.

Faeries with skin as white as snow and hair as flaming as the ceremonial bonfires outside the window giggle to each other, pouring overflowing cups of wine. Beside them, Faeries with jet-black braided hair and deep brown skin seem to be playing some sort of game involving the precarious stacking of wine glasses.

My curiosity rises, I nudge Viktoryn, and he slows his steps, leaning down so I can whisper in his ear.

"Can you point out The Courts for me?" I request in an innocent tone.

He eyes me suspiciously but concedes with a sigh. "If you wish. We have four elemental courts. Summer, Spring, Autumn, and Winter. The Summer Court will be seated with us or at the middle table. Then we have The High Queens of Autumn and their Court," he says, pointing to two women seated in deep fall shades crowned with golden leaves.

"*Queens?*" I ask, a small, pleased smile gracing my lips. Cressa did not allow such unions despite heavy protests from its people.

Vikotryn peers down at me. "Indeed. The black-haired Queen is Aluma, and her red-headed wife is Queen Sorrel. Laws on marriage differ from court to court, but Autumn and Winter have both fully supported all unions for centuries," he murmurs.

I catch the underlying meaning in his words. Summer and Spring must not support all marriages. The thought makes my stomach twist. I am left wondering how many Faeries have been unable to marry who they love because of such oppressive laws.

"How do they handle heirs?" I ask, a blush spreading over my cheeks.

"Consorts. Those are their children. Three daughters, two sons. Radley, Juniper, Ceadora, Brownyn, and Aki. Princess Radley is first-born, but their court chooses an heir by vote, not age of succession. Any of their children could be the next Queen or King," Viktoryn explains, his expression wrought with disapproval.

"By our table is Spring. At the head are King Atheron and Queen Laverna. You have met Princess Maylea, Heir to The Spring Throne. She is accompanied by her younger brothers, Aviv and Cadwell."

They are all crowned in fresh flowers that seem to breathe, bloom, and sway on their heads. May wears a moss-green gown that glimmers like the skin of a snake as she moves. She sees me and winks, eyes going distant when she notes Prince Viktoryn on my arm.

"How do you know Princess Maylea? There seems to be... *history* there," I whisper.

"That is a complicated question with a convoluted answer best left untouched," he replies, hand tightening on my arm.

"Has anyone ever told you that you have a talent for answering questions?" I coo.

"Certainly not."

"Precisely," I reply, and Viktoryn frowns.

I glance away from him to hide my smile. Only to find Princess Naenia in a sapphire blue floor-length gown glaring at me. I give her a conspiratorial grin, and she tenses, returning to her food.

"The Sea Royals and The Wandering Fae are not recognized as a part of The Seelie or Unseelie Kingdoms or as part of The Elemental Courts. We seat them together. The Wandering Fae do not claim a monarch. And as for The Sea Queen herself, she does not bother to attend these tedious little events. Instead, she sends her lovely daughter and her *wonderful* friends."

"How lucky for you. Is the male that looks so much like her, her twin? If so, is he not eligible for the throne?" I question.

"Yes, that is her twin. Bahari. He is not eligible for the throne as The Sea Kingdom only recognizes female heirs," Viktoryn murmurs.

"Interesting," I murmur, grinning.

Viktoryn narrows his eyes on me, I grin brighter.

"Finally, we have Winter. Our courts do not often *associate*. I am surprised they were brave enough to show their faces here. Usually, they avoid Seelie events. Their heir is a repugnant fool with a reputation for senseless cruelty. He and a few of his court were wandering about like unwanted strays earlier, but I do not see them now. That is for the best." Viktoryn rests his hand atop mine.

"Why—"

"They are unblessed *filth*," he spits, "worshipping The False Goddess of the Moon, The Bringer of Death." I blink and Viktoryn sneers. "The Summer Court worships The One True Goddess Cyrissa."

"Like the lake?"

Viktoryn nods. "We should take our seats, the King and Queen are shooting me glances to make haste."

I nod.

I take one final look at the room, taking in all The Courts. All of the Fae are undeniably beautiful, angelic, and unique. Too bad they look at me as if they wish their glares alone could turn me to ash. I wonder if they know, for the majority, the feeling's mutual.

As we approach our table, I smooth down my skirt and swallow my nerves. At the head of our table, a regal, middle-aged, crowned male Faerie lounges. An overflowing glass of blush pink wine in his heavily ringed hands, the liquid spilling over the edges as he boasts about his last hunting adventure. Atop his head sits a ruby crown perched precariously in his silver blonde hair, his hazel eyes meet his sons with a nod.

The Prince returns the gesture with a slight grimace as he eyes his father's ever-growing pile of emptied glasses. It makes me wonder how much time his father spends intoxicated, and I feel a small ache of unwelcome sympathy for Viktoryn.

On the King's right, a middle-aged, crowned female Faerie of great beauty sits. With gorgeous long blonde hair, shot through with streaks of white, pulled back into a sleek bun. Her golden eyes are a perfect match to Viktoryn's. She accesses her son and me, shaking her head disapprovingly.

"Father, Mother, it is my pleasure to introduce you to Willa of The Mortal Lands. Willa, High King Ambrose and High Queen Florence of The Summer Court." Viktoryn bows, and I follow with a slightly better-executed curtsy.

We sit. No one speaks.

The silence presses into my skin like dead weight. The Queen's gaze is surgical, while the King shoots me a lazy look, more interested in returning to his cups.

I fiddle nervously with my fingers under the table, and Viktoryn eyes the gesture. He runs his hand up and down my arm soothingly. The Queen notes the contact and shudders, a sneer creeping onto her features.

"You said she was pretty," Queen Florence remarks.

"Mother. You promised," Viktoryn warns tightly.

"I promised to be pleasant, not dishonest, dear. She is simply so…" Her eyes drag up and down my body, two twin blades. "*Ordinary.*" The Queen's nose scrunches as if she's smelt something foul. "A being so unremarkable does not seem worth all this trouble. I will be glad when we can be rid of it. I never understood your mother's thinking." She cocks her head at me.

"No matter, you mortal mutts did us a fine favour with your delicate little life spans. So easy to extinguish." She looks at her son. "It will be nothing more than a thorn in our side before it returns to dust."

I clench my fists below the table, nails digging into my palms as bitter words burn like bile in my throat, clawing to be freed.

"I made no such promises. If I may speak freely," I do not wait for permission, "I knew the Fae were obnoxious and unmannered, but I expected better of their royalty," I drawl, meeting the Queen's eyes with a tight smile. "If this is you pleasant..." I say, dragging my unimpressed eyes over her.

Prince Viktoryn chokes on his drink, eyes wide. I meet his gaze with an innocent grin. The entire table halts, the air filling with tension as all eyes swing my way. I wait, hand drifting to my dagger.

The King's laughter booms through the room as the Queen's eyes bore into me with a flaming hatred. I meet her glare, a smile pasted on.

The Queen rises and strides towards me at a vicious speed. My body tenses as she runs her heavily jewelled hand through my hair, tugging my braids so hard my scalp burns, sending diamond pins flying.

She snaps my chair back from the table, stalking around me like a predator. She leans forward, crowding my space. My heart kicks up, but I refuse to sink in on myself.

"Someone should teach it some manners," she declares, clucking her tongue as tittering laughter fills the room.

"Likewise," I counter.

Her eyes narrow, and the Queen reaches for me, but I snatch her wrist away. Her brows contort with rage. She bares her teeth as her free hand connects with my cheek in a slap that reverberates down my jaw.

I feel each and every one of her rings on impact. The slap echoes in the now hushed room. I drop her wrist, pressing my palm to my cheek. My eyes water, but I try to ignore the pain. The Queen grips my chin in between her thumb and fingers painfully. I attempt to rip my head away, but she holds steady.

"If you did not have your uses, I would stake your head to the Palace gates for daring to touch me. I would take pleasure in watching the birds peck your eyes from your skull," she muses, eyes bright with feral delight.

Her gaze drifts to Viktoryn and then back to me. "Do try to remember you will not be of use to us forever. Be grateful for my child's mercy, if not for him, you would be rotting in our dungeon. Not wasting valuable space dressed in a pretty little gown as his precious little *pet*... I do not have my son's fascination with you. And nor will he for long—young men get bored," she promises, patting my cheek.

Rage and humiliation brew in my stomach as all eyes in the room watch us with sick satisfaction. She steps back, straightens her gown, and turns to address her Folk.

"Someone forgot to teach the mutt manners before they brought their pet to dinner." She smiles too sweetly at her son. "No matter. It shall behave. As you were."

The room turns back to their tables, pointing and laughing as my eyes water. The Queen strides back to her seat, shooting me a cruel grin. Memories of my own mother's treatment hound my head, and I shut my eyes, drawing in a breath.

Viktoryn is rigid beside me, and I dare a quick glance at him. His eyes burn, but he keeps his expression bored, indifferent as he fiddles with a crystal decanter. My hand shifts to the dagger sheathed on my thigh instinctively.

Viktoryn reaches for me, squeezing my arm hard in a warning. A whirlwind of shock crashes into me; he knows I am armed. My heart pounds harder, sweat dampening my palms.

Do not be foolish. If you are, I will know. You will soon learn I always know.

My hand relaxes as I summon every slipping ounce of my self-control. As satisfying as it might be, attacking the High Queen in her own court—surrounded by her Folk and guards—will not get me far. I'll be dead before she hits the ground.

I scoot my chair back to the table and focus on picking at the food in front of me, avoiding anything I think might be cooked with Fae Fruit. Elle's journals warned of the dangers of Fae Fruit. For mortals, consuming it causes an almost hypnotic high that leaves humans vulnerable to suggestion.

It also mentioned that the Fae do not say *'Thank You,'* as their world runs on promises, swears, vows, bargains, and offers. Deals and favours must be squared as quickly as possible. The use of the phrase implies something is still owed.

Viktoryn's fork scraps across his plate, eyes churning with emotion as I watch him piece his composure back together.

"My siblings and your sister will be arriving any moment," he whispers, eyes flicking to my reddened cheek.

I nod. I will see my sister. She is here, she is safe. That is all that matters. I roll my shoulders and dig into my food.

As much as I hate to admit that any part of this night is good, the food is incredible. I shove some spiced duck into my mouth and moan at the flavours. Everything smells and tastes divine, and the Prince has to nudge me more than once for my bad table manners.

At home, we never had an abundance of food, and if we did, it was nothing of this calibre. I had only begun eating regularly once I joined The Queen's Royal Army.

I savour every heavenly bite of the various meats, cheeses, pastries, and other goodies that line my plate. The King and Queen pay me no mind other than to occasionally glare at me like someone brought a slobbery wild hound to their party. I find with a mouth full of gooey cheese, I don't so much mind their judgements.

Horns sound again, and my ears ring. Guards announce the arrival of Prince Viktoryn's siblings. Princess Daviana enters alone in a long, flowing, daisy-yellow dress with sleeves that sweep the floor. Trailed by Prince Archer, who is escorting my sister. I note with displeasure how comfortable she looks draped on his arm.

But the sight of her alive, unharmed, and smiling sends warmth to my chest. Her familiar strawberry-blonde hair is half pulled back in an elaborate hairstyle of curls and wildflowers.

Her blood-red gown has long mesh sleeves and a full skirt. Her wrists, ears, and neck drip in diamonds. She looks every bit as royal as the Faeries beside her. She flashes me a winning smile, and I feel one creep onto my lips as well.

She reaches our table, and I jump up to pull her into an embrace. Feeling her safely in my arms, I know all of it was worth it—the Knights, the Nixies. Knowing she is safe, I would do it one hundred times over.

Gasps and shocked murmurs rise from around us, and I release my sister to see everyone in the room bowing. The realization hits me that I have interrupted the Princess and Prince's entry.

Mortification is too kind a word to describe the feeling that slides down my throat. I scoot back to my seat as my cheeks burn.

"As you were," Prince Archer commands, a smirk on his lips as he surveys me.

He lets out a strained chuckle, and Princess Daviana breaks into full-body laughter. The room joins them. I force myself to laugh along.

"My brother said you were special. But you certainly know how to make a lasting first impression, mortal." Princess Daviana's voice is confident, cool, yet surprisingly friendly.

"I like her. She's got guts," Prince Archer chimes in with a chuckle, arm wrapped around my sister.

"Guts that should be strung up as decoration," the Queen mumbles, but to my surprise, Archer and Daviana only smirk, not seeming chastised in the least.

They look similar to Viktoryn. Golden hair, golden eyes. But Prince Archer's hair is longer, a curtain of wild curls, his body leaner, face set with a sharper nose. Daviana's is darker, a sharp bob of golden brown. It makes her look mature.

I nervously glance at Elle, who seems eerily at ease, until she spots the mark on my cheek. Her eyebrows shoot up, and I shake my head, but the concern does not leave her eyes.

"Do not look too mortified. Once, Prince Viktoryn got a little too far into his cups before a ball and stumbled in here without pants," Daviana drawls.

Viktoryn's face turns crimson. "Davi!"

Daviana flashes him a feline grin, so similar to her Mother's. Prince Archer bursts out laughing, and my sister giggles. A chuckle slips through my lips.

It's so wonderful to hear her laugh, the sound bathes my body in comfort. I want to pull her away and speak to her alone. I want to scoop her up and flee to the nearest exit. But I do not think for one second Viktoryn will allow either of us out of his sight.

"You should not dare laugh, baby brother. Last year at The Summer Solstice Ball, Archer choked on a piece of baked lamb after seeing a pretty Faerie. When she passed him, he spit the pieces all over her dress," Viktoryn remarks with a sinister smirk.

"Would you have preferred that I had choked to death, *dear* brother?" Archer spits, brows pinched.

"Depends on the day."

Dinner passes without any further incident, which feels like a miracle in itself. Being in the same room as Elle but unable to whisk her away from this place leaves me buzzing with pent-up anxiety.

The long tables are whisked away, leaving the ballroom open to dance. Lively music swells in the room, played by talented Faeries who manage to dance while playing their various instruments.

The music awakens something in my bones, flooding my veins with euphoric energy. I start gently swaying in time as drunken bodies twirl around the floor.

The room comes to life with each joyful, wild note. Something Fabelle's journal mentioned about Faerie music lingers in the back of my mind, but I can't seem to recall what it was as the alluring notes caress my ears.

I scan the room to find the Faeries I wanted to approach at the lake, but the music is a delectable distraction, and I find my mind drifting away.

Prince Viktoryn parts from me with a final whispered warning. The comment doesn't instill the normal rage in me. Instead, I brush it off like a stray piece of dust.

He joins Fabelle and Prince Archer in greeting some of the guests. A task I am more than happy to be excluded from as most of the said guests cheered for my imminent death earlier.

I cringe as I watch Elle fuss over Prince Archer, smoothing his clothes as they make their rounds. But it surprisingly doesn't cause the visceral reaction I was expecting. My eyebrows draw together in confusion.

The music picks up, spinning into a symphony of frenzied notes that beckon my body like a Siren call. A lightness blankets me, easing the tension from my limbs. I find myself floating towards the dance floor, ensnared in the melody.

A handsome, young, pale green-skinned Faerie with grassy hair and molten eyes spots me wandering and offers his hand. His easy grin is contagious as I place my hand in his.

"I don't know the steps," I admit, flushing.

"Worry not. I shall teach you," he chirps with a wink.

"Apologies in advance for the damage to your feet."

"I am certain you are worth the risk," he purrs.

He smirks, pulling my body into his. His warmth mixed with the music is a heavenly combination. We spin in circles, step by step, across the floor as the green-haired Fae patiently teaches me the choreography. Laughing with me when I do inevitably step on his foot.

After a few practice runs, the steps click, and the world melts away. Only my body, the music, and the green-haired Fae remain as I drown in dizzying bliss.

I don't think about saving my sister or escape routes or Viktoryn's betrayal. I don't think about all the things I need to do and all the unanswered questions piling at my feet. I don't think about the disastrous dinner or my brush with death at the hands of the Nixies. I don't think at all.

I let myself be swooped up and entangled in the giddy notes.

Time stops, passes, rushes by, and turns the clock backwards. We dance, moments, minutes, or hours passing.

The green-haired Faerie dips me, and I chuckle. Head back, my eyes find the skylight, the moon high in the sky—a spotlight to my revelry. My tongue is cottony in my mouth. My eyebrows furrow when I spot a large midnight black raven perched on the crystal chandelier, head cocked slightly to the side, thoughtfully, as it watches me with otherworldly eyes.

I meet its gaze, and a disorienting sense of familiarity floods me. I am pulled from my avian staring contest by a voice tickling my ear.

"It seems we have an audience."

I twist my body, following his gaze to find Prince Viktoryn. His arms are crossed over his chest as he glares holes in my head from where he leans against the side of a marble alcove. His furious eyes dart from my face to the way my body is suspended in the green-haired Faerie's arms.

The pure intensity in his eyes should startle me, but I simply smile. Entirely too engrossed in the music to care about his fragile male ego.

"Let him watch," I mutter.

The green-haired Faerie grins wickedly, placing a gentle kiss on my collarbone. I flush.

By the time we've made a full circle around the floor, Viktoryn has vanished from his alcove of brooding. A happy sigh leaves my lips, my tongue darting across them. I find them chapped and painfully dry. The green-haired Faerie notes the motion, and he snatches a glass of sparkly rose liquid off a servant's tray as we glide past. I grin as he hands it to me, grateful for something to quench my merciless thirst.

I desperately gulp, spilling some down my chin. The green-haired Faerie uses his thumb to wipe away the mess. The bitter-sweet flavour floods my mouth, and a burn chases its way down my throat.

The music changes, and the Faerie begins instructing me on the steps of the new dance. I follow along the best I can, but a pleasant heated burn has bloomed in my mind and stomach.

As he leads me through the steps, the liquid in my stomach becomes an inferno of wildfire that rages in my blood and bones, leaving a dizzying sense of euphoria in its wake.

The heat expands until it's coating my body in a honey-thick rapture of ecstasy. I cling to the green-haired Faerie, the only thing in the room that is not spinning.

The music becomes wind under my wings, my body flying higher while diving deeper into the never-ending bliss until I am nothing and everything. I am someone and no one, and the green-haired Fae is simply an extension of my joy, as natural as my own limbs.

My euphoria starts bubbling up and boiling over. A sheen layer of sweat builds on my skin as my body blazes like a bonfire. I am *too* hot, but the music is hypnotizing, ensnaring my panic in a net of luxurious bliss as soon as it rises.

My head feels faint, and I stumble over the next few steps on aching feet, but the green-haired Faerie hoists me back up with ease.

All I can think is I want to stay here, in this moment, forever. I never want to leave this freedom, this bliss, this never-ending pool of pure wonder. How, if I did, I would crave this feeling like a phantom limb for the rest of my existence. Never to be this full of light and joy. The idea sounds like its own special kind of tortu—

I am yanked from the green-haired Faerie's wondrous warmth by arms that wrap around my shoulders. The arms ignore my cries of despair, my desperate protests to not be separated from this endless heaven.

The music begins to fade. I whine objections as weight slowly settles back on my bones. I squeeze my eyes shut to stop the room from spinning.

The bright lights and bodies of the ballroom are replaced by a dimly lit hallway. My feet are no longer under me, and I find myself wrapped in strong arms. The cool night air is a slap. I gasp.

"Take me back to the ballroom! I want to dance," I plead, fighting the arms that cradle me.

They pay my pleas no mind, and I let out a disappointed groan.

"You have been dancing for hours, Willa," Toryn cuts through the haze. "You would have danced until you collapsed."

"But the music is wonderful!" I giggle as I lazily survey his face. "You are so beautiful. Faeries are so beautiful." My words arrive slurred as I pet the side of his pretty, sculpted face.

Toryn closes his eyes tight and takes a slow breath as I trail my fingers down the line of his cheekbone. He shudders.

"Did someone offer you wine?" Toryn asks gently—so gently, it's almost a caress.

"Why won't you dance with me?" I ask as my heavy head lolls into his chest.

"Willa, darling. I need you to answer me. Did someone give you wine?"

"I was thirsty from all the dancing," I slur. "A nice Faerie boy with green hair and skin like grass got me a drink. He was pretty. Like you. But green... you aren't green," I say with a crinkled brow.

Toryn sighs, his grip on me tightening. "You should not have taken it—I should have warned you. I should not have left you alone." He shakes his head. "I... seeing him hold you... touch you... you were driving me *mad*." His voice is rough, eyes heated as they drag across my skin.

"Do not fret. I feel great. Better than great—*wonderful*, perfect, the best. You should have some, too. Can I have more?" I ramble.

Toryn sighs, gently placing me back on my feet. My legs wobble beneath me, and I spin in circles away from him, arms spread wide like wings as I fly across The Palace Gardens. A whoop of excitement passes my lips and at some point, I lose a shoe.

"I am so hot," I remark with a giggle as my spins slow.

Toryn laughs and then huffs another sigh. "Yes. Yes, you are, my dear…"

"No, I mean. I am too *hot*," I mutter, pulling at the shoulders of my dress and the strings of my corset.

Toryn rushes over, grasping my shoulders, steadying me, and halting my hands. He seems suddenly solemn.

"Stop, Willa. *Stop*," he demands.

"What's wrong?"

"Willa, listen to me, darling," he pleads. "Look at me, please." He gently taps my cheek. "You drank Fae Wine. For humans, it induces a dangerous high. Combined with the music, which can be hypnotic to mortals… That Fae *knew*… " He shakes his head. "The wine is causing your body to run a fever. You must settle."

He shifts his hold, lightly grasping my chin with his thumb and finger. I wince, the spot still sore from the Queen's iron grip, and his hold lightens. Toryn guides my eyes to his own. Those breathtaking, heated golden eyes are as intoxicating as the wine.

My heart kicks up. His breath is close, so close, *too* close, and yet not close enough. And it seems to take a tremendous amount of effort for him not to close the distance between us, his chest heaving. He looks almost wild as his gaze dips to my parted lips.

I push onto my tiptoes, placing my knitted fingers behind the nape of his neck, dragging him closer.

I kiss hi—

He breaks away, stumbling backwards as his expression turns haunted. He shakes his head violently as if clearing it before running his fingers through his hair, knocking his crown to the ground.

I halt, my eyes roaming over the shiny gems. Toryn does not offer it a glance.

"Willa," he pleads breathlessly. "Do not. You cannot do this. I will not..."

"Don't be sad, let me fix it. Let me fix this." I smile, stepping towards him. He tenses as I place my hands on his chest.

"You cannot fix what I have broken," he mutters. "You cannot fix what I still must break."

I don't understand. I want to help. I want to kiss the pain away.

I lean into him, but he doesn't budge, staring at me like I have a dagger aimed at his heart. I throw my arms down at my sides in protest. He grips me when my legs wobble.

I reach for him once more, but he pushes me back. I stumble to the ground, rear planted in the grass. I grunt as pain shoots up my tailbone.

"*Do not,*" he growls. "It is but the effects of the wine. You do not want to kiss me, and I will not kiss you. Not like this. *Never* like this," he vows. Not unless it is real. This... *this* is not real, Willa."

"You do not want *me*. I know I am not the perfect male. But I will not allow you to kiss me when you are like this. You would never forgive me…" his voice cracks.

Toryn turns away from me and stalks off as if he cannot stand being near me. Like my proximity is painful. My mere presence is a plague from which he no longer wants to suffer. It should hurt, but my heart is still wrapped in a blanket of Fae Wine joy.

I sigh and lean back into the cool grass, letting the overwhelming warmth melt away. I shut my eyes, inhaling the sweet smell of sea salt and summer flowers. A soft grunt slips by in the wind, but I am too engrossed in my own blissful relaxation to pay it any mind.

I am scooped off the grass like I am weightless, endless, *flying*. The smell in the air shifts to pine trees and cranberries. I inhale deeply, and a pleasant hum parts my lips.

"Toryn." I chuckle. "You smell divine."

Toryn does not answer.

"Toryn, are you alright? Why are you so sad?" I ask.

"Not Toryn, Princess."

"Where is Toryn?" I question.

"Worry not, love. *Toryn* will be fine after he sleeps off the nice little bump I delivered to his head. Although, I have to admit that may be the least of his injuries. You managed not only to bruise but obliterate his ego. Impressive."

"Who would have thought The Golden Prince could be *oh-so-mortally* wounded by such a delicate little creature? It was truly a pity to interrupt the show." He chuckles delightfully. "I cannot say I find anything more pleasing than watching The Fire Prince marinate in his own self-made misery, but we, dear thing, have a schedule to keep," the voice drawls. "We are going on a little trip. A side quest of sorts." The voice sounds boyish, deep, and vaguely familiar.

I nod gently, the fatigue a blanket of iron coating my bones. I lean my head into the chest of the voice, eyes closed, bathing in the warmth and hard muscle. Their hand rubs soothing circles on my arm, and I hum a happy noise.

"Can I tell you a secret?" I murmur.

"Of course, Princess, do share with the group. I am always craving a delicious secret."

"Okay, but don't tell. You are so warm, and you smell delicious," I whisper, giggling.

"That is not a secret but a very well-known fact," the male purrs.

"This was not part of the plan, Raven," a snarky female voice I don't recognize warns.

"Amira's right, boss man. I do not like this," a velvet-deep male voice replies.

The disagreement is interrupted.

"Toryn stole my sister, but she looks so happy, and I am very mad at him. How can she be happy? She was kidnapped! She hardly looked at me... *Oh!*" I sigh. "Do you want to know another secret? He's still handsome, and I hate myself for loving him. I hate him. I hate his stupidly handsome face. I hate his scheming. I hate this place."

"You tell him, Princess," someone chuckles.

"Did you know I escaped? Well... tried to." I wrinkle my nose. "But I ran into a thief. A *gorgeous* wine thief. Oh! And the thief, he had stunning eyes, stormy eyes. Toryn would be so mad, and he should be! I want him to be. I want him to feel what I feel."

"I cannot believe he let anyone call him *Toryn*," the female mutters.

Someone laughs in agreement.

"No, it was not part of the plan," Raven answers. "But we will not argue when someone moves to make our job easier. And I always welcome some chaotic improvisation, keeps me sharp." A hand pushes my hair behind my ear gently. "And she will be fine, right, Princess?"

I hum cheerily. "See! The Prince got her cooled off, well... *mostly.*" Raven chuckles darkly, and the sound is so pleasant that as sleep beckons me into the darkness, I follow it happily.

I dream of Elle. She leads me through a forest, giggling. She's too fast, and I am stumbling across the forest floor, bare feet tearing open on roots and rocks, desperately pleading with her to slow down. She grins at me over her shoulder and winks.

Every time I catch up, my hand brushes hers, and she takes off at full speed, out of reach. Slipping through my grasp over and over. Exhaustion plagues my body, but I force myself to continue running. My legs ache.

Caleb, the Knight I killed, appears in the tree line with Brandon, both soaked in blood. Brandon, cradling his severed head in one hand, sword in the other, mouth open in a silent scream. I scream, begging for forgiveness.

"I am so sorry. I'm sorry."

Hot tears run down my face, and my bare feet burn, damp with blood and caked with thick mud.

A raven squawks in a warning. The forest around me bursts into blazing flames, corralling me as Elle continues to bound through the trees, un-

aware, dodging the flames with ease. Her giggling echoes through the trees hauntingly, the moon a spotlight to my desperation.

The air is filled with ash and smoke. Every breath is a battle of unbearable heat that burns the flesh of my lungs. Ash coats my body like an oversized coat.

The sky glows devilish red. Fire barrelling towards me in an unnatural way, boxing me in. My skin blisters, I open my mouth to scream, but nothing comes out.

I hear my father screaming for me to run. But this time, I can't run. I am trapped. I try to scream again, but nothing happens. A body forms in the flames... a body of flames. A feminine shape with long hair of red fire, blue flames forming a living gown around her.

She does not burn, completely at home in the blaze. Her gaze finds mine, curiosity and recognition flickering in her eyes. A familiar medallion glows around her neck, immune to the all-consuming flames. When she speaks, her voice is soft, kind, but strong.

"Don't be afraid of the flames. You were born to burn," she whispers, smiling, her voice reverberating off the flames, sounding from everywhere and nowhere. "Trust only yourself. Trust the fire. Do not trust another soul. Power corrupts them all."

Her voice is calm, but I am so afraid. I am trembling. Her words rattle in my mind.

You were born to burn.

You were born to burn.

You were born to burn.

The flames lick in closer, and I cannot move without being burned. This time, when I open my mouth to scream, the sound is haunting, inhuman.

I jolt awake with a scream, my chest heaving wildly. My hands brush over my skin as the feeling of my flesh bubbling and blistering lingers. My heart races at the vividness of the dream. It felt *real*.

Blinking the sleep from my eyes, the room around me comes into focus. The bed I am in is unfamiliar. My heart skips a beat or ten when I feel the medallion in my dress pocket, warm and thrumming. My hand slips to cover it, and the sensation dies.

The dazzling room is made of pure *ice*—intricate designs carved into each wall. Around me are shelves lined with gold-foiled books, a square window detailed with swirling designs of falling snowflakes, and rich, deep blue sheets swathed over my body. It is surreal and marvellous.

Based on the ice walls alone, it's easy to determine I am no longer in The Summer Court.

I move to slide off the bed, but my eyes lock on a pair of all-too-familiar stormy eyes. I swallow a yelp of surprise. In a dark blue velvet settee beside the bed, ankle over his knee, sits the wine thief. His default, smug expression plastered on his far too-perfect face. Hand instantly on my dagger, I leap from the bed and pin him, pressing the sharp blade into the delicate flesh of his neck.

"Is this how you say good morning in the mortal realm? Or am I so attractive you could not help but jump at the first opportunity?" he drawls, unaffected.

My blush is catastrophic, and I want to slice the smugness right off his pretty face.

He wears the same rings and earrings. Nails still painted black. But his cloak has been replaced by fine navy blue slacks, held in place by a chic silver belt and a creamy white tunic. A small, crown-like, silver band imprinted with snowflakes and tipped with diamonds sits crooked in his curly blue-black hair. Without the cloak, I can confirm what I believed. He is lean, sculpted, and ungodly, *irritatingly* handsome.

My heart pounds and my stomach flips. He does not struggle, completely at ease under my body and blade. I press into him further, securing my hold and ensuring he cannot break free. The contact knocks something in my memory free. A book fallen from a shelf, pages flying open as it lands on the ground. Flashes of a dizzying high and the events of the night return to me as a flood of open pages.

Oh, gods. I tried to *kiss* Prince Viktoryn and *strip* in The Palace Gardens. I wish for nothing more than to sink into the floor and vanish completely. Becoming one with the stone and never, ever having to think about that evening again.

The thief's body under mine is suddenly too much, too close, as the vivid memories return in increasingly embarrassing flashes. I shift, self-conscious of all the places our bodies meet. My blush deepens, but I force my features to remain neutral and cold. He smirks, one of his eyebrows raised as if he knows exactly where my mind has wandered.

"Who are you? Where am I? Where is Viktoryn?" I demand.

"Now, now, Princess," the thief *tsks*. "It is incredibly rude to stab someone with their *own* dagger. Especially when they so kindly gifted it to you in a time of *need*." His eyes find mine, amusement twinkling. He ever-so-slightly tilts his head. "On a first-name basis with The Fire Prince, I see. You must be very, very important. He is usually far more detached from his lovers."

I shudder at the use of *lovers* and ignore the sinking feeling in my gut that rises along with it.

"You think I worry about being rude? How sweet. And I have not stabbed you *yet*. Though the day is young, and my temper is short. Answer my questions," I hiss, increasing the pressure of my dagger, blood pooling under the blade.

He *chuckles*. And my anger flares. Blade to his neck, and he's *laughing* at me. His eyes glint with playful trouble as if this is all a game to him.

He wants to play? *Fine.*

I draw my dagger back, and his body relaxes—a mistake. I jam my knee between his legs, and he doubles over into me with a groan that fades into a breathless chuckle. I ignore the closeness of his lips. I return my blade to his neck, pinning him tighter.

"Just couldn't wait to get your hands on it, couldn't you?" he wheezes.

"That was my *knee*, and I would not be laughing if I was in your position. Answer me, or I will gut you like a fish and leave you here to rot, thief."

His eyes find mine, and a vicious smile grows on his lips. He smiles like he has a secret—like we are both in on an inside joke.

I jump as someone speaks from behind me. I curse myself for my foolishness, I should have ensured we were alone. I cannot think straight around this wretched being of stormy eyes and darling dimples.

"She really is *feisty,* albeit foolishly brave. Please do, gut him, you would be saving us an awful lot of trouble." She pauses. "I would, however, have to gut you in return, but I have no qualms with doing so," a female voice announces.

"You would be doing us a favour. He lives for trouble, and I am the unfortunate soul tasked with cleaning up his messes," a male voice groans.

Panic grasps me in both hands, twisting my stomach into knots. I cannot unpin the thief, but having my back exposed is a death wish. I might as well request they start playing a funeral song. I turn my head to meet the female's gaze, narrowing my eyes.

She's tall with deep brown skin and cat-like topaz eyes. Her pointed ears and glowing eyes mark her as a Faerie. Her thick, braided black hair is thrown over her shoulder, with features as sharp as the dozen of weapons lining her leathers.

My eyes slide to the male humanoid. I note right away the lack of glowing eyes or pointed ears. He towers over the female, nearly seven feet tall, broad as a bear, with brown hair and skin a cool greyish white. A light dusting of hair covers his chin and upper lip. With eyes so dark they gleam obsidian, my heart races as images of the Nixies' void eyes flash in my mind.

Most surprisingly are the curved *horns* sprouting from the top of his head like a ram. Despite his frightening build, his face remains thoughtful.

The thief takes advantage of my distraction and pushes his hips to the side, breaking my hold with remarkable skill and speed. Disarming me as he flips our bodies, pinning me in a hold identical to the one I had him in.

My dagger clatters to the ground, and a frustrated grunt leaves my lip as the tantalising smell of pine and cranberry invades my senses. He chuckles playfully, eyes full of challenge. I attempt to sweep myself out of his hold, but he maintains it, scanning my face.

The more I struggle, the deeper his smirk grows until it becomes a *devastating* smile. I can't decide if I want to punch or kiss that stupid, arrogant, infuriating look off his face.

"Are you quite finished, sweet creature?" he purrs. "This is no way to treat your heroic rescuers."

"I didn't need to be rescued."

He considers this, head tilting to the side, eyes assessing me with equal parts calculation and heat. He catalogues every visible scar and freckle, his gaze lingering on my green dress and the fabric covering the worst of my scarring from the Nixie attack.

"Your escape attempt in the cellar and all-out war with the Nixies seems to prove otherwise. Don't you think?" he queries.

"You were there. In the cellars. You could've helped me," I accuse.

"Who do you think left the daggers, Princess?" He raises a brow. "We both know you do not need a Knight in shining armour, and I have never claimed to be one. What kind of male would I be if I did not let a lady fight her own battles?" he muses, thumb rubbing distracting circles on the inside of my pinned wrist.

"Furthermore, my help would have made the whole ordeal far less entertaining. You put on quite the show... And if you recall, I *did* offer you my assistance. A very generous bargain on my part—but you refused." He grins, and I start regretting not slitting his throat when I had the chance.

"Generous? *Entertaining?* You mean to tell me you stuck around to watch me fight for my life as if it was some sort of cheap fair attraction?" I seethe, narrowing my eyes at him while wondering where he managed to watch from when I searched the room extensively.

He ignores that I have spoken at all, and somehow, that is worse than his arrogant quips. A white-hot blaze of rage shoots through my veins like a lightning strike, burning up my panic. My hands curl into fists, fingernails digging into my palms with a satisfying, sharp sting. His thumb stills on my wrist as he peers at my fists before resuming his circles.

He leans in, lips brushing the shell of my ear. "Relax, beautiful girl. No need to harm yourself. I mean you no harm."

I let my fists uncurl, and he leans back, tilting his head to address his companions. "Amira, darling, would you mind? My hands are rather... *occupied*," he winks at me, "and while she could not do me much harm, I would prefer to start my morning without a dagger in my chest. I usually prefer a strong herbal tea."

"Couldn't do you much *harm*?" I shout, exasperated. "Did you forget that mere moments ago, I had you pinned with a blade to your throat?"

"*Oh*, my sweet creature," he says gently as if comforting a child throwing a fit, lips twitching. "I could never forget that," he purrs. "Nevertheless, I *let* you pin me. I was curious to see what you would do." He shrugs. "And my morning has been rather dull. If I were trying, Princess, you never would have made it off the bed."

A string of rather foul curses slip from my lips as I let him know exactly what I think of him and his little games. His smile only deepens, sending me into a spiral of rage.

"I'm surprised that, with a mouth like that, Prince Viktoryn did not cut out her tongue. He is not known for his patience," the horned being notes, tone thoughtful.

Nothing to indicate he is mocking or joking—simply that he's making a factual observation. I shoot him a death glare anyway for good measure, and he holds his palms up in a pacifying gesture.

Amira scoffs at us, rolling her eyes so hard it's a wonder they don't plop out of her head. Moving with a silent, deadly grace, she unsheaths the dagger from the thief's belt, dangling it in the air in front of me.

The eerily silent way she moves reminds me of a wraith, and I make a note to stay on her good side. To my own damnation, the moon pattern on the dagger is a match to the ones left for me.

I sigh. If this group wanted me dead, they have had ample opportunity to make it so. And they wouldn't waste their time trying to prove we are on the same side. I still don't know what angle they are working and that leaves me unsettled. I eye the three of them suspiciously.

"Why?" I question. A single word that holds a landslide of questions within it.

Why help me? Why sneak into The Ember Palace? Why wait to take me from the ball? Why did you think kidnapping me was the only way to get me to leave with you? Why leave the daggers? Why try to prove to me I can trust you?

"What do you want from me?" I demand.

"That is a *loaded* question," Amira says, fiddling with a dagger she pulled from her belt.

"You don't say," I mutter, my gaze drifting to the giant horns on the head of the pale, bear-sized being.

"Is there any particular reason you seem to be unable to stop gawking at me?" the horned being asks.

"Apologies. I uh... like your horns," I try, clearing my throat.

The thief smirks and I glare at him.

"Have you never encountered a troll?" the being that is now confirmed to be a Troll asks as I attempt to wrap my mind around his existence.

I blink a few times. "I cannot say I have. The mortal world was sorely lacking in Trolls," I say carefully. "May I ask your name? All of your names, actually. If you wish for me to trust you, names would be a good start."

"I am called Olden, and this is Amira."

Amira waves at me with her blade, not bothering to look up as she begins to pick her nails with it.

"I have a proposition for you, sweet creature. Let's say I unpin you, retrieve your dagger, and in return, you wait to stab me until after I offer you an explanation for our... rather extreme methods. If you still wish to stab me after, I can arrange that for you. I do not deny that beautiful, vicious women with blades are rather appealing to me," the thief drawls, eyes wandering recklessly across my body.

"If that's true, there is something *very* wrong with you," I say coolly, even as my traitorous cheeks flush.

"Oh, you have no idea," Amira remarks.

Olden shifts on his feet.

"What do you say?" Raven asks.

I suck in a breath and consider my options. The thief has had ample opportunity to kill me and instead has offered me help. However minimal or unasked for. I was alone in the cellar, and the night of the dance, I could barely stand, let alone fight. If he wanted me dead, I would be.

If the ice walls and the blizzard roaring outside the window are any indicators, I am more than likely in The Winter Court. A court Viktoryn often regards with a suspicious amount of disgust. I may not know the exact details or politics, but The Summer and Winter Court are obviously at odds.

And I am in an unknown land without any allies. I do not have the luxury of being too picky.

Seated in the grand adjoining dining chamber, my dagger returned to my sheath in a show of good faith. I glare at the three potential allies sitting across from me. Food and drinks line the table as if the thief already knew what my answer would be to his request. And that I would need to eat and drink soon.

He's right. And I begin to fear that he plans to make a habit of it. He is tricky and clever and five steps ahead of me. I do not like it. I do not like him.

I scan the food, juicy plump berries with a fluffy white dip, various puff pastries, and a tray filled with a small army of cheeses. My stomach growls viciously, but I do not make a move to take any. Not risking the possibility of poison or more Fae trickery. The thief seems to read this as he watches my assessment of the table.

We sit in a silent standoff, both studying the other with a calculated gaze. He clears his throat and gathers a plate of food, picking at his selection. After a few minutes, when he remains alive, conscious, and breathing, I gather a plate of my own, unable to block out the rumbling monster in my stomach.

"We have not been formally introduced. However, I know exactly who you are, Willa Capri," he remarks, and my stomach tumbles at the way my name rolls smoothly off his lips. "But I fear you do not."

I narrow my eyes on him.

Games upon games. It is clear that's how he operates. His every action is a calculated move to ensure a desired outcome. Moves and counter-moves. Letting me pin him, the already-set table, and the use of my full name when it hasn't been provided.

All deliberate choices to feel out a potential ally or opponent. To see how I react, what I will let slip, and what manages to unnerve me. The look in his eyes tells me he knows the level of calculation spinning around in my mind too. He seems almost... *pleased*.

"I know who I am, and I would rather hope you do as well. Or do you make a habit of kidnapping... pardon me, '*rescuing*,' all the girls you corner and court in The Summer Court wine cellars?"

"He does not have to. Fae flock to him," Amira scoffs. "They all but skip into his bed like wide-eyed, love-sick puppies," she snarks.

"Amira, do not be so crass," Olden grumbles.

"When did Trolls become such prudes?" Amira snips.

"Shall we begin?" Olden asks with a sigh, avoiding Amira's question.

"We shall," Raven announces. "My name is Raven Winslow. I am The Prince of The Unseelie Winter Court, Heir to The Fierce Frosted Throne." Raven gestures dramatically at the extravagant ice walls. "Welcome to The Crystal Palace, Willa. This is my... associate, Amira, and my most trusted advisor, Olden," Raven declares.

I am pleased to be correct about my assumption that I am in The Winter Court. Less pleased that I am speaking with The Winter *Prince*.

I groan. "Of course. A *Prince*! Precisely what my life needs. *More* Faerie Princes."

Amira snorts a laugh.

"I understand your hesitation to trust us. Especially with your past... *associations* with The Summer Prince. But I swear to you we can be of help. How much has Prince Viktoryn," Raven chews on the vowels of Viktoryn's name like each letter is bitter on his tongue, "informed you about Elphyne's four Elemental Courts?"

"Past *associations*," I scoff. "That is one way to word it... Viktoryn has told me very little," I confess with a sigh.

"Yes. I understand you may have developed a certain... distaste for the Fae after what has occurred surrounding your sister and Prince Viktoryn," Olden murmurs.

"A distaste," I laugh. "Since meeting the Fae, I have been kidnapped *twice*, slapped, compulsed, drowned, strangled, and threatened. Distaste may not be the right word to describe the strength of my feelings... How do you know about my sister?" I question, shifting my narrowed gaze to him.

It's Amira who replies with a wicked grin. "It seems you have had quite the adventure. We know this because we have a network of spies in every court in Elphyne. *My* spies," she states.

Something occurs to me. "If you have spies crawling around every corner of The Summer Court, why in the name of the Gods were you sneaking around the wine cellars, *Prince*?"

"Exactly what I told you then, *Princess*. Summer Court wine is delectable. I guess you know that now. Don't you?" Prince Raven grins, tilting his head in a way that feels entirely too animalistic.

I do know. All too well. My breath stills as memories of that dizzying high rush through my head. My cheeks heat.

"And alas, sending my spies to retrieve wine would be an utter insult to their skills. And it would not leave me with the opportunity to bump into charming damsels in distress," Raven purrs, eyes drifting to my lips.

"I am not a damsel in distress," I hiss, rolling my eyes. "You're incredibly obnoxious! You kidnap me, insult my skill, and now expect me to sit pretty as you *ogle* me. It's like you're begging for my blade to find a home in your chest."

"Humour me, my sweet creature. I would love to see you try," Raven replies, lips turned in a taunting grin. "Come on, you can do it, come here," Raven curls his fingers, beckoning me forward and patting his lap. "Bring my dagger. I would love to see what you have got."

I force my eyes away from him as my heart flutters in my chest. Gritting my teeth, I huff out a frustrated breath and remove my dagger from its sheath.

Bringing my arm down in an arc, I slam the blade into the fleshy wood of the table while glaring holes in his head. The blade vibrates from the impact, swaying. The Prince looks dangerously amused, crossing his legs at his ankles, completely at ease as he shoves his hands into his pockets.

"So very angry," he taunts.

"*Beware*... we are in the presence of The Great Slayer of Tables," Amira drawls, trembling in fake fear. I glare at her, and she smirks.

My gaze returns to Raven. "Has anyone ever told you that you're unbearably arrogant?"

"You misspeak—you mean undeniably charming," he amends with a wink.

I prickle.

"Could you two stop your deadly courting long enough for us to get to the important issues at hand?" Amira snarks, still fiddling with a blade.

"I am not *courting* anyone. I wouldn't court him even if my life depended on it," I say, scoffing.

"That can be arranged," Raven drawls.

"Traditionally, the male courts the femal—" Olden signs. "Nevertheless, I second Amira's notion," he grumbles, rubbing his temples.

"Am I dreaming, or does Table Slayer have the Troll and I on the same page for once?" Amira says, and Olden huffs, but a small smile graces his lips.

Raven stares at me for a heated moment, but then he concedes, adjusting his crooked crown and diving headfirst into a history lesson, leaving me reeling with emotional whiplash.

Raven explains the basics of Elphyne. How The Courts are split into two kingdoms, ruled by four courts. The Seelie Kingdom contains

Summer and Spring, and The Unseelie Kingdom houses Winter and Autumn. The magicks of the lands are balanced equally between the four courts. And the power of Elphyne and of the Fae are simply an extension of nature, the land, and the balance between seasons.

When the power between courts is balanced, its Folk remain healthy and freely connected to magicks. When The Courts become unbalanced, the usually immortal Fae grow weaker and sick, aging more quickly. Unable to access their power without it costing them greatly.

Unbalanced magicks can cause unnatural disasters within the borders of the weakened courts. Magickally unstable events like dangerous storms, tornadoes, hurricanes, droughts, food shortages, and waves of incurable sickness. I nod along, wondering what any of this has to do with me, or my sister for that matter.

Olden hands Raven a map. He unrolls it, the worn parchment crinkling on the table. I scan the map of Elphyne—a singular large island. Hard to escape without a boat or the faintest clue where the mortal lands are, though. I am disheartened by that fact.

The land is divided into five main quadrants that all exist in their own unique weather patterns in direct correlation to their court. This explains how there is a blizzard raging outside The Winter Court window, but The Summer Court remains in perpetual sunshine.

The Spring Court sits on the northwestern side of the island, bordering The Summer Court, which sits in the northeast split by Cyrissa Lake.

The Autumn Court is directly below The Spring Court separated by a river that opens into The Bay of Renewal. The Winter Court sits under The Summer Court, separated by sprawling mountains and a river.

In between The Seelie and Unseelie Courts is a strip of farmland and forests that have been claimed by The Wandering Fae—thus named The Land of The Wandering Fae. These Fae have managed to evolve their powers without holding an elemental court. They do not claim any of the four elemental monarchs, choosing to govern their own people in alliance with The Fae of the Sea.

I try to hide my utter shock when they reveal The Fae of the Sea includes Mermaids and Faeries who live *underwater*. All ruled by the oh-so-lovely Sirens.

I simply nod, unsure of what to do with the slap of impossible but very real information. I have been swept away by a rogue stork and dropped into a land of make-believe. First Faeries, then Sirens, Nixies, Trolls, and now Mermaids. All *real*. All things, a few weeks ago, I would've believed to be beings of *fictional* fantasy stories.

I feel my mind fracture and split, adjusting to house an entirely new world, shattering through old beliefs of real and pretend, healing to account for my new reality.

Prince Raven explains that ten years ago, The Summer Court was overthrown by a group of radicals who believed that Summer should have more power and control over the four courts. They viewed Unseelie Fae as impure, lesser beings because they were not '*blessed*' by Cyrissa, The Goddess of the Sun, The Seelie God of Light and Life.

They viewed Esmerae, The Goddess of The Moon—The Unseelie God of Death and Rebirth—as a demonic force adopting the belief that anyone who was not a pure Seelie-born Fae as an inferior being.

They staged a coup, overthrowing High Queen Valda of The Summer Court and stealing her throne. They murdered her, her family, and anyone from her bloodline who may have a claim to the throne, or so they thought. Queen Valda was a wise ruler. She had spies and caught wind of the plan, leaving her a month to prepare. But the Queen had only enough time to create a contingency plan.

"*You,* beautiful creature, are that contingency plan."

I burst into laughter. He has to be kidding. "That's a joke, *right*?" I meet Raven's eyes first, then Amira's, then Olden's. They all carefully shake their heads. "Please tell me you're joking," I plead.

"I understand this is shocking. For your safety, Queen Valda ensured you would never know who you really were... You have grown up in the mortal world believing that your parents are the mortals who raised you," Raven says.

My mind is reeling, his words flowing into my head but refusing to settle like a mismatched puzzle.

"Whatever do you mean? Why would you say such a thing?" I snap, pushing away from the table with such force that the chair legs squeal and scrape as flashbacks of my mother's abuse slam into me.

A hailstorm of nightmarish memories pelt my skull, each more disturbed and painful than the previous. Ice-cold dread and confusion coat my mind until it's frozen solid, an impenetrable wall against these lies and manipulations.

Before I can recover, someone is speaking again, ripping my world apart like a loaf of bread, tossing the pieces away to be gobbled up by birds of prey.

A sweat breaks out along my neck, my hands tremble, and my heart beats furiously as it tries to escape the jail of my ribcage. As if it can run from this, protect me from this.

"The mortal woman you know as your mother was a human servant contracted to the Queen," Olden adds gently, leaning forward, his face twisted with concern.

"Why would a Faerie Queen pay some woman to pretend to be my mother? That is ridiculous. If what you say is true, why didn't my mortal mother tell me? Why didn't she leave?" My voice shakes.

I cannot seem to care that I am saying too much. Offering these near strangers too much about my life, too much leverage. This is not the smart way to play this game, but my head is spinning like a runaway dandelion seed caught in storm winds. And this isn't a game anymore—this is my life.

"The contract included an enchantment that prevented her from revealing the truth. For your and your sister's protection. The servant was not pleased to leave Elphyne for the mortal lands. But the Queen held her soul contract. She had no say in the matter," he continues.

"Was not *pleased*?" I shake my head. "For my protection?" I laugh in pure, wild disbelief, a manic buzz of fury settling on my crawling skin. "Does Valda know what her *protection* bought me?"

My chest cleaves open, a raging river of years of suppressed pain flowing freely into the open cavern between my ribs, turning crimson as it mixes with my hemorrhaging heart. Blinding, white-hot rage douses the pain and leaves me shaking.

The woman I believed was my mother, the very woman who spent countless years starving and beating me, is no more related to me than a stranger on the street. The woman who I spent years *pleading* to love me, to care about me, to see me, wasn't even my mother...

I lost *years* trying to figure out why she hated me so much. Years trying to be the perfect daughter. And she was nothing more than a disgruntled servant fighting against a life she never wished for.

A life she hated and raged against. A life raising me, raging against *me*. A child. A child who could not understand why *nothing* she did was ever enough. A child who spent all the hours of the day wondering what she did that was so terrible, so *unforgivable*, to deserve her mother's abuse.

A child whose identity had turned into desperately attempting to be smart, kind, quiet, and good enough to please her mother. Trying to please someone who never *wanted* her, never loved her, never cherished her. Who never would.

"You are a *liar*," I growl to no one in particular as the room spins—but some part of me, no matter how small, knows it is true.

"I sincerely apologise, Willa, that this is how you have to find out." Raven draws in a fortifying breath. "Your mother was Queen Valda Caprimore. Queen of The Summer Court and of The Ember Palace, a beloved and powerful Faerie before she was assassinated..."

A roaring has started in my ears, swallowing all the sounds in the room until all I can feel is how hard my heart is pounding in my chest.

"T-this... That is not possible," I whisper. "Valda was a *Faerie*. I am a human, mortal. Fabelle is human. I am not a Faerie," I argue.

"It is not that simple, Willa. Faeries can have human children. It is rare as most Faeries would never *want* mortal children." Raven winces, seeming to realize what he has said.

"Let me clarify, most immortals would never wish for their children to be chained to a mortal lifespan, to mortal weaknesses. But despite our long lifespan, Faerie women rarely bear children; it's an unfortunate deficiency of our species. To account for it, human women are often brought to Elphyne as brides to ensure that our bloodlines do not die out," he says, raising his palms in a pleading motion when my eyes meet his burning with rage.

My hand reaches for the handle of my dagger, still standing tall in the wood of the table at the mention of human brides. I yank it free, cringing as I think of all the young women who have disappeared in Mayfair. It is not an illogical leap to wonder if this is where they are ending up. My rage only builds at the thought of those poor families and girls.

Something strikes me suddenly. "Wait, is that why you call me *Princess*? Am I technically some sort of lost princess?" I gawk at him.

"Not technically. You *are* a Princess. By blood and birth, you are the rightful heir to The Summer Court Throne... But *I* call you as such because I like the way you turn beet red when I do." Raven winks, flashing me a lethally charming smile, but the action does not erase the wariness swimming in his eyes.

I have the sudden sensation that my life is a ball of yarn, being cut and unravelled in every direction. The threads of all I have known are being tugged away to nothing. A *Princess*. The thought is almost laughable.

I have spent my life resenting everything royalty stands for. Hating that some live elevated, luxurious lives while so many suffer. Hating that there seems to be no rhyme or reason to who gets to live in luxury instead of being battered on all sides by poverty. Only to be raised onto the very platform I have rebelled against.

My stomach churns, and I ball my hands into fists, nails digging into my palms until blood wells in their wake. I am barely grasping the last thing Raven uttered when he starts speaking again. And some part of me wants to scream at him, to shut up, to stop, to end this madness. To halt the sensation of my reality falling apart and being loosely sewn back together every time he opens his mouth.

"Queen Valda Caprimore fell in love with a human guard of The Unseelie Winter Court. When a human man and a Faerie mate, the result is almost always human. Hence why it almost never occurs—it is considered a grave insult to Faerie bloodlines. The radicals were already displeased with your mother's choice to take someone of Unseelie blood as her husband. Especially an Unseelie mortal. But she paid them no mind, she loved your father fiercely and thus ignored the warnings and unrest it caused in her court. The result was you and your sister..." Raven continues, seemingly unaware of the hurricane of horror his declarations are causing me.

"That's impossible, you said her entire line was killed," I mutter, grasping for any proof that what he says cannot be based in truth.

"*Almost* her entire line. The unrest caused by your birth pushed the radicals to action. They believed she had tarnished The Royal Summer Court bloodline with not only mortal blood but Unseelie blood. They viewed this as an unacceptable, treasonous insult to The Summer Thron—"

"My birth was an insult? *Wow.* I truly have been driving everyone mad before I could even utter a word," I mutter.

Raven narrows his eyes on me. "This is important, Willa..." He smooths down his shirt and continues. "Furious, the radicals spent years planning and growing in force. Queen Valda knew the forces gathering against her were strong. That it was only a matter of time before the rebels would move to overthrow her, but she had no idea just how far the plague of this sick ideology had spread. How strong they truly would be when they finally attacked."

"She began planning with your father, William, to find a way to protect her daughters and her court. She pleaded with The Goddess of The Sun to find a way to ensure your safety and the Kingdom's. The Goddess of The Sun granted her wish, believing your mother's intentions were pure. That she only wanted to protect her people and her family out of love. Thus, the Goddess transferred some of The Courts' power from the land into *you*. The power of The Summer Court lives in your very bones."

I want to call him a liar. To claim all he says is false, that he doesn't know what he's talking about. But Elle's journal confirmed that *Faeries cannot lie.* And in a deep, buried, forgotten part of my soul, it *feels* true.

A part of my soul sings every time he mentions my true mother's name. Like a glowing piece of me that's been missing all of these years. Hearing my father's real name aloud makes my heart ache, knowing I was named after the one Queen Valda cherished most.

But that does not stop the dizzying feeling of the ground slipping from beneath my feet. My body thrown from one truth to another, slamming into the ground only for it to slip away again.

I am falling.

Free falling from my own precarious sense of reality with each new truth revealed. My legs tremble, and a wave of dizziness slams into me. My fingers reach to grip the back of my chair for stability, nails biting into the wood, my legs rebelling against my weight. I have the sense that I cannot pull enough air into my lungs. I am not sure I am breathing.

"Woah, easy there, Table Slayer," Amira warns, standing and reaching for me.

"What does that mean?" I demand as Amira leads me back to my seat.

She helps me to my chair and I nod at her in thanks. I sit. No longer trusting my wobbling legs or the free-falling Earth to support the weight of my body.

The news continues to crest and fall.

"We understand that you have questions. We had no indication of how much The Summer Court told you, if anything," Olden murmurs, voice warm and cautious.

Any mask of calm or arrogance I walked into this conversation with has shattered. I have never felt more like a child. A terrified little girl in over her head. A brand new rage is birthed for Viktoryn and his trickery. His initial betrayal feeling so utterly insignificant compared to the real truths he was concealing.

"All Prince Viktoryn said was that I was *vastly important to the survival of The Summer Court and The Seelie Kingdom,*" I mutter bitterly, settling my hands in my lap to mask their trembling.

"A pretty spun half-truth. I am sure you have found the Fae are well-versed in those. The transferred power that now lives within your bones has destabilized their magicks and court. Remember how I mentioned that our magicks rely heavily on balance? Having a large portion of The Summer Court's power drained from the land and placed within you has weakened their land, bodies, and powers. Have you seen any of the summer Faeries use their elemental powers?" Raven asks.

"I didn't even know Faeries had powers."

"They did not tell you anything," Amira says, almost sympathetically, scanning my face.

The softness in the battle-ready Faerie's face causes my heart to burn. I do not want her tenderness. I do not want their sympathy. I do not want anything from Faeries. All they have done is taunt and tear and wreck and ruin.

I am distracted from the dark turn of my thoughts as Prince Raven lifts his hand and waves his fingers. Wide-eyed, I watch as *snowflakes* form and fall from the ceiling. Filling the room as they float lazily on a non-existent wind from invisible clouds. *Magick.* Instead of feeling wonder, my stomach lurches.

"No. I have never seen them do anything like that," I murmur.

"They would not want to risk her finding out. The less she knew, the easier she would be to control. If she knew the truth, she could try to rightfully claim the throne. Everyone believes the Caprimore sisters to be dead. Right now, no one knows who the Capri girls truly are. They have assumed you to be some type of temporary pets for the Princes to play with," Olden explains.

"*Pets to play with?*" I growl, and Olden cringes.

"It is the simplest rumour to spread, one a bored court will lap up. It makes for good gossip. They cannot risk the truth. Not while they try to ascertain how to transfer the power back," Olden adds.

"Though many did not resist the radical forces, that did not mean they agreed with the ideology they spewed. It is likely your mother had many supporters. She still may. She was a beloved Queen, even after the resistance she was shown during your father's introduction to the court. If the people knew of your existence or if you made a move to reclaim the throne, it would divide the court, risking a civil war. Furthermore, they would not risk using magick with the imbalance, the cost would not be worth it. The Goldynlockes are not dimwitted," Olden explains.

"I beg your pardon, claim the throne!? I do not wish to claim the throne! I just want my sister back. Why would I want to rule over a Kingdom of beings who stood by while my family was slaughtered? Who have treated me with nothing but hatred and violence? Once I have my sister, I am going back to Mayfair. They can have their damn power for all I care," I spit.

Raven looks at me with equal parts frustration and pity. "That is precisely the problem, Princess. You cannot go bac—"

"*Watch me.*"

Raven glances at the ceiling as if praying for patience before he continues, "Not only because of the ramifications it would have on my world."

"What are you talking about?" I demand.

"A day in Elphyne is the equivalent to three or more in the mortal world. Time moves differently between our worlds. Your mortal body will not age as long as you remain in Elphyne, but the moment you step back into Mayfair... the time will catch up to you all at once. The longer you are here... the less viable it becomes for you to return to the world you have called home," Raven mutters as his eyes search my face.

Unease pools in my gut as I attempt the math. *How many days have passed since I arrived? How many did I spend unconscious? How much of my mortal lifespan have I lost already?*

"Even if you did manage to rescue Fabelle and find a way back to Mayfair without being captured. They will never stop hunting you. No matter what corner of the world you run to. The people you love, those who help you, and anyone who might have information will be in danger. They *need* the power that lives in you. They are *desperate*. From the moment you disappeared, they have searched for you. Now that they have you... they will not allow you to go. Nowhere you go will be safe," Raven says.

"The Goldynlockes do not know how to reverse the Goddess's magick. All they have are vague prophecies and predictions, but one thing remains clear—*you* are the vessel that holds the power. You are the key. And the Goddess Cyrissa would sooner burn The Summer Court to ashes than allow the power to fall into the hands of the Goldynlockes. Cyrissa was furious that her descendant was murdered in the Goldynlockes' thirst for power. Your mother was part-deity, Cyrissa was her mother," Olden explains. "She is your grandmother."

"My mother was part... Goddess?" I shake my head in disbelief, the room spinning once more. "Why don't they kill me? If the power lives within me? If I am simply a vessel... if I died, would it not return to the lands?"

"They do not know for certain what your death would bring. The risk is too high that the power could die with you. Magick can be a fickle thing," Olden remarks, grimacing. "Magick this powerful..."

"Though the current High Queen of Summer recommended as much—she does not hold much fondness for humans," Amira adds.

I snort. "Yes, I reckoned as much when her hand connected with my face at the dinner table." Prince Raven stiffens. "Wait, if my birth mother was a Seelie, part deity, High Faerie Queen, and my dad was an Unseelie-born human... what does that make me?"

"Other than a mortal with a very confusing family history?" Amira questions.

Olden shoots her an unimpressed look. "A fine question. We think you are a mortal, a human. You have shown no signs otherwise. You look, smell, and behave as one."

"Smell like one? Humans have a *smell*?" I choke on the words.

"Faeries have *extraordinarily* powerful olfactory senses. Especially when compared to a mortal's. Humans smell differently than Faeries. Some of us can even scent human emotions. We are also gifted with advanced hearing and eyesight. Some of us with advanced speed or strength. However, that power is reserved for those of us with the strongest magicks," Amira confirms, scanning me for a reaction, my cheeks flushing as all of the various emotions I've experienced around Raven come to mind.

"What kind of emotions?" I hedge.

"Are you certain you wish for me to answer that?" Amira asks, pointing her dagger at me and then Raven with a raised brow.

A dangerously feline grin appears on her lips, and amusement glints in her eyes. Olden gives Amira a warning look, and she rolls her eyes, chucking one of her daggers at him. He catches it with a warrior's ease.

"Trolls have an even stronger sense of smell, hearing, and sight," Amira adds, crossing her arms with a smug smirk. Olden sends a warning growl at her, but she simply chuckles darkly.

"Has anyone ever told you that you can be rather unpleasant, Amira?" I ask.

"Has anyone ever said the same of you?" she replies.

"Fair point."

"If you will do me the honours, Amira. We must remain on the task at hand," Raven commands, and I am not sure if I am imagining it, but under his look of impatience, he seems a little *flushed*.

"That's rich coming from you, *lover boy*," Amira snarks.

Raven levels her a glare that would send lesser beings running. It has no effect on Amira. When he turns back to me, she rolls her eyes.

"I saw that. Do I need to remind you that I outrank you, Amira?" the Prince replies with a deadly calm.

Amira just smirks, leaning back in her seat, pulling a new dagger from her belt, and fiddling with the blade.

"Since you arrived in Elphyne, The Summer Court's power has begun to stabilize, if only in the slightest. Simply having the vessel within their lands has managed to re-balance some of the power. This alone confirmed that you are indeed the vessel. It is only a matter of time before they realize you have slipped their borders and come knocking. But I assure you, you are safe here," Raven vows, his eyes finding mine with a confident, reassuring gleam.

"Attempting to remove you against your will from either of The Unseelie Courts, be it Winter or Autumn, would be viewed as an act of war. We are praying they are wise enough to not invoke a war while they remain weakened. But they will do anything to restore power to their court. Desperation makes Folk stupid," Raven finishes.

"Why now? What has changed? And why bring Fabelle if I, alone, am the vessel of this power?" I question.

"The Queen hid you well. It took nearly ten years for Prince Viktoryn to locate you. Longer for him to gain your trust. Though I do not think he expected you to put up such a valiant fight." Raven adjusts in his chair and clears his throat. A slight crack forms in his unabashed confidence, he sees me mark the change. And in a single breath, the mask of arrogance and composure returns.

Strange.

"A few years ago, one of the Goldynlockes scouts located your city and neared your home. Your father spotted the scout and led him astray. He knew he could not allow the scout to locate you. From what we have gathered, it is believed he sacrificed himself to kill the Knight and protect your location. Though neither body has been recovered," Raven explains.

The confirmation that my father did not abandon us like my mortal mother tried to convince me warms some of the hollowness that set up shop the day he did not return to us. I never believed he simply left, relief and grief mixing within my soul.

"Until Viktoryn located and manipulated me into trusting him, you mean."

Raven nods. I swallow down the rage that alights at the thought of my father's sacrifice being in vain because of Viktoryn.

Him and I meeting... Viktoryn choosing me. It had nothing to do with luck or love or fate. Nothing to do with him seeing something in me worth loving. I was simply a pawn in a game I was not aware was being played. I was an object to be moved and manipulated.

A piece in a long-played game started by a Queen who desperately sought to be able to love who she pleased. Is it possible to *hate* a mother you never knew? To hate that her choices led you to have none? A mother who abandoned me with a woman who abused, starved, and tormented me? A mother who left me with a broken Faerie Kingdom thrust at my feet like a cursed inheritance? The feet of a girl who didn't even know Faeries or Elphyne existed a week ago? To hate her and yet *admire* her?

Admire that she was fierce and wise and brave. That she was a leader who would surrender her life to protect the lives of her family? Someone who would die for a cause they believed in so unabashedly?

I shove down the feelings and banish the thoughts. I will allow myself to grieve the person and life I thought were mine when lives do not depend on my ability to adapt to the world-altering responsibilities I have inherited.

I find myself wondering if the power within me is a gift, a burden, or a curse. If my choices could lead to something better, a Kingdom my mother would be proud of? I spent years hating these systems, silently rebelling against them... but what if with this power, this gift, I could work to change it? What if this is my chance to climb to the top and topple it all from within? Yet a part of me knows my choices could just as easily doom us all...

"This power, you said I am its vessel... what does that mean?" I ask.

"Around your eighteenth birthday, you shall be able to access the power that lives in your bones. Faeries call this The Calling. A point where your power reaches maturity and can be wielded. We hope that once this occurs, you will be powerful enough to reclaim the throne, overthrowing the Goldynlockes. Though there is a risk that when you reclaim the throne, the power will return to the lands—"

"To the lands *and* the Goldynlockes," I finish for him, taking a steadying breath.

"Ideally, they wish to avoid you ever attempting to reclaim the throne. Or your power," Raven says.

"Wait, what is the power? You can wield snow, what powers will I possess?"

"Snow, among many other impressive and powerful things." Raven smirks, a hand pressed to his heart in mock offense. "I am not but a snow cloud in a crown. Though what a lovely cloud I would be. I happen to be one of the most powerful Faeries in Elphyne. Even when the Goldynlockes were at full power. I was second only to your mother."

"Not the time to show off, lover boy. You can woo the Princess with your fancy powers and win her heart later," Amira snips.

"Can someone please answer my question?" I demand.

"The truth is... we do not know." Olden scratches his head. "Every Faerie's power is different, unique, related to their home court but not exclusively. Your mother could manipulate light, heat, and fire. She was also a gifted healer. She had unmatched power, thanks to the blood of The Goddess of the Sun coursing in her veins. Your father had no such power, though he was a skilled warrior. We have no way of knowing how his Unseelie, mortal blood will affect you," Olden says.

"And as of now, there is not a single account of a mortal with elemental powers. I scoured our libraries extensively but found nothing. We are uncertain how your powers will manifest and how your mortal body will handle being the vessel of such significant power," Olden replies solemnly.

"The Calling... This power could kill me. There is a chance I will not survive it, that I will not survive past eighteen."

No one responds. The room goes uncomfortably quiet, taut with a strained tension. I scan their faces, but they all avoid my eyes.

Olden adjusts and clears his throat. Amira stares at the dagger she fiddles with. And the Prince, for the first time since I have met him, cannot meet my eyes as he smoothes the fabric of his tunic. They will not say it, but it is written all over their faces, screaming within the silence.

There is a possibility that I will not survive The Calling. That this power could kill me. I could be dead in less than a year. This all could be for nothing. My death could doom my sister and an entire court of living, breathing beings.

Just as I am about to suffocate in the silence, the door to the room bursts open and a handsome, heavily-armed Faerie strolls in. His gait relaxed yet still fixed with power.

"Am I late? What did I miss?" The Faerie's grey-green eyes meet mine and flare a little. "If you would've mentioned she was cute, I definitely would not have been late."

I watch this overwhelmingly tall male saunter past, all bulk warrior, toned muscle, and confident swagger. His skin is dark, with a strong jaw and black hair faded short on his head. He is wearing a relaxed smile, arguably his most dashing feature. His eyes dance as he watches me study him.

"Why bother asking if you are late if you know you are, Raith?" Amira snaps.

Raith messes her hair as he passes, and she curses, taking a swipe at him with her blade. He easily dances out of its reach, peering over his shoulder to wink at her.

He slows his steps and studies the table.

"Ooh. I walked in on some *tension*... maybe I should have been later," Raith drawls, palms raised. "Raith Stefanovich, milady, a pleasure to meet you."

He crosses to me, dipping into an over-elaborate bow and kissing the top of my out-reached hand.

"Willa Capri," I reply, shaking his surprisingly large hand.

"Willa Caprimore," Olden corrects, and I glare at him.

"Why the long face, Willa Capri... more?" Raith drawls, raising a brow at Olden.

"You really do have impeccable timing, Raith," Olden grumbles.

"Oh, you know, I just found out I am the long, lost heir to The Summer Throne. A throne that is now ruled by my mother's murderers, the same murderers who now have my sister captive as bait. So that I will hand them over the power that was transferred into my veins by a

Goddess who is also my grandmother, apparently. A Goddess who has vanished and refuses to tell anyone how to return the power to The Magickally Unstable Summer Court as vengeance for my true mother's death and to prevent the power from falling into the hands of those very same murderers."

I pull in a deep breath, running out of air before continuing. "The same power that might very well kill me before I have a chance to fix any of the mess they managed to create during a time when I couldn't walk or talk yet."

"Oh and also that Faeries are even real and that Elphyne even exists and that this is indeed not all a terrible dream," I mutter. "Oh wait, did I remember to mention that my mortal mother, the one I thought was my mother my entire life, isn't actually my mother at all? No matter. That seems almost insignificant now, compared to the whole kingdom, powers, dead real Fae mom thing."

Raith doesn't miss a beat or lose a single drop of his swagger as he drawls. "Sounds like you need a drink."

"Is there a reason you have only now decided to grace us with your presence, Raith?" Raven asks dryly.

"Ah yes, I come bearing bad news," Raith says, straightening to bow to his Prince.

"Aren't you supposed to soften the blow and say you have both bad and good news?" I ask, pointing at him.

He points back.

"Ah, yes! I come bearing bad and good news," Raith corrects. "Which would you like first?" he asks Raven.

"Both. Out with it, Raith," Raven commands, crossing his arms over his chest as if creating a barrier between him and the news.

"Good news, Willa Capri... more?" Raith shakes his head as if he is still not sure.

"I do not even know."

"Fantastic. We can indeed get you a drink! Bad news, it will have to be later as Prince Viktoryn Goldynlocke, accompanied by fifty Summer Court Knights, waits at the gates demanding entry to search for their missing Princess." Raith gestures to me and winks again. "He claims that if we kidnapped a Royal Seelie Princess, we would be in violation of The Great Treaty, which would void the Kingdom's peace agreement. Which would, in turn, allow him to go before The Elemental Council and request the right to declare war on The Winter Court. This is why I didn't offer good news—it's mostly bad news." He shrugs.

"Wait, peace treaty? War? The what council?" I ask, glancing between the four of them.

"Elemental," Olden corrects.

"We do not have time to explain. We need a plan," Raven remarks, pushing up from his seat.

He does not seem worried in the least. If anything, he seems reenergized, powered by the chaos. Calculation and mischief dance in his eyes as he pulls Raith aside, whispering to him.

Amira materializes out of thin air beside me, and I flinch.

"Someone needs to put a bell on you," I hiss, and she shrugs, tossing her dagger in the air and catching it effortlessly.

"See that." She points to Raven's face with the tip of her blade. "*That* is his scheming face. Pretty Prince Viktoryn should be shaking in his overly expensive boots, Table Slayer."

"Stop calling me that."

By some miracle, Raith buys us enough time for me to change out of my soiled solstice dress. I put on a thick navy blue dress with a matching fur-lined cloak that Amira stole from Raven's sister's room. The dress is tight in the chest and hips but it works.

As we exit the grand main doors of The Crystal Palace, I get my first real look at the sprawling ice fortress.

The Palace has been built into the side of a sprawling set of snow-capped mountains. Towers of sparkling crystalline ice reach for the sun like blooming flowers, the lights of life visible through the semi-transparent walls. It is monstrous and wonderful and ethereal. Snow falls in thick fluffy flakes all around, transported on a sharp north wind that causes me to shiver in my cloak.

I school my expression, squaring my shoulders and lifting my chin. In my mind, I repeat the plan over and over. We have one chance to get this right and little room for error.

The gates come into view, tremendous shimmering jaws of slick icicles gleaming like a beast's sharp teeth. Behind them, on horseback, sits a smug Prince Viktoryn, flanked by fifty Summer Court Knights. They look out of place here—too gaudy and loud in a place of quiet, gentle wonder.

On my right, Prince Raven is the picture of calm, unbothered arrogance, nothing more than a spoiled royal annoyed to have his day so rudely interrupted. On my left is Olden and the small walking armoury that is strapped to his back and sides. The look on his face would send lesser beings running like their pants caught fire.

Raith trails behind us, a silent, menacing force. No longer the goofy, charming Fae I met but an army commander. Fifteen black armoured Knights follow him, waiting on his orders. More hide in the tree line.

As we come to a stop, the smugness melts from Viktoryn's expression, his chest so still I wonder if he's breathing. A flash of surprise appears on his face as his eyes land on me. I guess he assumed he would march up to the Palace to find me taken prisoner, shaking and pleading for him to save me. Not standing beside his adversary in a show of unification.

"Prince Viktoryn, to what do we owe the displeasure?" Raven greets, with all the entitlement of a bred and born royal.

"Do not insult me, Unseelie *filth*. You know why I am here," Prince Viktoryn growls, trying and failing to cover the rage rampant in his eyes.

Where Raven seems to thrive with delicate word games and courtly cunning, Viktoryn does not bother with such subtlety or royal posturing.

I study the princes, head to head with Raven the cracks in Viktoryn's royal facade are obvious. Where Raven is elegant, calculated, and poised, Viktoryn is forceful, demanding, and opposing. Raven fills space with a dark, understated power that can be felt in his every word choice. Whereas Viktoryn dominates with rippling tremors of power that seem to pulse from his predatory posture.

Opposite sides of the same coin. Two types of rulers who approach their role in complete opposition to each other.

How different would our lives be if they were born into a legacy of allies instead of enemies? How much could they have accomplished if fate had dealt them different cards?

"Oh dear, The Pretty Little Fire Prince is spitting insults, whatever will I do?" Raven gasps, flattening the back of his palm against his forehead. "What a shame it is all he can do. I am so aching for a good fight." Raven flashes Viktoryn a devilish grin, slipping his hands into his pockets as if he sees The Fire Prince as no real threat. Viktoryn notices, going rigid. "As you know, a Prince's time is extremely valuable. What can I do for you, *Prince* Viktoryn?"

I try not to smile as I watch Raven present and pummel multiple of Viktoryn's insecurities in but a moment. I never considered court games a battlefield, but as Raven unravels Viktoryn with a simple sentence, I realize that, when it comes to ruling, wars are won with words *and* weapons.

Prince Viktoryn dismounts his horse and the white stallion lets out a huff. Viktoryn clenches his fists at his sides, one hand drifting to rest on the pommel of his sword. In answer, Olden takes a thundering step forward. Viktoryn eyes the troll cautiously, disgust dripping from his gaze as his hand drifts back to his side.

"We both know, *bird-boy*, that you are no match for me in swordplay," Viktoryn announces. "Willa, my dear, move away from them. I do not want my Princess to be associated with Trolls and Unseelie dirt. They cannot be trusted."

Despite his words, I stay by Raven's side.

"You would have to, with the lack of magicks and all. What a *pity* to be castrated from your power. It must infuriate you that a mere mortal is set to accomplish what your family never could," Raven coos, voice laced with mock pity.

"She may be a mere mortal, but she is *mine*. My Princess. And I say we are leaving. Come, Willa, now," Viktoryn demands.

The leash on my tongue slips further every moment I stand here, positioned like a prop while Viktoryn's words dig under my skin and spread like angry fire ants.

How dare he? How dare he use the fact that I am a Princess to further his cause? When he refused to tell me until it served him.

I am no Raven, so when my lips slip, I am not nearly as calculated, but I still do the trick.

"*Your* Princess? I am not your anything, or was me trying to escape your castle not clear enough of an ending for you? You are nothing to me. *Nothing*, Viktoryn," I enunciate the word slowly to let it settle in his thick skull. "And you will watch your tone when you speak to Olden. I will not tolerate disrespect. I would trust him with my life. I cannot say the same for you, can I, Your Highness?"

Viktoryn shifts, taking a half step forward like he wants to vault over the gate to steal me away. I've never seen him look so angry, so unravelled. Fury bleeds from every inch of his being, his hands shaking with rage, one drifting back to the pommel of his sword. He ignores my comment as if I have not spoken and instead glares at Raven.

"If you kidnapped her from Seelie Lands, a Seelie Princess with Seelie blood, you have violated The Great Treaty," Viktoryn growls, giving me the opening I have been waiting for.

"Funny," I spit in a way that makes the word sound like a curse. "You failed to mention that I was a Princess with a claim to your throne. Interesting how such a thing slipped your mind, Viktoryn. How *did* that happen, do tell?"

"I did not tell you for your protection, Willa. And I was right to! See what happened the moment someone knew of your true identity?" Viktoryn pleads with a sudden softness that makes my organs recoil.

I watch him transform in front of me. His body relaxes, his eyes softening as he attempts to make himself look smaller, less threatening—moulding himself to appear as the Toryn I once knew. And I see what I did not previously—the horrifying manipulation of it all as he goes from monster to man.

He scans my body as if it will tell him what I am not saying. I only tip my chin higher, unrelenting. All his transformation accomplishes as

I witness the snake shedding its skin is a solidifying wave of knowing that the person I loved never existed.

So, I choose.

"Prince Raven did not kidnap me, Viktoryn." I scoff. "What would cause you to make such an outrageous, baseless accusation? I cannot say the same for *you,* but he rescued me. I was drugged by someone in *your* court." I point an accusing finger at him, and he shrinks back.

"I could not think straight. The Fae Wine had scattered my emotions, I was confused and furious at you for all the lies. So when you turned, I saw my opportunity. I hit you with a rock and ran into the forest. As you know, in my state, I could not make it far. Thank gods, Prince Raven found me wandering and so kindly brought me to The Crystal Palace to recover. He was worried that someone in The Ember Palace had drugged me with the intention of harming me. Which seems likely now, doesn't it?" I sneer down my nose at him. "It seems your protection is not worth much after all."

"Oh, *please.*" Viktoryn scoffs back. "You could hardly *stand*, Willa. Do you think me an insipid fool?"

"Do you really wish for me to answer that?" I chirp.

Viktoryn narrows his eyes on me.

"I am *not,* and I do not believe you were able to deliver the blow that knocked me unconscious or that you were able to make it to the forest."

"That is perhaps your problem, isn't it? You *always* underestimate me. Perhaps it is time to abandon such a limiting mindset, Prince," I reply, condensation dripping from my tone. "Correct me if I am mistaken,

Prince Raven. But am I not half Unseelie? Meaning by *blood*,' I glare back at Viktoryn, "the blood your court seems to care so very much about, Viktoryn, I am a member of The Unseelie Courts as well."

"You are correct, Princess. You are as much Unseelie as you are Seelie." Raven nods to me and then turns to Prince Viktoryn. "I only intended to protect the Princess from those who wished to harm her in your court," Raven confirms, primly, staring down The Summer Prince.

Viktoryn flinches at the subtle accusation in the words as a look of utter disgust flashes on his features at the mention of my Unseelie bloodline.

I tilt my head to hide the smirk that grows on my lips at Raven's clever play of words. It is not a lie to say he intended to protect me from The Summer Court. Raven's plan left all the outright lies to the human. Genius, if I do say so myself.

"I know what she is," Viktoryn spits like admitting it tastes foul. "An unfortunate truth, but a truth nonetheless. However, now that she has recovered, she can return to The Ember Palace, where she belongs. Come now, Willa. I've had enough of bird-boy's *beak*."

"As tempting as that offer is," I smirk, fire in my eyes, "I do not think I'm ready to return to *my* Palace just yet. The Winter Prince has been such remarkable company. I think I'd like to remain here a while longer," I remark, smiling at Prince Raven, whose returning smirk makes my stomach dip. His eyes sparkling with dark promise.

I turn back to Prince Viktoryn as a montage of emotions tears across his face. He seems to be using a tremendous amount of energy to keep himself from lunging at the gates. Viktoryn grips the pommel of his sword so tightly, his knuckles go white at my not-so-subtle claim to The Ember Palace. Or maybe it is my blatant flattery for The Winter Prince that pushes him over the edge.

It seems his Knights also sense the escalation in his emotions as they reach for their weapons.

Olden steps up to my side, hand on the pommel of his sword as he lets out a warning growl. Raith and his Knights take a thundering step forward.

My eyes catch something glinting in the trees behind the group of Summer Court Knights. I squint to locate the source and find Amira, bow in hand, high in a tree, an arrow aimed at the line of golden Knights. Another armed female I don't recognize hangs in the branches beside her.

Raven simply *tsks* at The Fire Prince like scolding a child as rivers of ice and wisps of dark shadow begin to flow up the gates in a startling show of power, some slithering across the ground like living vines. Raven does not seem to be affected in the least by his use of magicks, hands still stuffed in his pockets, a reprimanding look on his face aimed at Viktoryn.

The Summer Court Knights begin to murmur to each other, shifting on their feet uneasily. The fear in their eyes is undeniable as they peer into the true power of The Winter Prince.

"Now, now. You do not want to do that, do you, Viktoryn? You are wise enough to know if you or your Knights strike on my land, the treaty is void, and all you will be leaving with is fifty frozen bodies." Raven drawls, looking Viktoryn up and down, unimpressed. "Make that fifty-one."

A Knight in the front row lets out a shout as his lips turn blue, veins of ice spilling from his mouth. I fight to keep my expression neutral as he drops to the ground in a lump, skin blue. A second later, another yelps as ropes of shadow wind around his limbs.

Viktoryn watches, eyes slightly wide as he turns back to Raven. He is seething as he slowly gives The Winter Prince a single curt nod. Raven smirks, drawing his powers back from the gates, the shadows and ice retreating. The Knight on the ground begins to gasp, but no one pays him any mind as he twitches in the snow.

"I can assure you, Prince Viktoryn, that I will arrange the Princess' safe passage back to her Palace whenever she pleases. She is no prisoner here. You will find that no harm will come to her in my Palace." Raven steps up to my side, flanking me with Olden. "As for you, Princess Willa." He takes my hand, placing a gentle kiss on each of my knuckles.

I shiver at the heated look in his eyes as he glances up at me through his lashes.

"You are too kind. The feeling is mutual. We are happy to host you. You are welcome at The Crystal Palace at all times," he vows.

Something in Viktoryn snaps, his mask shattering before my eyes.

"If I find out you laid a single finger on her, I will burn your fucking Palace to the ground, Raven. I swear to The Goddess of the Sun, you will burn!" he shouts, all of his composure melting away with the fury of his flaming jealousy.

Raven steps back, dropping my hand.

I expect him to pull his powers back out and cause mayhem. But instead, Raven looks Viktoryn dead in the eyes and bursts out *laughing*. Rolling his eyes and waving off his threat as if nothing more than some pesky cobwebs.

"You always did have a flair for the dramatics, Fire Prince."

Raven smirks, taking my hand in his once more as Viktoryn tracks the movement with predatory intent. The direct disobedience of our touch leaves him gawking in disbelief. Eyes as wide as a full moon as he opens and closes his mouth like a gaping fish.

It feels so wonderful that I lean into Raven's touch. He tugs me gently, and I stumble into his chest, my breath catching as he wraps his arms around me. My back meets his solid chest, and I am enveloped in his warmth.

His lips find my ear as he whispers, "Just go with it."

I nod, finding it extremely satisfying to witness someone who has always gotten their own way so publicly distraught by a small act of disobedience. Prince Viktoryn's control and claim of me crumbling before his eyes. And Gods, does it feel *good*.

Raven's hand finds the nape of my neck. He squeezes reassuringly, and a bolt of lightning shoots down my spine. His presence is so grounding and yet electrifying. He tilts my head, applying a gentle kiss to my neck as he stares Prince Viktoryn down. A surprised hum leaves my lips as goosebumps rise down across my body.

Raven presses another gentle kiss below my ear and whispers, "I could do this all day. Look at him… you like this, don't you? Taunting him? Holding all the power? Watching him struggle? How naughty, indeed."

My heart flutters like a thousand bees have been set free in my chest, my cheeks warming as I nod. I meet and hold Viktoryn's furious gaze as Raven tightens his arms around me.

"Very good," he mutters, placing another kiss on my neck.

"I will kill you for this," Viktoryn vows to Raven.

"Well worth it," Raven promises.

Viktoryn's glare finds me.

"I hope you know what you are doing, Willa. You are but a foolish little mortal mutt who does not have the slightest idea of what you are up against. Do not forget who resides in The Ember Palace. I would not wish for your sister's stay to be cut short." Viktoryn shakes his head. "You play with fire and forces much bigger than you could ever know."

The condescension in his tone snaps something in me. I will not be spoken to like a child. I will not allow him to make me feel small. I am not his possession. Not when I am standing with someone who, despite being endlessly annoying, has not once made me feel less than. No, Raven makes me feel *powerful*.

The lock on my emotions shatters, walls crumbling to ash. Pieces fly in every direction, sharp shrapnel, embedding shards of my rage, grief, pain, and sadness in my very flesh. Everything I have suppressed since

Viktoryn decimated my life floods me, and as overwhelming as it feels, it also feels a lot like *freedom*.

He betrayed me, broke me, used me. He took the one thing I cared about and twisted it into a threat so I would play his obedient pet.

He made me love him. He touched me and held me and watched as the woman who was not even my mother beat me. A woman he *knew* was not my mother. And did nothing.

He never protected me—*I* did.

From the start, I fought for myself and my sister. And for the first time, I am realizing it was never him, it was *always* me.

This newfound power may very well be as much a curse as it is a blessing, but I will not allow it to become another weapon in *his* arsenal.

He can taunt me, take from me, but he truly does not know me at all if he thinks I will just lay down and take it.

All the fire and fury I've held back rears its ugly fanged head. A cobra ready to strike and drain all of its venom. The grief, the pain, the anger, and the fear begin to boil beneath my skin—igniting my emotions into a blazing fire. A fire in my soul, that's been *begging* to burn, pleading for oxygen for years. And for once, I do not hold back. I drop the match and let the power hum within me.

I will not be a pawn in anyone's game. Not anymore. Not ever again.

The gold medallion in my pocket thrums in agreement. Raven stiffens as he senses a source of power, but he quickly recovers.

"I was born to burn. I do not fear you. I will burn your Palace to the ground if a single one of your Faeries even dares to *look* at her wrong." I step forward, freeing myself from Raven's arms.

"If any harm comes to my sister, Viktoryn, I will move my coronation date up and have traitors to the throne punished for treason. I have something you need, and I will *die* before I allow a single member of your family to wield it."

"Everything you have? Everything you've done? It will mean nothing when I am finished. You will be nothing. I would be grateful if I were you that your future Queen is merciful. If I felt like counting the sins of the past, your mother and father's heads would already be lining the Palace gates. They would make a *stunning* addition to the decor, don't you think?"

"How unfortunate would it be if the heir to The Summer Throne, The *Cherished* Golden Prince, never got the chance to rule," I retort with a sinister coldness I did not know I possessed, but my chest lightens with every word. "Watch yourself, Viktoryn. For I will be in every shadow, every nightmare, waiting around every corner. You will never escape me."

I pivot on my feet, boots crunching in the snow as I march back towards the entrance of The Crystal Palace, not giving him the courtesy to reply.

The cool wind nips at my cheeks, but all I feel is the rising heat in my chest, a *purpose*. For the first time in my life, I feel a sense of freedom. Power thrums through my veins that does not feel as if it stems from magick at all. I let everything I feel feed the fire that blazes in my soul, pumping it full of fuel and oxygen and rage. A rage I plan to hone into a blade, a purpose, a power.

I am done being a pawn, an object for everyone to manipulate. Gods help the next one who dares to try.

"That was not part of the plan, Princess," Raven whispers once we're out of earshot of the gates.

I let out a soft hum. "Wasn't it? Guess I got tired of being moved across the board like a pawn," I reply, staring straight ahead.

Raven says nothing, surveying me with renewed interest. Looking at me like he's really *seeing* me for the first time. And behind his practised mask of calm, it is hard to tell if he likes what he sees. I decide I don't care. But I do, just a little.

We are about halfway back to the stunning ice-carved entrance when Viktoryn shouts over the howling wind.

"Your sister was upset that you missed her engagement. Prince Archer got her quite the ring."

I halt, and Olden collides into my back, not expecting the stop. Raith and his trailing Knights come to a stop behind us. But my centre of gravity shifts and I start to plummet, feet losing purchase on the ice. Olden's reflexes save me from a nose dive into the snow as he scoops his arms around me. I find my footing, and he releases me. But I still feel off-balance as I huff down a deep breath, trying to reign in the need to sprint back to the gates and slit Viktoryn's throat.

"Keep walking, Willa. He wants you to react. He wants you to go with him," Olden warns. "You do not bend to his whims. Head high. Keep walking."

I struggle to keep from physically vibrating with rage. The resolve I felt only seconds ago snuffs out. My hands fist at my sides as I draw in a swallow breath.

"My sister is engaged to my enemy's brother. She's a *child*," I grit. "As long as she is in their grasp, they will manipulate and use her to get to me. I can't let that happen. I cannot allow this wedding to happen."

"I know. But this is not the way. Go with him now, and we lose all of the power. Do not bend. We will figure this out *together*," Raven says gently.

I nod numbly. They are right, I cannot walk back into the trap Viktoryn set for me.

"*Together*," Olden echoes the word.

"Together," I whisper.

No one speaks for a long time once we've settled in the lounging area attached to the bed chamber. The silence in the room grows more stale with each moment it remains. The room contains a plush navy blue settee and wing-backed armchairs settled around a hearth roaring with a crackling fire. Shelves carved from the dark mountainous stone are filled with extravagant books that line either side of the grand fireplace.

I wander mindlessly by the shelves, fingers brushing over the spines of dusty books, trying to block out the roaring of rage in my ears. The smell of worn paper and smoky pine lingers in the air.

I can feel Raven's eyes tracking me from where he sits, ankle over his knee on a wingback chair. Olden, the ever-stoic protector, lingers a few feet behind me, book in hand, as if he's worried I will suddenly collapse. He pretends to not be shadowing me, and I pretend not to notice him shadowing me.

Amira paces back and forth behind the settee, tossing her dagger in the air. I wonder if she is ever truly still or if something in her blood screams and thrashes if she settles too long, spurring her back into motion.

Raith is sprawled across the entirety of a settee, leaning back on the arm he's tucked behind his head, ankles crossed. The picture of relaxation, he is the one who breaks the never-ending silence.

"Whiskey?" he questions.

"*Whiskey*," Amira, Raven, and Olden echo.

Raith doesn't waste a second, leaping up from the settee to grab a crystal decanter of amber liquid from a hidden compartment in the bookshelves. He pops the cork off with a grin.

"I like to always keep some handy, never know when you might need it. And I promised the lost Princess here a drink," he remarks with a wink in my direction.

"I did not even know that was in there, and this is *my* room." Raven scoffs, earning a dark chuckle from Amira.

"Wait, this is *your* room?"

"Indeed."

"You mean, I slept in *your* room last night? Your *bed*?" My heart stutters. "Where in the name of the Gods did you sleep?" I demand, arms crossed.

"Precisely where you saw me this morning when you attempted to *stab* me." He smirks. "She's not much of a morning person," he warns his cadre with a mocking yawn.

"Wait, you do not jest, the Princess here, tried to *stab* you?" Raith lets out a roaring laugh, and Olden grunts in confirmation.

"She did. Maybe if you showed up on time for once, you would not have missed it," Amira snarks, then grins. "It was *quite* the show."

"Amira, even with a face like this," Raith gestures to his handsome features, "I still require my beauty sleep."

Amira rolls her eyes. "I would gladly carve that pretty face of yours up if it means you'd attend meetings on time."

Raith has the good sense to look a bit horrified.

"I did not try to stab him. Alright? I only threatened to stab him," I correct, exasperated.

"Oh, because that is *so* much better," Raven adds with a playful eye roll.

"I do not think the distinction matters much," Olden mutters, rubbing his temples like he has a raging headache.

"I think it does! There is a difference between trying and failing to stab someone and threatening to do so," I add.

"If you say so, Princess," Raven purrs. "It sounds like you are upset that you *failed* to stab me."

"I am not!" I lie. I was, just a little.

"Raven, you failed to mention that the lost princess was quite so," Raith eyes me appreciatively, "spirited... and radiant." He grins, meeting my eyes with a heated look as he gathers four glasses and fills them to the rim.

I blush and turn back to the bookshelves to hide the redness rising on my face.

Raith rounds the room, handing everyone a glass. He lingers as he slips mine to me, brushing his fingers across mine. He places one finger under my chin, applying pressure until my eyes meet his. He notes the redness in my cheeks, shooting me one of his smug smiles as he returns to the settee.

"Oh Goddesses, save us," Amira groans, covering her face with her hands. "Not this again." She huffs, pointing her dagger accusingly at Raith and Raven with narrowed eyes. "Does this alliance mean I am going to have to put up with the two of you constantly courting? Need I remind you, the last time you two fought over a girl, it ended with a destroyed building, three missing horses, and a minor political scandal?"

"Now that is a story I am dying to hear," I say, laughing.

"I have to agree with Amira." Olden nods, taking a tentative sip.

"Things must be truly dire if those two are agreeing. And yet..." Raith murmurs, his eyes dragging over my body from head to toe *twice.*

"Didn't I?" Raven interrupts. "I wonder what could have possibly possessed me not to mention it, Raith," he drawls, hand pressed against his heart in mock innocence.

Despite myself, I laugh. One of the first real laughs I've had since my entire life changed. The sound renewed with a lightness I haven't felt in a long time. Raven's gaze finds mine and a bright smile beams on his cheeks. Those captivating dimples are even more pronounced with his genuine smile.

"Scared of some healthy competition, boss man?" Raith remarks, sending Raven a taunting smile.

"I am not sure what competition you are referring to unless they have yet to arrive." Raven raises his brow at Raith, a challenge in his eyes.

Raith chokes on a sip of his drink. "Rude."

"You two are insufferable. Willa, will you stab me, please? I cannot do this with them again," Amira pleads, holding up her dagger for me.

I give her a mischievous look, grinning with a dark laugh, and slowly shake my head.

"I would like to think that them fighting over me would be enough mayhem to destroy *at least* two buildings, to cause four horses to go missing, and create a major political scandal," I tease, causing Raven and Raith to burst into a fit of laughter while Olden and Amira eye me wearily.

"Okay, alliance off," Amira declares, stepping back to glare at me. "They are already enough trouble."

Raven sends her a look that seems to say, "*You wish.*"

Remembering the glass in my hand, I look down at the liquid, swirling it. The light makes it appear like molten gold as its rich, smoky scent fills my nose. I hesitate, thinking of the night that landed me here in the first place. My history with alcohol thus far is not entirely positive. *Especially* in Elphyne.

Olden notes my hesitation. "It is whiskey from The Mortal Lands."

"If you do not want it, I will *happily* drink it for you," Amira grumbles. "Especially if Raith and Raven are about to be back to their insatiably competitive ways."

I wave them off, taking a big sip of the liquor, my face contorts as it burns my throat. I sputter a bit as the liquid settles like a thick, honeyed heat in my stomach.

"Not a big whiskey drinker, are we, sweetheart? Stick with this group, and you'll be a pro in no time," Raith drawls, lifting his cup in a toast and draining the entire glass.

Raven downs his entire glass, letting out a long breath, challenge glinting in his eyes as he asks Raith to pour him another. Olden looks weary as he takes another small sip, no doubt wondering which of the males he will have to carry out of the room later if they keep at it.

Amira joins me at the bookshelves, leaning as she whispers in my ear, "They tend to be a *bit* competitive. Girls, booze, battles, it matters not." She pauses, studying me with scrutiny as something wars in her eyes. A decision settles in her gaze.

"Raven has three little sisters, but they grew up together. Raith lost his family young, and the King took him in as one of his own. Raith is the closest thing Raven has to a brother. And Raven is the closest thing Raith has to family," Amira says with unique tenderness as she surveys the unlikely group. "They drive me mad, but in our own way, we are a family. Olden may pretend he hates playing mother hen, but he loves it."

"A *bit* competitive?" I tease, and Amira smirks, bumping her shoulder into mine.

I smile at the little group before me and the ease I feel with Amira at my side. They look so comfortable and at ease with each other. Longing pinches in my chest. *A family.*

37

The sun has well past set, the moon rising high by the time Olden and Amira half-drag a drunken Raith from the room. He slurs something about Olden being too much of a mother hen, which causes the Troll to sigh defeatedly.

The door shuts, leaving the Prince and I in silence. My head feels lighter with the whiskey swirling through my blood, some of the heaviness of the day lessened. But worry still gnaws at my gut as I think of my sister.

The Winter Prince, since finishing his second glass, has been uncharacteristically quiet, his eyes fixed on the navy blue and silver patterned rug that sits in front of the fire. Not even speaking when Raith and Amira started making jokes at his expense.

"Are you alright?" I ask.

Raven's elbows are braced on his knees, glass cupped between his hands. He snaps back to reality with a wry laugh that sounds more like a puff of defeat. When he finally turns his head to me, his eyes are haunted.

"I should be asking you that," he says roughly with a half-hearted smile.

I do not know what to say to that. I have never been good at *this*. Whatever this is. I fiddle with my empty crystal glass, staring at my hands. After a few minutes of silence, I refill my cup, downing it all in one quick gulp.

"I like your friends," I try.

"Do they count as friends if they are paid to assist you?" he asks jokingly, but I do not miss the hint of truth in the statement as he runs a hand down his face.

"I have not known them, or you, long. But based on tonight alone, I do not think they are here for the coin," I say, and he shrugs.

Unable to stand the haunted look in his eyes a moment longer, I move to sit beside him where he resides on the settee, hoping to ease some of the heavy tension from the room. He shifts his body, settling to face me, and I watch as he pieces his charming mask back into place brick by brick. His default smirk plastered on his features even as shadows hang in his eyes. The shadows dance across his features, sharpening his angler cheekbones.

He relaxes a little, tension melting from his shoulders, and he lets out a deep sigh. We sit in companionable silence, accessing each other like we did earlier this morning but with softer eyes. It's hard to believe that it was only this morning when it now feels like a world away. In a way, it is.

My entire life has since shifted on its axis, shaking free new truths and old pains. Tombstones from my past collide with the uncertainties lurking in the shadows of my future. And in it all, while I stare into his stormy eyes, it feels like something has shifted between us, too.

Even though nothing feels concrete, the ground ever-shifting, *he*... he feels grounding, right, *steady*. When he looks at me with that unyielding intensity, it feels as though his gaze alone is tethering me to the Earth. It is terrifying.

I shake myself from my thoughts and the ache in my heart, breaking Raven's gaze as I watch the flames in the hearth.

I need to be careful. I know I need to be careful. I have been down this road before, and it led me to nothing but betrayal and destruction. And right now, I cannot afford another mistake. Not when my heart has yet to mend from my last.

And yet...

My eyes find his again, and my breath catches. Raven watches me so intently that it feels as if he can read every wayward thought rushing around my head. As grounding as it is, it also leaves me feeling entirely too exposed. Like his eyes have stripped my mind naked, memorizing each freckle and scar.

"Let's play a game," Raven mutters, breaking our silence.

"A game?" I echo, surprised.

"Indeed. A *game*. I will trade—a truth for a truth."

"How very Faerie of you. Of course, even your games must be a bargain," I drawl, crossing my arms over my chest.

That earns me a full grin and a soft, dark chuckle. I find myself grinning back, my stomach releasing a plague of butterflies.

"Precisely, you first," Raven remarks, leaning back into the arm of the settee, one knee propped up, arm braced on top.

I ponder my options. For a head that's been spinning with questions, my mind is suddenly, painfully blank. It is hard to think when Raven watches me like that. And I know whatever I choose to ask will mean something to him—ever the strategist.

"How old are you?"

Raven chokes on the whiskey he was sipping, sputtering. I smirk as it seems nothing surprises him. I find I like the feeling of surprising him a bit too much.

"I gave you the option to ask me *anything* and this is what you choose?" He shoots me an incredulous look. "My age?"

I chuckle at the sight of him in such disarray. "Yes. Stop stalling. This is your game, Raven. A truth for a truth."

"Dreadful creature," he remarks.

I chuckle.

Raven watches me a moment longer and then sighs. "Very well. Fair is fair. A truth for a truth." He clears his throat. "Faeries are practically immortal. But we age and mature differently, at least in comparability to human life spans. We mature slowly, remaining a child with child-like whims and wishes for the first eighty or so years of our lives. We then enter adolescence for anywhere between fifty and sixty-five years. Though it does vary a great deal for each Faerie. But we can live thousands of years in a balanced court," he explains, face concealed in a neutral mask.

"*Thousands*?" I gawk at him.

"Thousands," he confirms with a curt nod, hiding his smirk behind his whiskey glass. "My turn."

"Oh no. Not so fast." I narrow my eyes. "You still haven't answered my question."

"Ah, you caught that, did you? Clever thing." He clicks his tongue.

"You are rather dreadful at this game," I challenge, and he rolls his eyes. "Only one rule, and yet you manage to break it."

"Patience, beautiful creature. Rules are meant to be bent and sometimes broken." My cheeks flush at the nickname. "I do not wish to unnerve you." He rubs his thumb across his bottom lip, and I roll my eyes. "I am 119, considered very young in Elphyne. An adolescent... I probably appear not much older than a mortal, at say, seventeen. Our aging slows rapidly once we reach 100," he says, scanning my face.

"You are quite old. Kinda gross," I tease, and I swear he flushes. "If you were mortal, you'd already be dead."

"So eager to be rid of me, now, are you?" he teases. "I am the same age as you, or even younger in equivalent to your lifespan. I simply got to remain a child much longer. My turn," Raven purrs, and by the absolutely wicked smile that overtakes his face, I know I am not going to enjoy his question. But those dimples almost make the apprehension worth it.

"Do you really think I am *gorgeous*?" He drags out the word.

My entire body flushes, cheeks burning bright red. I sputter, opening and closing my mouth like a fish. He watches me, that stupid grin on his face, eyes darkened with pure satisfaction. And I start to wish for the hundredth time today that I slit his throat this morning.

"Well?"

"*Yes*," I hiss through my teeth. "But your *obnoxious* personality ruins it."

I didn't think he could possibly look *more* smug but as soon as *yes* leaves my lips, he oozes it like a mortal wound. I shake my head and desperately attempt to redirect this dreadful game.

"It's strange," I ponder, and he hums. "They are scared of you. Terrified, really. Viktoryn, his Knights. I have never seen Viktoryn fear anything. Does it bother you?"

Raven shrugs and is quiet for a moment, expression thoughtful. "I have earned their fear. Are you scared of me?"

I chuckle, looking away to the fire dancing in the hearth. "Not nearly as much as I should be."

He smirks at me, his gaze dipping to my lips then slowly trailing a heated line back to my eyes. My redirection is going *dreadfully*.

"And you are wrong, Willa. He fears nothing more than what you may become."

"He does not fear me. He only hates that he cannot control me."

"Oh, how wrong you are," Raven says, but I roll my eyes.

"It was strange," I admit, "to see you like that. I have not known you long, but with me..." I clear my throat and correct, "With your friends, I mean. You are so... relaxed." It does not feel like the right word, but I do not know what would be.

He cocks his head, considering, pointer finger tapping his glass. "It is part of my duty. Being a ruler means wearing many masks. Knowing when to wear them and how to wield them."

"How do you not get lost in it? How do you not lose pieces of yourself in all of the masks you wear until you cannot separate them from yourself?" I ask, genuinely curious as it seems such a weight to carry.

"You do lose pieces of yourself," he answers, clearing his throat and fiddling with his glass.

"Oh."

"Were you hoping for a more optimistic answer?" Raven chuckles.

"I... I do not know." I shrug. "I do not envy you, it must be a tremendous weight to carry."

Raven simply shrugs back.

"My turn. A truth for a truth." I nod. "Do you still love him?" Raven asks, remaining the picture of casual calm as if the answer will not affect him either way.

But the tightening of his fist around his glass tells another story. I just do not know what tale. If I wasn't studying him as intently as he was studying me, I might've missed it.

I hesitate and immediately know that my hesitation is answer enough. The wrong answer. Something like disappointment flashes on Raven's face before he can shutter himself.

The answer *should* be a resounding *no.* And yet... it isn't. Feelings do not operate on a system of should and should nots. If only it were that simple.

Toryn came into my life and became what I needed most. He held me together when I was only pieces of myself. And because of that, I fell in love with him.

Even though I know now that man was a lie, it doesn't make my feelings a lie. Emotions cannot be discarded like a worn-out coat. Emotions stick to us like glue, sinking into our skin and wrapping around our bones. Drying down around our hearts to be slowly, painfully peeled away bit by bit.

Do I love who Viktoryn is as a Prince? No. *But do I love the man I thought was my light in an otherwise endless dark?* Yes. And though I have slowly started to peel away strips of our love, he is still all over me.

"Not in the ways I once did," I answer, dipping my head to watch the fire, unable to watch whatever reaction crosses his face.

I expect Raven to recoil. But instead of pulling away from the ugly truth I've let spill from my bleeding heart, fingers close around my chin gently, tugging until my eyes collide with the thunderstorm raging in his.

I am *enraptured* in his spell, bewitched by those eyes as my heart starts to pound like it wants to flee from this vulnerability.

My inhale catches in my throat, and I find myself afraid that if I breathe, I will shatter this moment, this intensity, the heat of his body in front of mine.

I think of all the times I have thought of his eyes as a storm, but that wild energy seems to thrum through his entire being. Always restrained, waiting to break free and be a beautiful disaster. I find myself wondering what it's like to be caught in the eye of his storm. If the ruin would be worth a view.

I find myself wishing to be the one who unravels him. The one who shatters his calm, freeing the storm.

He leans in further, lips brushing my cheek as he whispers into my ear, "Are you ready to make your third mistake?"

For a moment I do not understand his meaning, but then it hits me like a lightning bolt. Our very first conversation back in the cellar when I believed him a beautiful wine thief.

Your first mistake was trusting the Fae. Your second mistake was trusting The Summer Court Fae. I look forward to seeing what your third mistake will be, sweet creature.

I am all at once mortified and enthralled. My lungs have forgotten how to breathe as his exhale dances across my skin. My stomach runs away and joins the circus, doing backflips and somersaults.

A breathless, "What?" is all I can manage.

"I said, do you want to make another *mistake*?" His voice is a deep, wicked whisper.

"I heard you the first time," I murmur breathlessly.

"*Hmm.*" He hums in my ear, the vibrations tickling my skin.

My mind slowly tries to work through the fog that's blown in with his nearness.

Do I want to make a mistake? When everything currently hinges on me not making a mistake? On me being able to handle this new world and the maelstrom of razor-sharp emotions that come with it.

Do I want permission to make a mistake that won't cause a Kingdom to crumble or my sister's life to be extinguished? Maybe. *But why does the offer feel like so much more than a simple mistake?*

"No. *Yes.* I do not know," I murmur, wondering how my heart hasn't given out when it's beating *so* fast. My eyes find his lips, and I swallow.

"*Mmmhmm.* Those are the choices. Which one do you *pick,* sweet creature?" Raven purrs, lips ghosting my pulse point. "There is no audience now. No eyes to witness..." He chuckles a satisfied sound when he feels my puttering pulse.

Gods, I know I *should* say no. But I am so far past shoulds and should nots. And his chuckle is as intoxicating as his smile. His lips are a poison designed specifically for me. I would die a thousand times over, only to return to this moment. I've become tall grass in the wind, unable to bend anywhere but into his touch.

"Yes."

Like a leash snapped, he does not waste a second, peppering hungry, reverent kisses along my neck, towards my jaw. I remember how to breathe only as a ragged gasp escapes from my mouth as he tortures me with his.

Another bewitching chuckle follows my gasp, and my head *empties* like a plug pulled on a bathtub. All I can do is *feel...* his lips, his breath, his warmth, *him.*

And Gods, I want to make so many mistakes. I want to *drown* in mistakes. I want to eat and drink and *die* in mistakes.

Raven's hands explore my body, mapping each dip and swell. My hands dive into his soft curls, anchoring his lips to my skin. Fingertips brush my bare skin—

A knock at the door causes us both to tense. Raven pulls his lips from my neck and my chest rises and falls like I've sprinted a mile—his isn't much better. His wild eyes meet mine and then whip to the sound.

"Go away!" he shouts. "*Now*. If you value your life, walk away while you still have legs."

"It is urgent, Your Highness."

"I assume you do not wish to continue with an audience?" Raven asks, and I laugh, shaking my head. "Very well."

He sighs, studying my body as if memorising it. Then he leans back in, lips inches from mine, and whispers, "Come find me *anytime* you want to make a mistake."

I manage a lame nod, tucking my clothes back into place.

"This better be good. If you value your head," he growls at the door, rising to answer it.

A quick, heated conversation has him at the door for less than two minutes. I cannot make out what is said, but when he re-enters the room, the tension has returned to his shoulders. The grim expression on his face makes me shift uncomfortably on the settee.

"What is it?" I question, trying to sort out the knots of anxiety blooming like weeds in my stomach.

"The Ember Palace has sent you a formal invitation to Prince Archer Goldynlocke and *Princess* Fabelle Capri's wedding. It was personally signed by Prince Viktoryn who has requested he escort you."

232

Suddenly, I am not in a storm but sinking to the bottom of the ocean with weights attached to my ankles. Seaweed entangles my limbs, growing until the vines are a noose around my neck. I cannot breathe. There is nothing beautiful about *this* disaster.

Deep down, I was praying that Viktoryn was bluffing, that this was some sort of convoluted move to manipulate me into returning with him. The reality of Raven's words, of the formal invitation, settle on me like an iron weight.

Panic flares in my lungs, and they burn, a sense of utter helplessness washes over me. The walls of the room begin to spin and then close in around me. Every breath brings them closer to boxing me in like the fire in my dreams.

"I need to get out of here. I need to find my sister." I do not mean to say it aloud.

Mindlessly, I rise, grabbing my cloak off the chair it was haphazardly thrown on earlier, securing it around my shoulders.

"*Woah*, Princess. Slow down. What do you think you are doing?" Raven demands.

I ignore him as the sound of my own rushing blood roars in my ears. I suck in too-shallow breaths, reaching for my dagger to ensure it's secured on my thigh. I charge to the door.

Raven moves directly into my path. I dodge him, dipping under his arm. With irritating speed, he is there again, blocking the door with his body.

"Willa. Stop, talk to me."

I take a few measured breaths as a fire ignites inside me, churning with fury. I huff, trying to ease the burning in my lungs.

I stare at the centre of his chest, but I do not meet Raven's eyes—I know if I do, I won't be able to do what needs to be done. My sister won't be safe until the Goldynlockes' bodies are six feet under. They will pay for this.

"I do not want to hurt you. But if you do not move out of my way, I will not hesitate to plunge this dagger into your chest, Raven. *Move*," I snap, pushing him with my palms.

He does not stumble. He only sighs, smoothing down his tunic.

"You cannot stab me whenever you do not get what you want."

"*Watch me.*"

He hesitates, eyes contemplative, but he relents, moving aside. I rush past him, out of the room and into the hallway. Desperately, trying to remember the path we took to the front gates earlier but this castle is an endless winding maze of ice and cave. I turn left and right, marching down the halls, passing stoic midnight black armoured guards, who, to my surprise, make no attempt to stop me. I peer back as I round a bend and am glad to find Raven has not followed.

Except that he has, when his voice sounds beside me, I jump, surprised by his sudden nearness and stealth.

"Willa, you are smarter than this. Think." Raven taps his temple. "What is your plan? Huh? Storming into The Heavily Guarded Ember Palace as an army of one?" Raven questions, voice coated in frustration. "I know you are a lovely vicious thing, but not even you can take them all."

I keep stomping, trying to orient myself in these endless halls. Raven stomps after me, running a hand through his hair.

He rounds on me, trekking backwards in front of me with disturbing grace while attempting to get in my line of view. I duck my head and keep storming forward. But he doesn't relent and I glare at him. He watches me expectantly, waiting for my reply, my grand plan.

I do not have one.

"Smarter than this? You hardly know me. All I am to you is a *mistake*," I spit, tossing his own words back at him.

He flinches, hurt flashing in his eyes. It is quickly replaced by frozen-eyed fury. And I swear the temperature in the hall plummets.

"Do you know how to get to The Ember Palace from here?" He gestures around wildly as he watches me fail to navigate the Palace.

I try not to outwardly cringe.

"Have you travelled in Elphyne at all? Do you know how dangerous it is even for the Fae to travel at night? Do you know what kind of creatures prey on humans?"

When I don't respond, he takes a deep breath.

"Fine! Let me tell you, *mortal*. Creatures that get inside of your mind and lead you into the forest by preying on your darkest desires. Creatures who skin and eat humans alive. Creatures that torture you until your heart gives out by showing you your greatest fears. Creatures who steal the face and voice of your loved ones and lure you astray."

I do not stop. His eyes grow angrier, more desperate.

"What is your plan? *Huh*? Storm up to the gates and demand to see the royal family? Take them out with a single dagger? The Fae are *immortal*, Willa. The Royals are especially powerful, even when weakened. Do you think I will *let* you? This is a suicide mission," he hisses. "I would never ask you not to defend yourself but *think*. Be reasonable."

"*Let* me? I do not require your permission, *Prince*. And I certainly do not recall asking for it!" I shout, continuing to barrel down the hall. "I have a plan! The Fae may be immortal but I imagine even immortals need their *heads*," I snarl, feeling less human and more feral animal who is resisting being caged, acting only on survival.

"Forgive me," he breathes.

"For wh—"

The answer is clear when my back is slammed into the wall of the hallway, the air whooshing from my lungs in one swoop. Raven cushions my head with his hand, ensuring it does not hit the wall. Then he pins my arms to my side.

I thrash under his grasp, flailing, a scream of frustration echoing down the halls. My chest heaves as I try to kick his knee and dislodge the hold. But he places his knee between my thighs, pushing his hips into my waist, caging me in.

"Let me go!" I shriek.

"I am afraid I cannot do that, my love," Raven says with a heartbreaking gentleness.

My head droops, the exhaustion of all that has happened weighs me down like a blanket of boulders. My rage melts into an all-consuming dread and helplessness that turns my bones to iron.

I stop fighting, his grip loosening. *I am so tired.*

It is not until he releases one of my arms to wipe tears from my eyes that I realize I am crying. I risk a glance at his eyes, expecting to see rage, but they are filled with a gentle pity. And somehow, that is so much worse.

"I need to save her, Raven. I can't let them do this to her. She's *everything*. She's all I have left," I plead, voice barely more than a hoarse whisper.

"I know. Alright? I hear you. And I want to help you. But I need you to trust me. You are no good to any of us dead. I... you... you are too important to The Courts to die," he whispers like he is afraid his voice alone could shatter me.

"The Courts?" I ask, voice raw.

What did I expect him to say?

He does not know me. I do not know him. I cannot trust him any more than I can trust Viktoryn. But at least with Viktoryn, I know exactly where I stand and what he wants from me.

I know that Raven cares about his Kingdom. His *duty*. But I want someone to care about *me*. Not what I can offer their courts or kingdoms or magicks. Not because they believe I am some kind of solution, living on borrowed time. But because they see something in me worth loving, worth saving. But I will not wait for that.

I am so tired of being everything. I am so tired of knowing that if I falter, if I stop pushing myself forward—

No—I will continue to be my own Knight in shining armour. Like I always have been and always will be.

I must focus. I need to save my sister. To do that, I need allies. I need Raven and the resources he can offer. His loyalties and feelings cannot affect what I need to accomplish.

"Look at me." I do. "Whether you trust me and my motives or not. Trust that I want the Goldynlockes to pay for what they have done," he murmurs.

I nod and fight my discomfort in him seeing me break down. He pulls me into a tight embrace like he can sense that internal struggle. I stiffen but then melt. We stand in the hall, in each other's arms, for a long while.

"When is the wedding?" I croak.

"Four weeks from tomorrow."

"Let's burn it all down."

"As you wish, Princess."

The next morning, I shift out of bed and make my way to the bathing chamber. When I look in the mirror, a gasp slips my lips. My skin looks ungodly pale, dark half-moon circles sit below my too-wide eyes, giving me a sunken look. Despite getting a full night's sleep, I feel as though I haven't slept.

I bathe, washing my hair and braiding it back into two plaits before returning to the bed chamber. Raven shifts sleepily in the settee, his neck at an uncomfortable angle.

"Sorry about stealing your bed again." I sigh. "You can find me a guest room for tomorrow..."

"No need."

"*No need*?" I question, crossing my arms.

"Unlike The Fire Prince, your safety is my top priority. I would not be of much use to you if you were in the guest rooms on the opposite side of the Palace," he explains, stretching out his limbs in a catlike manner that causes his shirt to ride up. I can't help but steal a glance at his toned stomach and I hate myself for it immediately as he notices. "And perhaps I like being this close to you."

A dangerous gleam twinkles in his eyes as he lengthens his stretch, revealing more toned stomach. I look away. "Though I am a little surprised that you are staying. I thought for certain you would be running back to The Ember Palace."

"As much as I loathe to admit it, Raven. You are right." I cringe. "I cannot do this alone. I need someone who knows the ins and outs of Elphyne."

Raven clears his throat, eyes widening, lips twitching up. "I think I misheard you. Could you repeat that? I fear my ears are not working correctly..."

I toss a pillow from the bed at him, he dodges it with irritating ease. "Has anyone ever told you you are insufferable?"

"Oh, more times than I care to admit," he muses, running his thumb across his bottom lip. "But it has never sounded as pretty coming from their lips."

I roll my eyes and shoot him a glare, but it's much less threatening with the deep blush I can feel blooming on my cheeks.

"Are you going to help me, or are you going to spend the entire day irritating me? I am not going to beg."

"A little begging never hurt anyone but we can save that for later." Raven leans forward, placing his elbows on his knees as he studies me.

"Splendid. So glad I asked for your help. Totally not regretting it," I mumble under my breath. "I am taking the settee tonight."

"Absolutely not. You will be sleeping on the bed. The only way I will let you sleep on the settee is over my dead body."

"If you keep talking, that can be arranged."

"Oh! How you wound me, Princess." Raven clasps his chest in pain.

He rises, stalking towards me as he quickly closes the space between us. Pinning my back against the bedpost, his fingers slowly skim my hips and waist, eyes pinning me in place with a whirlpool of intensity.

"Did I ever tell you how irresistible you are when you are mean?" he murmurs in my ear.

Raven's hands settle on my waist with a tight squeeze, not hard enough to hurt but firm. Almost as if he is trying to convince himself that I am still here. That I am not running back to Viktoryn.

I am breathless, aware of every cool pass of his fingers as he brushes them across my exposed skin. My tongue ties.

"Nothing to say now, Princess? I so look forward to your pointed remarks," he whispers, breath tickling my neck.

"You're the *worst*," I mumble, trying to ignore the way his breath dancing on my skin makes me squirm.

"You do not really believe that, do you? *Hmm*," he mocks. "Do not answer that," he hums, nipping at my ear. "I like it when you spin such pretty, pretty lies."

"Oh, hush," I snap.

"Your wish is my command."

The sudden touch of his soft lips on my neck elicits a gasp as my body automatically arches into his. A soft groan hums across my neck when our bodies meet. He trails feather-light kisses across my neck and jaw, my body filling with a dizzying heat. A quiet moan escapes my parted lips, and he smiles against my neck.

All of my worries about what's to come melt away with each gentle touch. My breath hitches when he kisses the corner of my lips.

He slowly draws back and I immediately miss the contact of his lips. He hovers close enough that if I took a deep breath, our lips would meet. And then, just as quickly as he was against me, he's gone, leaving me dazed.

"Best we get on with it, Princess. We have a lot of work to do if we want to be ready in four weeks," he says with a wink.

"Did I ever tell you I hate you?"

"Not nearly enough."

The following day, Raven gathers a small group of those he trusts the most and summons them to one of the Palace's many meeting rooms.

Amira arrives first, dressed head to toe in black, weapons strapped to every part of her body. I wonder how she manages to not tip over by the sheer weight of the armoury on her back.

Eight chairs line the dark wooden table in the room. To my shock, Princess Maylea of The Spring Court, the Faerie who saved me from the Nixies, wanders in next, planting a kiss on Amira's cheek. Colour stains Amira's cheeks, and she clears her throat as Maylea takes the seat beside her.

"So we meet again. I am glad to see you made it out of the Nixies' attack in one piece," May beams, blonde hair braided into a crown atop her head, filled with wildflowers. "Though I had little doubt."

"All thanks to you," I grin and hesitate. Wondering if it's better if I simply keep my mouth shut. I don't. "Not that I am unhappy to see my valiant protector, but what are you doing here? Aren't you Seelie and heir to The Spring Court? Does that not make you Raven's mortal enemy?"

May glances at Amira, a pained look on her face.

"A long story for another day," Amira answers a tad sharply.

"I heard we are crashing a wedding. I am so in!" Raith announces, bounding through the door with a wild grin, a sword and large axe strapped to his back as he takes the seat beside me.

I lean over to Raith and whisper, nodding to Amira and May as they are caught up in one another. "Are they...?"

"Maylea may be The Spring Court Heir, but she is also our best archer and Amira's fiancee," he whispers, and I grin.

Amira catches me staring and scowls at me. If you had told me that *deadly,* taunting Amira could blush like a schoolgirl, I would've said you were mad. But she softens with May at her side, melting into the bubbly blonde. Amira's gaze shifts to Raith, and her scowl deepens.

"You are on time for once, Raith. A *miracle.* To what do we owe the pleasure of your punctuality?" Amira drawls with a feline grin that doesn't meet her eyes. "Does it perhaps have anything to do with the Princess on your *left?*" She uses the dagger I wasn't aware was in her free hand to point at me.

"Can't a male choose to simply better himself, Amira?" Raith drawls.

She rolls her eyes, and Raith shoots me a lazy but heated grin that causes Raven to clear his throat a little too aggressively.

Olden trails in next followed by another troll that looks nearly identical to him. The surprise must show on my face because Olden and the Olden that's *not* Olden exchange a look.

"Twins." Not Olden that looks like Olden glares at me. "The name's Fredrick, but friends call me Ricky. *You* can call me Fredrick," he remarks, demeanour the opposite of his brother's.

Alright then. Real friendly fellow.

I ignore his comment, studying the twins. The only difference is their horns, Olden's are much longer and curled, whereas Fredrick's are shorter with a point. Without them, I doubt I would be able to tell them apart.

"I refuse to believe we are going to all this trouble over a mortal who will be dust and ash in the blink of an eye. What an utter waste of time," Fredrick mumbles.

Raven's fists slam into the table with a deafening crack. Instinctively, I jump. Ice spreads from his fists, coating the wooden table as it crawls and grows in crystalline webs. The temperature in the room plummets, and my gasp of surprise clouds in the air.

Raven's eyes light, shifting from stormy blue-grey to a deep sapphire filled with barely contained power. His body is deceptively relaxed, expression almost bored.

The Troll, to his credit, hardly winces, but his breath stalls. The tips of my ears begin to sting.

"Care to repeat yourself, *Fredrick*?" Raven speaks with a quiet calm that promises violence.

All eyes in the room turn to Raven, but no one other than Fredrick looks the slightest bit afraid. Raith is hiding a smirk behind his hand. Amira glares at Fredrick as if she can incinerate him with her thoughts.

Olden looks inconvenienced, as if this is a regular occurrence where his twin is involved. May doesn't even attempt to hide her grin as Raven firmly puts the Troll back in his place.

"My apologies, Your Highness. I meant no offence. I only mean to question if it's wise to allocate so many resources to The Summer Court and its unseated heir. We do not normally involve ourselves so publicly in opposing court politics. Especially for something as futile as the wedding of a mortal who we have no claim over."

The temperature in the room continues to drop with each word out of Fredrick's mouth. He doesn't hesitate to continue speaking. I'm not sure if he's brave or stupid.

"Humans are not even considered *full* citizens under our Elphyne's laws. And as she is currently a Princess without a throne and the lifespan of humans is no more—" Fredrick's speech is cut off by a choking sound, his face turning blue as he gasps. His hands fly up to claw at his chest, eyes widened in panic.

Not brave, definitely stupid.

"I addressed your *concerns* privately this morning, Fredrick. You were warned to drop the issue. I can only believe that your inability to follow orders is an attempt to undermine my operation. And to instill doubt in our ally about her worth not only as a future ruler but as a being *you* see as lesser than Fae." Raven leans forward, towering over the table.

"You have been warned that this type of thinking is not welcome in my Palace time and time again. You would think living with the prejudice Trolls face from the Seelie, you would be wise enough to understand the harm in these ideologies."

"Are you too moronic to process the commands of your future King, or are you attempting to prove your inadequacy as a member of my Inner Circle? Your lack of critical thinking is a liability. I have allowed you plenty of leniency in your past missteps. But no more. Willa, despite being *mortal*, has more claim to any sort of power or throne than you could ever hope to grasp. If you are unable or unwilling to do the job assigned to you, speak now, and I will relieve you of all your duties and happily banish you from my lands."

He must pull his power back because Fredrick chokes in a gasping breath and begins shaking his head frantically.

"No, Your Highness. I apologize."

The ice theatrics are interrupted by the arrival of a muscular, short female Faerie with buzzed brown hair, warm mahogany skin, and shimmering golden-brown eyes. Her expression is neutral as she takes in the room.

"Is there a problem here, boys?"

"Is there a problem, Fredrick?" Raven asks, with a razor-sharp grin that holds no kindness.

"None, Your Highness."

"Glad to hear it. The name's Kaali," Kaali says, giving me a two-finger wave and a crooked grin.

I recognize her as the other female who was in the trees earlier with Amira, when Viktoryn stormed the gates.

Raven gives a final warning look at Fredrick as the ice recedes.

"What an exciting way to start the morning," Prince Raven drawls. "Let us begin. As you all know, this is Willa Caprimore." He gestures to me, and I wince a little at the use of my true last name. "Willa, these are the members of my court or fellow courts," he corrects when his eyes meet May's, and she gives him a respectful nod, "that I would trust with my life. They handle the tasks I trust only them to complete. I expect them to extend the same level of loyalty and protection to you."

The room nods in agreement with a bit of annoyance. Fredrick cringes at the statement. I get the impression this isn't the first time *they* have heard this speech regarding my safety. Or maybe they aren't overly pleased to be on nursemaid duty for a lost mortal Princess of a rival court.

"This is my Inner Circle. We are known by many names, not all kind. They report directly to me. They have sworn an oath to protect the best interests of The Winter Court and its heir. We all agree—" Raven glares at Fredrick with a look that dares him to challenge his claim, "that it is in the best interest of my court to have you as an ally. This meeting is to determine what we can do in regard to Fabelle's upcoming wedding within the laws that govern The Seasonal Courts. Anything discussed within these walls is to remain between us. I trust you all to use the utmost discretion."

For some reason, at the discretion comment, Raven sends a look in Raith's direction, and he responds by holding his hands in the air, pleading innocence.

"One time, Raven, it happened one time," Raith mutters.

"Three," Amira corrects.

Raven ignores them both.

"Olden, as you know, is one of my Royal Advisors. Fredrick commands The Crystal Palace's Royal Guards. Raith is the Commander of The Crystal Palace's Army. Kaali is our Head Combat Instructor. Amira is my Spymaster and Second in Command. Princess Maylea, though she may not be directly from The Winter Court, has proven that she is a trusted asset and ally. And she happens to be our best sharpshooter. Any questions, Willa?"

So many. But put on the spot, my mind blanks, so I shake my head. The meeting runs all day. Decisions are made regarding the training I require, the wedding, basic strategy, spy placements, and required weaponry.

By the end of the day, my brain feels ready to overflow, spilling out all the topics of the day onto the meeting room floor.

Back in The Prince's room, I rub my head, trying to soothe the ache that's set up shop, pounding against my skull with hammers.

Plopping down on the bed, I let out a sigh and shut my eyes. It's mere moments before I hear the door, Raven strolls into the room, settling on the bed beside me as we stare at the ceiling, shoulder to shoulder.

"Can I ask you a question?"

"Of course, my beautiful creature."

"Viktoryn said that he used compulsion to get me to sleep on the journey here. And I believe that Princess Naenea used it to get me into the water with the Nixies. Is there a way for mortals to resist compulsion?"

The temperature in the room drops as I speak. I glance over to Raven to see he's gone rigid, the good humour gone from his expression.

"Compulsion is a type of glamour that crosses the line of free will. It should be used sparingly, if at all." Raven swallows. "There are ways to resist it. Two, to be exact. Mortals can train a mental shield to resist compulsion, but this can take years... and for some, it never works. The second way is to acquire and wear a ronan berry and iron charmed necklace or bracelet on your person. I have seen mortals sew them into their clothes. We will acquire you some before the wedding."

"Alright."

"Can I ask about your scars?" Raven says, surprising me with the direction of his thoughts.

My hand instinctively runs over the raised scar that runs from the column of my neck to the start of my collarbone.

"Why?"

"The Nixie attack..." He pauses. "Faerie healers tended to the wounds, correct? They should have been able to fully heal the wounds, leaving no scarring. Any decent healer could have. However..."

He turns to me, leaning his weight on his elbow and placing his head in his hand. Gently running his fingers across the visible scars on my arms and neck. "All of your injuries left scars..."

A wave of ice-cold shock slams my stomach.

"Why would Viktoryn's healers leave scars then?"

"They *wouldn't*," his eyes fall closed for a moment, "well, they shouldn't." Raven shakes his head, studying my eyes as if looking for an anchor for his next words. "Unless *commanded* to do so. I assume he informed the healers to leave them. As some sort of sick reminder to you of what happens when you try to rise against the Fae or in some hope that it would make you seem less desirable to others or to convince you that you required his protection..." he says evenly, but his jaw is strained. "I do not know. All I know is that you have scars when you should not."

He traces the scar on my neck. "I refuse to consider what would have happened if Maylea had not been there." His eyes fall shut. "I sent her to watch you... but."

"I have been hurt many times before you and will be many times after you, Raven. You are not at fault," I mutter quietly, staring at the ceiling.

I try to recall all of the events of the attack and Viktoryn's reaction following.

Did he order them to leave me scarred? I wish I could say that the idea sounds preposterous. But after seeing the cruelty and trickery of the Fae first hand... I would not put it past Viktoryn to permanently disfigure me to prove a point.

"I think you might be onto something." I sigh, running my hands through my hair to free it from its braid. Raven's eyes follow my fingers as they work.

"I should be more upset by the notion, but I've always had scars. Either from my mother or training with my father. They feel like a map of all I have endured and overcome. What's a few more? It will take a lot more than a few Nixies to stop me," I say, half-jokingly, but I mean it.

"I could have my healers remove them if you wish it. I hate that he allowed you not only to be attacked... but to go as far as to permanently disfigure you." He shakes his head. "I did not prevent it, I should have."

"Erasing them... it feels like letting him win. These scars are proof that no matter what the Fae throw at me... I will go down fighting. And it wasn't your fault. I didn't even know you then... But to know you were watching out for me... That means a lot, that's what matters. You do not owe me anything, Raven," I murmur.

Raven goes unnaturally still, and the temperature of the room plummets again, this time almost painfully.

The tips of my ears start to sting as I turn to him, confused by his reaction. His eyes swim with emotion before he masters his expression, shutting me out. It feels like he has slammed an ice wall between us.

Raven pushes up from the bed, mutters something about royal business, and stalks out of the room, slamming the door.

The next three weeks fly by. My mornings are spent being drilled with Elphyne history and court etiquette until my head aches. My instructor is an ancient-looking female Faerie named Olga with snow-white hair and brittle aging bones.

When my curiosity gets the better of my manners, I ask her how old she is. In response, I get whacked with the wooden, silver-tipped cane and cursed at. I grow fond of her much more quickly than she grows fond of me.

In the afternoons, when I have a few free hours, I pretend to scour the library, using it as cover to meet with Princess Maylea. May pulled me aside during my first week here and suggested we meet privately to discuss matters of The Seelie Kingdom without the presence of The Winter Court's Inner Circle.

As much as it felt like a betrayal to our friends—and that is what they have become... *friends*—there was a very real possibility that we would end up ruling The Seelie Kingdom, together. Making us extremely powerful allies. And I really did like her. We had become more than allies. We had become close friends.

During one of these initial meetings, May had proven her worth as an ally separate from The Winter Court.

Hidden behind the stacks in the romance section, May waved me over with a conspiratorial grin.

"Are you certain you weren't followed?" I asked. "Your future wife is a spymaster."

"Precisely. So you see, I have learned how to be very sneaky," she remarked. I laughed as she cast a bubble of magicks to conceal our voices. "Did you get the key?"

"The key?" I echoed, schooling my expression to neutral as the gold medallion whispered to me from my dress pocket.

"The rains of May will be your guide," Maylea said with a wink, and I hid my shock.

She smirked at me, not buying my fake nonchalance. "I snuck it to Alice. She's a... friend of mine.

"Wait! You were the one who gave me this crazy thing? It almost lit my bed on fire," I whisper shouted, exasperated.

"Ha. So you do have it."

"Maybe."

"I am going to teach you how to use it."

"Use it? Why? Why are you helping me? Why risk betraying Amira's and Raven's trust?" I questioned.

"I owe your mother a lifetime of favours. Fae do not like leaving things owed."

After our secret meetings, my evenings consist of combat and defence training with May and Kaali. Occasionally, when her duties allow, Amira joins us, mostly to send not-so-subtle flirty glances at May. And to insult my skills.

I soon learn that the Fae's definition of *'combat and defence training'* is synonymous with borderline torture. They throw every type of weapon and fight style that they can dream up at me. They decide that, despite their superior Fae abilities, I should fight all three of them at once.

Still, I find that my time with the ruthless and determined ladies of The Winter Court becomes my favourite part of the day. I find myself admiring them. Being surrounded by such strong and capable females bolsters my belief in myself.

I bond with May over our shared love of animals—and our shared Seelie alliance.

Kaali—though the quiet, broody type—happily shows me every way to make a man crumple to the floor with only my bare hands with unmatched enthusiasm. A skill she encourages me to attempt on every unfortunate male soul who wanders past our training sessions. I do, happily.

May lets me know that, for a human, I have excellent accuracy with a bow—high praise coming from the best sharpshooter in Elphyne. While Kaali drills me about how my wavering focus will get me killed and takes great joy in demonstrating all of those ways, it very well might until bruises cover me like a second skin.

I find myself subconsciously searching the room for Raven, but he never stops by. And then I find myself hating that I am looking for him at all. A few times, I swear I can feel his eyes on me, but when I turn, he is never there.

And though they may be brutal, they are brutally effective. I am improving daily. And if I have any hope of surviving the coming months, brutal is exactly what I need to be.

My long days end with strategy meetings hosted by Raven, where we iron out all the details of our coming mission. Other than these meetings, I don't see much of him. I start to get the feeling he is avoiding me but decide that might be for the best.

Sometimes, I see him before I fall asleep—he's taken to sleeping on a cot on the other side of the room. As if he cannot get far enough away from me. It makes me feel like I truly was just a mistake to him. One he's regretting making.

I cannot bring myself to feel the same way.

Less than five days remain until Elle's wedding, but I try not to think about it, banishing any thoughts of the event away as soon as they appear.

Raven isn't back from wherever he goes during the day when I sink into bed. But that's not abnormal.

Exhaustion has become my self-assigned best friend and I am slipping in and out of sleep when a piercing alarm sounds. My heart is racing by the time my mind drags itself out of the fog of almost-sleep.

I sit up, crossing to the window to see if I can locate the source of the commotion. I spot a small fire by the front gates in the endless falling snow. Knights in midnight black-plated armour run towards the flames. *How odd.*

A click and groan snags my attention from the fire, dragging it to the wall near the bathing chamber. My hand instinctively swipes the dagger off the side table as my heart kicks up into a sprint.

I blink a few times to clear my eyes as *Viktoryn* prowls out from an opening in the wall. A sickening smirk plastered on his face, a bloodied green head crowned in marigolds in his hand.

"Hello darling, it has been too long," Viktoryn purrs. "I brought you a present." He holds up the severed head like a prize.

I feel sick.

"Not long enough." I swallow. "Is that...?"

"The Fae who drugged and danced with what was mine? *Yes.*" Viktoryn grins. "It is also a reminder of what I do to those who touch what does not belong to them. I want you to think of him every time you let that avian mutt touch you. I want you to know what happens when you do not behave," Viktoryn says, eyes gleaming with pleasure. "*And* now that the threat has been extinguished, you have no reason to delay your return."

I try to ignore the unseeing, gory head in his hands as he places it gently on a decorative side table. A marigold falls from its grassy hair to the floor, and bile burns my throat. He begins to walk around the room as if he knows it well, lighting wall sconces and candles.

"You have two seconds to tell me what you are doing here or I'll stab first and ask questions later," I spit, taking a confident step towards him even as my body trembles.

"I am so glad I do not have to pretend I find your mouth endearing any longer." He sighs, running his hands over his chin. "Other than my special delivery, I have information that you may find *enticing*."

"How did you know I was in this room? How did you get past the guards?" I demand.

"Oh, always so naive. If it was not so tragic, it might be sweet. Are you to tell me you believe that bird-boy is the only Prince with spies?"

Someone has been watching me.

He crosses the room to stand in front of me, eyes scanning the space. "*Curious.*"

"You didn't answer my questions," I say, lining up my blade with his heart.

He smirks, glancing at the blade.

"Are you really going to try and stab me?"

"Are you really willing to stick around and find out?" I counter, glaring. "I think when I decide to kill you, I'll opt for something more public, befitting of a treasonous murderer."

"I so look forward to seeing you try," he mocks, patting me on the head like a child.

I grit my teeth and consider cutting his hand off. "Cut the pleasantries, Viktoryn. Why are you here? What do you find so *curious*?"

"I only find it curious that you are sleeping in his bed. Was it so easy to forget me, darling? It is impressive. Who would have thought a mere mortal could hop from one Faerie Prince's bed only to land in another? What a scandal."

He gestures to me and then to the bed behind me, his eyes blazing. "A downgrade, but impressive nonetheless."

"So very easy," I purr. "Do you really think I could ever love you? Or *want* you?" I spit. "You would not be calling it a downgrade if you knew how good 'bird-boy' is with his hands." I smirk.

He doesn't need to know that Raven and I have done very little in reality. *Humans can lie.*

Viktoryn's body goes from relaxed to rigid in a breath. His hands forming white-knuckled fists at his sides. He presses into me so quickly that I don't have a chance to react, fingers pressing into the soft spot in my wrist, causing my dagger to drop to the stone with a clang.

His spare hand grips my throat as he slams my back into the wall with a force that causes a yelp of pain to escape me as my head connects with the wall. At the sound, he *smiles,* squeezing tighter as he lifts me onto my tiptoes.

The panic I expect to feel never arrives—instead, bolstered resolve settles within me as I think back to the training Kaali has instilled.

"Remember, you *useless* little thing," he growls, shaking me slightly, "you were mine first. I might be tolerating your adventures with that scum now. But *I own you.*"

Viktoryn crowds over me until we share breath, or until we would if I could breathe.

"I have the one thing you care about most in the world. The one thing we both know you would leave him and his little friends for in a heartbeat. The thing you would *crawl* on your knees before me to get back. I have played your little games, darling. But they will be ending soon."

"You wish."

I connect my knee to his groin. Following the movements I've been taught with ease, even as the grip on my throat causes my head to spin.

My knee slams into him, a groan slipping from his lips. His grip loosens as I bring my arms up between us, forcing my elbows down into his arms, breaking his grip. Bracing my back on the wall, I bring my feet up to his chest and kick, sending him sprawling backwards.

A wild look paints his features as he flies back, colliding with the stone floor, knocking the table his *'present'* was on over and sending it flying.

Viktoryn rises slowly, never letting his eyes wander from me. He grabs the head and backs towards the open passage. I can't help the slight smirk that rises on my lips as he watches me with a new uncertainty. I retrieve my dagger from the floor.

"Someone's taught the mutt some new tricks. *Interesting.* All I am saying, *pet,* is he must not have told you the truth yet. If he still has you snuggled in his bed... can I really blame him? A male does enjoy a bitch as a bed warmer," he snaps.

I stifle a gag. But his words do as he intended, planting a seed of doubt in me about Raven.

"Get out. Take your present with you," I growl, taking a step towards him. "This bitch has teeth."

At my step forward, he smirks, but the delight that was in his eyes upon his arrival has faded. As he steps back, I throw my dagger; it misses the tip of his nose by a hair, implanting itself in the wall. Viktoryn turns to me with slightly wide eyes.

"And a *dagger*."

My heart races as I wait for the adrenaline to leave my body. I fix the table and chairs, grabbing the stray marigold and shoving it into a crevice behind Raven's wardrobe.

I lock myself in the bathing chamber as I hear Raven return to the room. The ache around my neck becomes a necklace of pain as the green-haired Fae's decapitated head appears in my mind.

Seated with my back pressed into the cool door, I run my fingers over the hand-shaped mark blooming on my skin, watching my fingers move in the large, gilded, full-length mirror.

I sit, unable to move because I don't know what to tell Raven. Viktoryn could not have gotten into the Palace without help. And he has spies within the Palace, watching me, reporting where I *sleep*. Which means I cannot trust anyone here. On top of that, I don't know what Raven is hiding. But he is hiding something.

My mind keeps hitching on the fact that Viktoryn *cannot* lie, and he seems to believe that whatever secret Raven has kept from me is severe enough that I wouldn't want to be close to him.

Trust only yourself. Trust the fire. Do not trust another soul. Power corrupts them all.

I replay all of our conversations, searching for something I missed. I think about how I haven't seen or met The High King or Queen of The Winter Court. How that should've struck me as odd earlier. But I've been too busy with issues of The Summer Court to question much of how The Unseelie Kingdom operates. But his parents must be alive if Raven hasn't ascended the throne.

A knock on the door causes me to jump.

"Willa? Are you alright? There was a small security breach," Raven calls, voice coated in concern.

I almost scoff at the question. This is the most he's said to me directly in *weeks*, and it took a *security* breach.

I take a deep breath. I *should* tell him about Viktoryn's visit, but he will want to know what was said. And I keep picturing his head in the place of the green-haired Fae. Plus the knowledge of that passageway could prove useful, but I won't be able to hide this bruise for long...

"Fine. Just having some stomach pain. Could you send for a healer?" The lie glides all too easily off my tongue.

"Of course. Can I come in? Check on you?" he requests.

This time, I do scoff under my breath. Annoyed that *now* he wants to pretend he cares.

"No. I do not feel well. Can you please just send for a healer?" I plead.

He sighs. "Very well."

All I can think as we communicate with this door between us is that it feels like so much more distance than a door. A cavern has split the Earth, shattering our precious trust, and somehow we have ended up standing on opposite sides. The distance is insurmountable.

Have I repeated the same mistake as before? Handing over my heart and trust like spare change to whoever will take it? Switching one wicked Prince for another? Maybe Viktoryn was right when he said I was desperate to be loved.

Has that made me an easy target, walking from one trap into another? Or is Vikoryn messing with me? Trying to cause rifts in my alliances? If so, I fear it's been all too effective.

By the time the healer arrives, I have formulated a plan. A slightly stupid, definitely reckless plan, but a plan nonetheless.

When I first allow the healer in, her eyes widen at the sight of my neck, and she immediately insists that the Prince come in and see. I hold a finger to my lips to shush her, not wanting Raven to hear us with his pesky Fae ears.

I manage to spin a half-convincing lie about the injury occurring during training. I tell her I am embarrassed for Raven to see it. The healer doesn't seem to fully buy it but she relents, healing the bruising quickly and letting me know that it might be a bit tender for a few days.

I exit the bathing chamber with her. Raven gives her a nod of appreciation, and her eyes dart nervously from him to me as she bows and scurries from the bedchamber. She chose the right career path—she'd make an abominable spy.

"Are you alright?" he questions, eyes narrowed as he studies me.

"Fine," I murmur, and he eyes me suspiciously but eventually sighs.

We prepare for bed and settle in. It is not long until Raven's breathing deepens and evens out. I find no such luck, staring at the ceiling as questions that only breed more questions wrack my mind.

An insatiable nagging that I've stepped out of one trap only to find myself in another, filling my body with panic and dread.

Once I am sure Raven's heavily asleep on his cot, I slip out of bed to gather supplies.

With a heavy cloak slung over my shoulders and a pair of fur-lined pants on, I brace myself for The Winter Court weather. My dagger is secure on my hip, gloves tugged over my hands, and in my pocket lies the golden medallion, a map, and a compass I '*borrowed*' from Raven's office.

A thunderstorm of conflicting feelings rage inside me as I dare one last glance at Raven's sleeping figure and I pray I am not making a mistake.

I pop the secret passageway door open with a quick click. Wincing at the sound, I glance back to see if Raven's moved, but his chest rises and falls evenly. I blow out a breath and step into the dimly lit hall.

The cramped passage isn't lit, and I hesitate, my claustrophobic tendencies begging me to turn around and go back to bed.

But I need to do this. I need to get to Elle before anyone knows I am gone. Viktoryn won't be expecting me. Raven will assume I got up early and went to training.

If I can find The Royal Stables I passed a few days ago with Amira, I can get a horse and get my sister and me out of here before anyone knows we are gone. Far, far away from these Princes and their never-ending, life-threatening complications. I can do this for her. I *have* to.

I pull the door gently shut behind me, darkness consuming me, and my breath hitches. *One foot in front of the other*, I repeat in my mind as the panic tries to rise in me like a phoenix. Placing my hands on either side of the freezing walls, I guide my blind steps forward over uneven rock.

I've been walking for a few minutes, counting the seconds in my head. Still yet to see any light. And I start to wish, more than anything, I found a way to bring a lantern or a torch as I continue to step into the never-ending blackness, my chest tightening into knots.

A thin strip of light appears along the ground, like a threshold to a door. A huff of relief leaves my lips as I quicken my steps towards it. I feel around blindly for a latch or door knob. My hand hits an empty wall ornament that would be fit for a torch, and following pure instinct, I pull down. It clicks, the door creaking open a crack.

I grin, surprised that it actually worked. I listen through the crack in the door for guards or any sign someone has caught onto my escape attempt, but all is as still and silent as the snowy night.

I push the door open to step through, and my heart leaps into my throat as I walk directly into a body cloaked in black.

"Isn't this familiar... Going somewhere, sweet creature?" the hooded figure coos.

My heart flutters. I would know that voice anywhere.

"R-raven... I thought..."

He ignores my attempt to speak, dropping his hood. His expression is unreadable, but when I see the pure fury storming in his eyes, I suck in a breath and resist the urge to step back. Unlike mine or Viktoryn's anger, which burns hot, his is brittle and ice-cold. A frigid, angry wind.

"We really need to stop meeting like this," he intones, stepping back to lean against the wall, lit only by wall sconces—half cast in darkness, he looks formidable.

I say nothing, staring at him like he's a figment of my imagination and this is all a bad dream. Anything I can say will only incriminate me further. The accusation in his eyes is painfully clear.

I take a step back towards the passageway only to collide with another body, a gasp escaping my lips. I whip around to meet a second shadowed figure.

"Hello there, sweetheart," Raith drawls, arms crossed, a smirk plastered on his lips, but his eyes are filled with accusation.

I am good and truly trapped between them. Raven in front of the only exit, Raith blocking the passageway back.

I turn back to face Raven, but my mouth has run away, and my mind has emptied in my panic. Nothing I say will fix the look in his eyes—a look of pure betrayal. And nothing he says will fix the distrust in mine.

"Not going to attempt to explain or deny what you were doing?" Raven asks, his voice a deadly calm as he stuffs his hands into his pockets. "You can lie, after all."

"I do not owe you an explanation," I hiss.

He glares down at me, waiting for one anyway. I stare up at him, crossing my arms over my chest and widening my stance. Praying he cannot see the way my hands tremble or hear how hard my heart is racing.

"*Hmm*," Raven replies when I say nothing. "I have to say, I am disappointed. Where did all your foolish bravery go, little firebird? So ready to fly away without a farewell?"

I do not answer, and his eyes narrow.

Raven moves quickly, pinning me into the wall beside the doorway, ripping my dagger—his dagger, his gift—from my sheath and tossing it to Raith, who catches it easily. My hands form tight fists at my sides.

"I thought I was not a prisoner. I thought…" I trail off because I do not know what I thought. I do not know what to think or how to think when he is near me.

"You thought *what*? Sweet creature? *Hmm*?" His cool fingers skim my cheek. "You thought you could sneak out of my bed and into this passageway and somehow find a way to The Ember Palace? You thought I would stay soundly asleep while you snuck off to get yourself *killed*?"

He tilts his head and pulls the crushed marigold flower I hid behind his wardrobe from his pocket. He twirls it between his fingers.

My heart kicks into a run as I stare at that cursed flower.

"You thought I did not know Viktoryn made it to my room earlier, revealing the passageway to you before filling your pretty little head with his poison?"

He sounds so brutally calm. The kind of calm that warns you of the coming storm. And I am about to be trapped in the eye of it.

I stare into Raven's cold, accusatory eyes, searching for any of the normal, playful warmth he radiates. I find none. But I do not back down, hoping the fire in my eyes rivals the ice in his.

"You thought my healer would not inform me of the hand marks *he* left around your neck?" His voice is no longer calm—it's a frozen razor-sharp knife of hissing rage.

The hallway's temperature plummets, and chills run up my spine. My next exhale comes out frosty.

"*Hmm*? You thought what, my dear? *Do tell*. I'm endlessly curious about the inner workings of your mind." His icy finger taps my temple.

"Especially when they mean running directly towards the male who *strangled* you this very evening. I cannot for the life of me find the logic in that. So please, go ahead and grace me with your superior thought process."

Raith lets out a quiet chuckle, and I hesitate, shame filling my cheeks, painting them crimson. I look away, unable to meet the anger and frustration in his gaze. My fury fizzles out, leaving me with doubt.

My hand subconsciously reaches up to brush my fingertips over the still-sore skin around my throat. I wince, trying to swallow the guilt caught in it, but find I cannot.

Taking a deep breath, I locate my absent resolve. I will not allow him to shame me for doing what needs to be done to protect what's left of my family.

"Do you really want to do this with an audience?" I spit, nodding my head towards Raith, who is casually leaning in the opening of the passageway, looking dangerously amused.

"It did not bother you that day at the gates," Raven drawls. "If I do recall, you quite enjoyed an audience then."

I scoff, cheeks heating as I remember the feel of Raven's lips on my neck.

"Pretend I'm not even here," Raith says, shooting me a wink

"Silence, Raith," Raven commands.

"Do you really need him here? Two versus one doesn't seem entirely fair."

"She's got a point, Rave. Unless you think she can take you now that Kaali's taught her all those funky moves," Raith reasons, doing a weird half-dancing movement with his arms that looks like uncoordinated mock fighting.

"*Funky* moves?" Despite myself, my lips twitch up.

"Raith?" Raven says calmly but firmly.

"Yes, boss man," Raith drawls, mock bowing for Raven.

"What part of *silence* was not clear?" Raven sighs but somehow manages to make it sound like a threat.

"Fair point," Raith responds, miming zipping his lips.

I blink at both of them for a moment, wondering how I ended up here. I turn back to Raven to deal with the more pressing issue.

"Let me go, Raven. Or did you not mean what you said to Viktoryn? That you would let me go back to The Ember Palace whenever I wish. Well, I *wish* it," I hiss, pushing him back.

Something in his expression shifts as he steps back. Part of Raven's icy rage melts, leaving behind watery amusement. His ability to go from furious to amused in seconds sends my head spinning.

He beams like the sun at me, smiling wide, but none of that warmth reaches his eyes. I find myself trying to swallow, but my throat has gone dry.

"Do you?" Raven coos, brow raised.

"Yes."

His grin is all-teeth, predatory.

"Do you really?" he challenges.

"Yes," I push.

"I think you are spilling lies right to my face, sweet creature."

He leans in, but I refuse to cower back.

"I do not care what you think."

"I am sensing a pattern here," Raith interrupts, hands over his heart. "You do not owe us an explanation, and you do not care what we think. You wound me, sweetheart. I thought we were friends."

"Shut up, Raith!" Raven and I hiss in unison.

Raith sinks back a bit at whatever look he sees in our eyes. The temperature in the room plummets further, and I am so glad I am fully dressed for a winter storm as I shiver. Even if the storm I ended up in wasn't the one I prepared for.

"*I* care about what you think. Tell me what you thought," Raven says, attention fully on me and seeing the intensity in his eyes I understand why Raith recoiled.

When I do not start to speak, he grips my chin in between his fingers, forcing me to maintain eye contact with him. I shake my head, the picture of defiance. I can't. I can't tell him what I think. I can't tell him anything. I can't trust anyone. Even as this conversation digs into my body and eviscerates my heart. And the space between us continues to expand, every inch pure agony. *I can't.*

Raven shifts his free arm, caging me to the wall. He leans down until his face is an inch from mine. His frame consumes my space, my air, my being. I momentarily forget how to breathe. And I am suddenly and vibrantly aware that I should be very, *very* afraid because I am cornered by an apex predator. The most dangerous and powerful Faerie in all of Elphyne.

"Tell me," he says, this time a whisper, scanning my features, waiting.

I do not speak.

He *tsks* three times.

"Stubborn as always. I admire that you stick to what you know, Princess." Raven shakes his head, sliding his other hand to my throat, gently pressing into my pulse point. I wince. And he *smirks* when he feels my pounding heart. "Oh, how your heart sings for me."

"Let me tell you what *I* think, Willa. I think you thought that I did not notice or care about the change in your behaviour this evening. I think you thought I believed you when you said you would wait for my assistance to rescue your sister. I think you thought you could sneak out of my bed through a passageway you should not know exists and, by some miracle, find a way to The Ember Palace without meeting an early grave," he growls the last word.

"Which is both fascinating and unendingly foolish. Your bravery is something else, beautiful girl. Unparalleled, really." He tilts his head, amused.

I attempt to pull back from his grip, feeling entirely too vulnerable as he lays out all the assumptions he's made that come far too close to the truths hidden in my mind. A smugness lies in his eyes as if he knows it, too.

He glides his hands across my skin until they cup each side of my neck. The movement is gentle, but I am overtly aware of how easily he could snap my neck. My breath hitches, as Raven slowly runs his fingers up and down the tender skin left behind from Viktoryn's attack.

I tense under his hands. He sighs, eyes dancing with a sick combination of amusement, disappointment and anger. And maybe... just maybe, a bit of *hurt*.

"I think you thought I would be so careless with your safety that I would not notice the scent of another male in my room. Followed by your suspicious need for a healer. I think you thought I had no idea that you have your own schemes afoot."

I swallow.

"I think your precarious trust in me is justified based on what you know about my world. Yet your refusal to inform me that you had been injured is utterly ridiculous and *childish*."

I find I am all out of good ideas and patience, so I replace them with bad ideas and anger. I grit my teeth and do the single stupidest thing I can think of, even though a dangerous otherworldly being has its hands around my neck.

But I need to get out of here. I can't breathe.

Bringing my foot up, I drive my heel into the top of his foot. His grip loosens, and I slap his arms away. Turning to stomp off exactly like the child he has accused me of being. He hisses in pain but then baffles me by starting to *laugh*.

I've heard that laugh before, and the sound sends a wave of icy spiders down my spine. I halt, hesitating and Raith steps forward to block my path. I glare at him with as much hate as I can muster. He just grins, that stupid, charming Raith grin.

I feel the warmth of a body press into my back. Steadying the trembling in my legs as gentle fingers come from behind me, brushing my hair over my shoulder. My eyes fall shut from the soft touch.

"So stupidly brave." Breath kisses my neck. Then lips. I shiver.

"Let me go, Raven," I hiss.

"No. I am not done telling you what I think. And until I am, you are going to stand here, like a good girl, and *listen*. Are you capable of that, firebird?" It is worded like a question, but it is not one.

I nod.

He turns me to face him, scanning me like he is looking for something specific, but I do not know what. His face softens, and yet all I want to do is run.

Raven re-grabs my chin and forces me to meet his eyes. All I can think is how much I hate him for this. How humiliating it is to be scolded like a *child* with an army commander as the audience.

"I think your actions insult my intelligence and defame my character. And I think that if you knew what was *good* for you, despite whatever The Fire Prince planted in your sweet little mind, you would stay with me." He pauses, watching, waiting and yet my voice has run off because my legs cannot.

"But you don't, do you, sweet girl?" Raven's lips ghost my hairline. "You do not know what is good for you. No one has ever been good to you. Always so ready to race into danger to protect that little sister of yours." He studies me. "Who protects *you*, firebird?" His voice softens, and my heart... *shatters*.

The question so *foreign*. His voice is so quiet. But the truth is so deafeningly loud.

Who protects you, firebird?

He sounds so genuine, it physically hurts. And for the first time since Viktoryn placed those seeds in my mind... *I think I have made a mistake. A horrible, terrible, undoable mistake.*

But Raven's behaviour is so confusing and all-consuming. Around him, I do not know the difference between up and down. He's under my skin and inside my mind like a burrowing parasite. Digging into my thoughts and shifting through my feelings. And I do not understand.

He calls me a mistake, he rages at me for not thinking about my own safety. He kisses my neck, he storms out of the room and avoids me for weeks.

I do not know what to believe, and my head is scrambled from all of the betrayal and games. I wish I could simply ask the world to pause. I wish I could beg for a few minutes. To let me unscramble all the puzzle pieces being flung at me.

But the pieces have become a shattered mirror reflecting all my failures and mistakes and choices right back at me. And in them, I see a little girl plagued with questions, in over her head and full of wide-eyed terror.

I so badly want to stick the pieces back together. But I am *drowning* in puzzle pieces and broken glass. They are being shoved down my throat and branded into my skin. And I am bleeding faster than I can drown.

"You've been avoiding me," I whisper.

"Yes."

"Why?"

He shuts his eyes, leaning his forehead against mine.

"I wish I had a good answer for you," he whispers.

I nod once, pretending that the answer doesn't hurt. Then I pull away, and he lets me.

"You said I'm not a prisoner here. But if I am not free to go when I please, what *does* that make me?"

Raven shakes his head, a smile on his lips as he stares up at the ceiling like he's praying to The Goddess of the Moon for patience. When his eyes meet mine, they are haunted and angry. But they are also defeated.

"You want to go, *go*. I will not stop you. If you think you have got a better shot out there, all alone, than with me... But when you make it less than ten paces outside the gate before you are swallowed by the forest and tortured by the creatures keen to skin you alive, do not say I did not warn you, Willa."

He leans down until his lips brush the shell of my ear, words dropping into a whisper, "But do you know what I think? I think you want to stay, and *that* scares you more than anything. Do you know how I know this?" I inhale so quickly it sounds like a gasp. "Since the moment you arrived here, you have not made a single inquiry about returning. Leading me to believe you do not wish to."

I do not know how he manages to make his spoken truths into sharpened daggers that cut me into pieces, but he does.

I care about what you think.

Who protects you, firebird?

I think you want to stay, and that scares you more than anything.

Just to spite him, I want to turn and go. But I know he's *right,* and I hate him for it. I hate how he can read me like this after only knowing me for a short while. I hate how, around him, my innermost thoughts are inked diary pages on my naked skin, pages he consumes greedily, without remorse. I put up walls and he rips them down with single sentences.

I've spent my life hiding behind those walls. It was the only way to survive. To survive signing my life over to an army I did not believe in, to survive the abuse I was dealt with daily, to survive handing over my childhood in exchange for my sister's.

I had to cauterise my own bleeding heart, ice the bruises in my consciousness until the walls I kept around my thoughts and feelings were *impenetrable.* I did not have the luxury of cracking or stopping or breaking down. If I fell apart, my life did, too. Not only my life but my sister's. So, I built and reinforced those walls. Over and over and over.

Yet, with one look, he's brought a battering ram to them. Shattering my walls, unravelling my feelings, and prying open my mind with his bare hands. Every time I try to reinforce those walls, they crumble before the grout can settle. And even when he leaves them standing, I can feel him crawling all over them. Tangles of ivy creeping up stone, embedding itself in the cracks, both holding me together and ripping me apart in unison. And it's *madness.*

I cannot be falling apart. I cannot be crumbling when now, more than ever, the world would relish in me breaking apart. I hate this. I *hate* him. I hate that I do want to run. I hate even more that I wish to stay.

And yet, *I do not run.* Not as he steps back and motions to the exit. Not as minutes pass and we stand there in loaded silence. Not when I finally sigh and slide down the wall to the ground, folding in on myself.

Not even when he mumbles, "Thought so." And I want to run all over again. Or when he turns to go, hesitates and says under his breath, "You'll always be my favourite mistake."

And my walls incinerate themselves and I burn.

I burn, but I do not run.

The dreaded day of Fabelle's wedding arrives too quickly and still not quickly enough. Viktoryn has a gown sent for me, and Raven makes his displeasure that I choose to wear said gown abundantly clear.

The cut and colour would not be my first choice for myself. Blood red and dripping in rubies that cascade down my curves to the floor. Catching the light in a mesmerising twinkle, a panel of lace between my chest where the gown opens and dips low.

I know for Viktoryn, this is some kind of sick power play meant to unnerve me. But as I catch my eyes in the mirror, the attempt he's made to claim me if only in his court's colours, feels futile.

The blood red of the gown feels like a premonition of what's to come. A silent promise of the chaos and destruction I will reign on his family for the torment they have enacted on mine. A reminder that I may be mortal, my lifeblood much easier to spill, but I am not afraid to spill it to reign triumphant.

"I think it suits me." I shrug.

"It's a beautiful dress on a beautiful girl. But I can see *him* all over it."

I simply shake my head, rolling my eyes.

Raven helps me pin my hair back, and when I ask him where he learned to do this, he smiles and says, "I have three sisters." He hesitates after securing the last pin. "I got you something."

"Oh?"

"Close your eyes."

I do. His fingertips brush my neck, and I shutter before I catch myself. I curse his softness. These moments will only make whatever comes next so much harder.

His fingers return, and the weight of a cool necklace settles on my skin. He fiddles with the clasps and steps back to secure a ronan berry and iron charmed bracelet on my wrist, meant to allow mortals to resist compulsion. He places a glamour on it so the charm remains invisible.

Looking at the necklace in the mirror, a sense of awe fills me as I take in the details. It's a perfect combination of our... *my* courts.

A diamond-bejewelled crescent moon intertwined with a shining sun of shimmering red, orange, and yellow stones that reflect the light. I run my fingers over the charm and smile.

"It's lovely. No one has ever given me anything like this before."

Raven brushes a thumb over his lips, looking as if he wants to say more, but he just nods and rushes off to finish getting ready.

On the ride to The Ember Palace, Amira uses her air magick to muddle our voices so that we can finalise our plans.

"Ready to kick some Summer Court ass or die trying?" Amira snips.

I manage a tense half-smile, running a hand over the built-in trousers and tie pockets in my dress. An ache of longing swells in my chest as I realize how much I miss Alice and Beatrice.

"Amira, would it kill you to have some optimism?" May chuckles.

"Optimism is your job, my sun," Amira drawls with a wink, May flushes, biting her lip.

"If this plan works, no ass-kicking will be required," Raven corrects. "Quiet in, quiet out. We should have Elle before they even start the wedding harps."

"I would not mind a little ass-kicking," Amira says, her hand shifting to the sword on her side.

"That's because kicking ass is the only thing that has ever brought you joy, Amira. It's sad," Raith remarks.

"You are one to talk, muscles," Amira spits.

"Quiet in, Quiet out? Why do I feel as though it is never that easy?" Olden grumbles, rubbing a hand over his face.

"Because things rarely go to plan," Amira says.

"Hey, things occasionally go to plan. Especially if I plan them," Raith announces with a smirk.

"Raith, your plans, unless they involve pointy objects, flexing your muscles or blind luck, are unabashedly terrible. That is why I am the spymaster, and you are the mindless muscle," Amira retorts.

Raith gasps in mock hurt, pretending he has been shot in the heart.

We near the edge of The Summer Court's land and the Inner Circle mulls over some final details. Amira leads her horse beside mine, pitching her voice low.

"If you do not stop fiddling with that damn charm." She tips her chin to my wrist where my hand is subconsciously fidgeting with the bracelet as I grip the reins. "No glamour is going to hide it from anyone with a minuscule bit of common sense."

"Right," I reply.

She gives me a look that does not instill any confidence in me about what is to come and rides off.

Hidden in the woods, outside The Ember Palace, the team disperses, leaving Raven, May, and I to approach the front gates. I run over the phases of the plan in my head, focusing on what I need to do.

Phase one is making it past the gates, where guards wait to check each guest's invitation. The hope is that they don't look too closely at mine, which does *not* invite Raven. The only plus one I was offered was *Viktoryn*.

We reach the front of the line and I hand my invitation to the guard. He hardly looks it over, opening it and skimming in with a bored gaze. The guards scan me and Raven, Maylea already bounding on ahead. Raven's face betrays nothing, the perfect mask of collected calm as the guards give us the once-over.

When they notice that they are in the presence of The Winter Prince, they draw up straighter, and I swear a bit of terror flashes in their eyes as they bow and wave us forward.

We head towards the grand front doors of The Ember Palace, and for the first time, I really take it in. The central double doorway stands behind a stunning archway that is screaming with obnoxious luxury. Gold and white marble twisted into an overly elaborate design of The Goddess of The Sun leaning to touch her lips to the land as flowers explode from her touch.

The Palace itself is tremendous, with long wings and four sprawling, pointed towers of gold. Giant windows of yellow and orange stained glass in the shapes of the sun line the walls. The doors to the verandas are set with white, gauzy curtains that blow in the wind, the summer sun casting shadows across the lush seating.

The giant entryway swallows us. And I feel as though I've walked directly into the belly of a beast, jaws snapping shut behind me. I force down my panic and roll my shoulders.

I may be a pawn in a game I don't fully understand, but today, I am making a move of my own. I remind myself that I am infinitely more equipped for the challenges that lay ahead than I was a month ago.

May breaks off towards the wedding venue with a nod to Raven and me. I meet her gaze and give her the confirmation signal we agreed on. Raven and I venture off alone, finding the servant's hallway with a stairway that leads to Elle's floor.

A few stray wedding guests roam the halls, chatting with the guards. But most of the activity in the Palace has been condensed to the wedding venue itself.

Raven and I wait until we are sure the halls are clear, slipping into the servant's hallway. We begin to climb the dimly lit stairs.

When we reach the top, I lock down my fear as Raven leans his ear against the door. He waits a few moments and then nods, signalling it's clear.

"Amira dealt with the guards, right?"

"They should be soundly asleep. You have fifteen minutes before more round. Be smart, be swift, firebird."

Raven leans in, then retreats and I stare up at him with an aching heart. It feels like hundreds of unsaid words hang between us. I force myself to turn away, to accept my fate, *our* fate.

I push open the servant's door entering a golden hallway, the first left is safe, I sigh a small breath of relief. I turn around the second but hear voices and halt.

My heart leaps into my rib cage, I survey the hall as the voices get louder. Quickly pulling a pin from my hair, I unlock the door nearest to me. Praying it isn't occupied, the lock clicks open seconds before the voices round into the hall.

I push the door shut, leaning against it to steady myself. My chest heaves, but to my relief, I find myself in an unoccupied library with floor-to-ceiling books. If I wasn't on a rescue mission I'd love to take the time to browse the shelves. I press my ear against the door and listen. Two female voices giggle brightly in the hall.

"I cannot believe that Prince Archer is marrying a mortal girl! Has he lost his head? Who would choose that slip of a dust-destined girl over one of the Fae?" the squeakier of the voices gossips.

"You are notorious! Prince Archer could do so much better. Me, perhaps." The voices giggle.

I roll my eyes as the voices fade, sneaking back into the hall. I quickly round the next corner and locate what, according to Olden, should be Elle's room. I pick the lock and enter a dark parlour room where three Knights lay in an unconscious heap on the ground.

Stepping over splayed limbs and armour, I pick the lock on the second door. It clicks, I look down at the guards worried they will awaken, but none of them move.

I step inside, the room larger than the one I was placed in when at the Palace. But the design and detailing are almost identical except for the addition of a large open veranda.

I assume I wasn't allowed one for fear I'd jump off to escape—a *wise* assumption.

The bed chamber is empty, and for a moment, I worry I am in the wrong room. But then, in a gown of striking golden fabric, a head of strawberry blonde curls walks into the room from an adjoining bathing chamber.

My sister gasps when she sees me, crossing the room in seconds. She throws her arms around me with a squeak. I cling to her, afraid to let go, silent tears streaming down my cheeks.

"Willa! You're alright! I was terrified that The Winter Prince harmed you. You should hear the things they say about him. I was worried you wouldn't come. You don't know how happy I am to see you," she squeals, squeezing me so tight it hurts.

"Elle, can't breathe."

She loosens her grip, gently moving her hands to my shoulders as she surveys my face.

"I missed you so much. I was so worried. I couldn't lose you, too," I mutter, searching her for signs of harm.

"Oh Wil, don't cry," she murmurs, wiping the tears from my cheeks.

"I am so happy to see you, and I will explain everything soon, but we need to go," I say, clutching her hand to lead her towards the door, but when I pull, she stands stiff. "Now, Elle."

I turn back to her, trepidation knotting my stomach from the guilt dripping in her eyes.

"Willa... please forgive me but... I-I can't go with you. I want to marry Archer. I love him."

"Love him? Elle, you hardly know him. You have known him for what... a *month*? I know the Fae can be tricky and charming, but you are not safe here. We have to go," I state more forcefully, grasping her shoulders.

"That's not true."

"What's not true, Elle?"

"He's been visiting me in Cressa for months."

"What? That's... that's not possible."

"It is."

I grab her wrist more forcefully, practically dragging her towards the door. She wrenches her hand free and plants her feet. Lifting her chin as she rolls back her shoulders and suddenly I feel like I am not looking at my little sister but at someone else. A *stranger.*

Gone is the little girl who read Faerietales, replaced by someone who thinks they've found their happily ever after and refuses to give it up.

I glance back at the door. Then, at Elle, whose eyes swirl with grit as she stares down at me like *I* am the enemy and not the villain she's about to tie herself to for eternity. It tears me in two. I can't believe I didn't see this sooner.

"Willa, please let me explain. Prince Archer has been visiting me in Cressa for months. He brought me books from all over the world and asked me to read all I had written to him." She giggles. "I started falling for him. And when he offered me an out... a life that wouldn't consist of so much pain and suffering, I leaped at the chance," Elle explains.

"When, how—"

"Well, it was hard for us to find time to talk, and I knew Mother wouldn't approve. I worried if you knew... you'd go all overprotective on me... So Toryn would hold you late at practice some days to give us more time."

My voice returns as the pain of my sister's betrayal rips through me like a tsunami of icy knives.

"What have you *done,* Fabelle? You mean to tell me Toryn would hold me late at practice, so you could court your secret Faerie suitor? Knowing that I would be *beaten*? *Starved*? As a result of being home late... you let... I *trusted* you. I can't believe... Do you know what they are? What they did?"

"I... I am sorry. But I love him, and I wanted to see him. Once I realized how Mother was reacting to us being late, I begged them to stop delaying you. I swear it. That is when Archer started coming over in the evenings... while Toryn," she hesitates, "talked to you." Her voice quiets. "And now it is too late... I do not have a choice."

"Talked to me? You mean distracted me so you wouldn't get caught. Whatever do you mean you do not have a choice? You *always* have a choice."

"I entered into a soul contract with him." Elle winces. "I didn't understand exactly what that entailed when I signed it. I just wanted *out*. Out of that house. Out of feeling helpless. Out of having to watch you slowly work yourself to death. Out of feeling like life just *happened* to me. I was tired of being the weak one, the one who couldn't help... and I love him. I really do. I made him promise that we would find a way to bring you with us. That was my one condition. That you would never have to go back to that house."

She reaches for my cheek as if to console me, but when her fingertips brush my skin, I leap back as if burned. A thousand realizations batter my skin at once, sharp and thin like paper cuts.

"Were you even kidnapped? Or did you skip off to Elphyne with your Faerie fiancee willingly?" I seethe. "You have *no* idea what you have done."

She flinches at the accusation, refusing to meet my eyes. Confirmation enough.

"We... we had to make sure you would com—"

"I would *always* come for you." I step backwards, heart roaring in my ears. "I risked my life for you. I was worried you were dead. And all along, you have been playing Faerietale Princess..." I shake my head.

"I never asked you to. I never asked you to do any of it. I am sorr—"

"You're *sorry*?" An unhinged chuckle escapes my throat. "How did he get you to sign the contract? You're a smart girl... You should've known better! He is manipulating you, Elle!"

"*Known better*?" Her eyes fill with rage. "He promised he could make *everything* better," she spits, pointing an accusatory finger at me. "That he could take me away to a world full of magick and adventure like my stories. Archer promised that he would make me a Princess." She gestures to her gown.

"Like the ones in my books. And he promised Toryn would save you from Mother, that she wouldn't be able to hurt you anymore. He said we could be safe and happy here as long as we behaved. I couldn't stand there and do *nothing* while Mother beat you senseless. I knew that if I did this, I could *help*. I could finally be the hero instead of the victim. And I could have power, real power, the kind of power *no one* can take away. The kind that would ensure no one could ever hurt me or you again," she hisses, throwing her arms in the air in frustration as if *I* am somehow missing the point.

Heady disbelief and pain weigh on my bones, encasing me in an endless well of dread as she explains her reasoning, but I can't help but feel a twinge of compassion for my little sister. Despite her flawed choices, part of me understands.

It's why I joined the army. In a way, signing my life away just as she signed hers. For a chance at a better life, one where I could protect her. But the feeling is fleeting as the reality of our situation comes crashing back down on me.

"Did you know that your betrothed's family slaughtered *our* family when you signed that cursed contract? Did you know who our real Mother was?"

"It's not like that." She looks at me exasperated. "They explained." She holds her hands up before her. "Queen Valda wasn't a good ruler. She didn't uphold the values needed to protect the throne and The Folk. They did it to protect the Seelie," Elle pacifies.

I scoff. "You believed that? Are you really that naive? Do you hear yourself? You sound like a lovesick child," I spit. "This isn't some Faeire-tale, Elle. The reality of this world isn't happily ever after. The world is a cruel place full of manipulative, power-hungry, self-serving beings, and you've happily skipped right into one of their traps. This, all of this," I gesture around the room, "proves why you need to be sheltered from everything this world really offers."

Elle flinches as if slapped. My stomach recoils with guilt, but my unrelenting rage consumes it.

"They murdered our birth mother because she married our Unseelie mortal father. They tried to murder *us*. Father died protecting us from *them*. They deemed him unworthy, a lesser being because of his mortal and Unseelie blood. The very same blood that lives in *our* veins, Elle. The blood that pumps through the heart you willingly handed over to their killers," I shout. "Did they explain what *values* they needed to protect? The values they believed were worth slaughtering a family for? They see us as impure, half-breed freaks. The only thing they were protecting was their own hateful self-spun, extremist ideology and thirst for power. How could you be so stupid?"

"I... no... that... can't be true," Elle mutters, eyes wide, hands now shaking at her sides as she squeezes them into tight fists.

"It is. Do you really believe I would tell you something that wasn't? Archer manipulated you into that contract so he could control not only you but *me*. They need me to balance the court's power because Valda transferred it into my body to keep it from them," I say, and Elle shakes her head.

"How are you making this about you? Why can't you just be *happy* for me?"

"Did you not hear me? Knowing all of this, you would stay? You would be his bride? His *wife*?"

Elle winces and then straightens to her full height. Her eyes light with fire and darken. She draws in smooth, deep breaths. And I watch with horror as she builds up walls until she barely resembles the sister I know.

Nothing human remains in her eyes, nothing kind or sweet in her stance. She looks like one of *them*.

"I'm not asking you to understand. Nor am I asking for your permission," she says, primly. "You don't control me. I am marrying Prince Archer whether you like it or not. You will come to my wedding and be pleasant and pretend to be happy, or I will alert the guards that you need to be removed from the premises," Fabelle commands with all the authority of the Royal she is about to become.

"*Who* are you? What happened to you?" I whisper, voice breaking.

"Who am *I*? I am the girl who is tired of living in a hovel and wanting everything I could never have. I am the girl who can't stand to read one more Faerietale knowing that I could never live a story so *epic*, so memorable. I am the girl who refuses to be nothing for a single second longer. I am about to be more powerful than you could ever wish to be. More important, more *untouchable*. I am done being a poor, pathetic, powerless girl."

She steps closer to me, our faces inches apart. "That girl? That *weak*, needy child is *dead*, Willa." She scoffs.

"What happened to me? I grew up and realized that not everyone gets a happily ever after. But if I wanted something close, *I* would have to make it happen. Sometimes, you have to sacrifice to get what you want. You could've had this, too. If only you would have behaved for *once* in your life." I flinch. "So, who am I? The future Queen of The Summer Court if all goes to plan. But you? You are *nothing*. You are nobody," Elle states, planting her hands on my shoulders and shoving me back.

My eyes widen with shock, hurt, and rage as I stumble back to find my footing.

"You dare tell me about *sacrifice*?" I hiss as some integral part of me shatters. My voice comes out more ruthless than I ever thought possible. "I sacrificed *everything* for you. I starved so you could eat. I endured punches and pain so you could be protected. I joined an army that's as good as a death sentence, so you didn't have to live on the streets."

"Oh, please, dear sister," Elle coos, eyebrows knit with annoyance. "Spare me the holier than thou speech. I understand. You're a little miss perfect who did everything to save her family. And I am the naive, stupid little dreamer who needed to be protected. Too lost in her silly little stories. Not anymore. I don't need you. I need nothing from *you*. Now, get out!" she shrieks, cheeks flushing red with anger. "I'd prefer not to have you thrown out of the Palace on *my* wedding day. You will not ruin this for me. Leave, or I'll make sure the guards find you safe accommodations in the dungeons."

You are nothing.

You are nobody.

You will have no one.

I don't need you.

Each word thrown in my face is a pot of scalding water, my sister's words a special kind of venom injected straight into my heart.

My ears rush with the sound of my own blood, heart pounding violently against my ribs. Until that roaring is the only sound in my head.

My lungs constrict and squeeze, an iron fist clenching them with no mercy. Time seems to slow and stop.

I stare at the woman who looks like my sister and sounds like my sister. But has become a monster of her own creation. A girl who would abandon her family for prestige and power. For a crown dripping in my slain mother's blood. And for a second, I think I might hate her. Or maybe I hate myself for letting this happen.

Trust no one. Power corrupts them all.

The dream's premonition feels like a sick taunt in hindsight. I did not consider that the person who would allow power to corrupt all of the goodness inside them would be my own kin. My own sister.

I turn to go, but Elle grips my elbow, dropping her voice into a whisper. Her eyes are filled with warning, "You've forgotten. You've forgotten so much."

"I have not forgotten a thing," I snap, ripping my arm away, glaring at her.

She steps back, shaking her head. "Get out."

I glance at the clock on the wall and mentally curse. A part of me shrivels up and dies as I realize all I can do now is leave her to the fate she's crafted. While I sit back and watch her march head first, crown on her head, into a trap. Grinning at the bars of her gilded cage as they drip with Valda's blood.

I make it back to the servants' hall where Raven waits with no real understanding of how I got there. My head feels disconnected from reality. Like someone has chopped the head off a doll and made her dance on puppet strings.

Raven peers behind me, eyebrows knit as he asks me something. The words do not meet my ears. All that rings through my mind are the killing blows that Elle spit as the part of my heart she owned corrupts and rots.

I watch Raven's lips move, his eyes wide with worry, but I hear nothing. A chant begins in my mind, a taunt that holds a razor-sharp knife to my heart.

You are nothing.

You are nobody.

I don't need you.

The words have never felt more true. My heart is hosting its own funeral, and my thoughts become a death march of misery. Before I know it, I empty my stomach on the floor. I am dimly aware of Raven's fingers wrapping around my arm and his lips moving to form sounds my head refuses to register.

I wonder if this has all been some kind of cruel nightmare. At any moment now, I'll wake up in my bed back in Mayfair, ready to start another unrelenting day of training. Elle, safely in her bed, writing in her journal, thrilled to share the tales she's spun. I'll help her braid her hair for school like I have done a thousand times before.

But no matter how hard I blink my eyes or pinch my skin, the dim stairway of The Ember Palace remains.

It feels like the walls are laughing at me as they close in—taunting me. This is a *nightmare*. And I cannot wake up. I cannot run. I am trapped because I cannot save her—not from herself.

I am aware that my breathing is too shallow, too short. But I can't seem to command my lungs to fill. My hands and face start to feel like static, and a fizzy sensation builds under my skin.

And then I am falling.

Cool fingers brush my cheek, and I can feel my head propped up on something warm. My eyes open at the bottom of a dimly lit stairway, a damp musty smell overpowering the familiar smell of pine and cranberries.

I blink, a blurry form materialising above me to reveal Raven gazing intently down at me. His eyes clouded with fear and worry, his fingers still brushing my cheek gently. I push to sit up, but my head spins, and I plop back down into his thigh.

"Easy," he warns. "Easy there, sweet girl. Look at me." I do, and when I meet his eyes, I can breathe again. "That's right. Right here, nothing else matters." My body eases. "Good girl. I need you to breathe. Can you do that for me?"

Raven's voice is a calm lifeline, cutting through the panic and confusion. I suck in a breath and then another.

"What happened in there?" he demands.

"I... I... she..." I stutter, but in all truth, *I* don't even know what happened in there.

I try to form words, but everything spins and then collides into a clear but horrifying picture. Elle wasn't a pawn. She was a player. And I was just brutally forced into checkmate.

I was the obstacle to be moved for them to all get what they wanted. And while she may have not been aware of *all* of their motives, she still assisted them in orchestrating her own kidnapping knowing how badly it would wound me.

She let them use me... *helped* them use me. All so Elle could secure the crown, Viktoryn the power and throne, and Archer, the human bride that would be able to manipulate me. And it worked. They did not win, they *obliterated* me. Ten steps ahead of me at every turn for months.

And in part, it's entirely my fault. I didn't *see* her—I didn't see my sister. I didn't see her as the girl who can trap, trick, and plan on par with the Fae. I was too busy seeing her as weak, naive, and in need of protection.

My sister had always been quiet and cunning and sweet. A scholar more suited for bookshelves than battle. The one who had been able to keep a grasp on her girlhood when our lives had been reduced to ashes.

I had always been stubborn and spiteful and strong. Blunt and broken. A sword made to protect. A weapon to be aimed. Forged in the flames of our losses, built to withstand the storm. And yet, my reality had been turned inside out.

I knew Elle was driven, intelligent, imaginative, and capable. But I missed that she could use the brilliant mind that created epic stories and shaped great adventures to manipulate the life she wanted into fruition. And maybe, just maybe because of that... I deserve the outcome of her victory.

I had taken on the role of protector. And unknowingly forced her into a role she never wanted to play. I became the one who would sacrifice and scrape by and chip away pieces of myself. So caught up in the role that I missed my sister chipping away pieces of herself to become the kind of person who could scheme her way into a crown.

I never once considered what *she* would sacrifice to obtain the life she dreamt of. What pieces of herself, of her life, of her family she was willing to shed to escape. I had assumed my sacrifices were enough. I had assumed that what I could offer her was enough. That she would happily settle into the life I carved out for her. Never stopping to ask if she had plans of her own. Or if she even *wanted* the life I had given up everything for.

I had spent my life mastering the art of being underestimated only to be beaten at my own game.

And now...I did not know who I was without the burden and blessing of being Fabelle's protector, provider, and sister.

Who was I if not the girl fighting for a better life for my sister? Who was I with a sword and soul of fire but no one to protect? What would my father think if he could see me now?

I was now nothing more than the daughter who had failed to protect her father's family. The fighter he trained, defeated by her own kin. *How utterly disappointed would he be?*

And yet, part of me still admires that all of these years she, too, had been planning and scheming and working. If only she thought to include me as an ally instead of pinning me as the enemy.

I manage to pull myself together enough to relay what happened in Fabelle's room to Raven. He listens without judgement. His eyes occasionally distant as he processes. Sometimes flitting around the room as if mentally mapping all of the moves and counter moves.

My heart aches knowing this might be the last time he sees me as an ally. This may be the last time he ever holds me and looks at me as if we are an unstoppable team. After tonight, he may never forgive me for what I have to do.

If I wanted to win, I needed to stop playing by their rules. The game I thought I was playing had shattered into millions of irreparable pieces. Broken pieces I wouldn't fix but sharpen into knives. And I wouldn't win this by playing fair.

It was time for a rematch. This time, I wouldn't be a pawn, I would be the Queen and I would win. And if I couldn't, I would burn it all to ashes. Leaving nothing but dust behind.

I made Viktoryn a promise that day. If anything happened to my sister, I would burn his Palace to the ground—a promise I intended to keep.

Though they forced me into a corner, slowly tearing away all of the things that mattered to me, they had failed to calculate one thing. Thanks to them, *I had absolutely nothing left to lose.*

But they did.

And I would take it all away.

Piece by piece, pawn by pawn.

If I was nothing, I would leave nothing in my wake. And then, I would take what's rightfully mine. This night would end in blood, and it wasn't going to be mine spilled...

I still had a few cards up my sleeve.

The room around me is a blur of golden banners hanging from marble-beamed ceilings and lines of decorative white chairs filled with excited, chattering wedding guests. The throne room—a room I had yet to visit until today.

I watch the wedding as if underwater, disconnected. My sister is about to tie herself eternally to the family that rose to power in the blood of mine. A family that slaughtered my true mother.

And I cannot stop her. And yet, I feel nothing.

I have retreated into the safety of my mind, into the emptiness of my grief, to plan. My body is a hollowed vessel. In the place where my emotions should be thrashing furiously is nothing but a deep well of black-inky nothingness. A river ran dry in a year-long drought.

And all I can think is good.

This is good. Because what I have to do next would demolish me if I had to feel the consequences—or maybe it wouldn't. Maybe, now, I do not care who I hurt—or what I have to burn.

Raven sits beside me, all decked out in his best finery, swaths of mid-night blue and silver thread. His storm-blue eyes seem brighter against the deep blue of his tunic. His curly blue-black hair is tamed, and atop his head sits a silver diadem inlaid with sapphires. He looks polished, perfect, princely.

Two talented, iridescent-winged Fae play fiddle-like instruments in a tune that is meant to be lively but somehow manages to seem ominous. Fitting, I think.

At the front of the room, on a raised dais, standing in front of an extravagant throne, a rather nervous-looking Faerie officiant with bright copper hair and freckles stands beside Prince Archer. The Fae who will be the ruin of not only my sister but my family's legacy.

Raven watches me like I am a bomb—like I am an apocalyptic disaster waiting to happen. I do nothing to change his mind. His weary glances assess me as he tries to figure out if I am on the verge of shattering like glass or killing everyone in sight. Both feel likely.

But instead, I hold onto that hollowness and choose to feel nothing at all.

You are nothing. You are nobody.

They do not know it yet, but I hold all the power. I am not nothing. I am everything. And I am ashamed to admit it took me far too long to realize it. So, I am going to take away the one thing they all need. The one thing they all crave—only second to oxygen. Power.

The world seems to have a sick sense of humour. My sister is to marry into the family who took everything from us—in the room of the throne we had fallen from. It was almost funny—in the way that it wasn't funny at all.

Prince Archer watches me with a taunting grin. But when his eyes lock on mine, he blanches, and I wonder if I look as brimming for bloody vengeance as I feel. I can practically feel the red-hot thrumming need for revenge vibrating from my bones.

He recovers quickly, smoothing down the front of his fancy wedding tunic that gleams as if sewn from pure gold. A crown full of blood-red rubies perched on the golden brown curls that frame his unnaturally handsome face. Beside him is the Faerie whose downfall I will relish in the most. Viktoryn.

Viktoryn has been many things to me. A teacher. A mentor. A friend. A lover. And now an enemy. A betrayer. A traitor. He is a shapeshifter, transforming into my most delighted daydreams and horrific night-mares.

My mind fills with all the ways I will make them pay. With their blood, their minds, their crowns, and their oh-so-precious power. The very power that is worth more than my trust, my love, my heart, and even my life. The power that corrupted the last truly good thing in my life.

I trust Raven, but I learned long ago to always have a backup plan. I have never been one to sit back and hand the reins of my fate over to anyone.

So I have plans of my own afoot, ones that involved a Spring Princess whose loyalties lay as much with Raven as they lay with me—not that he knew it. In a world where males on thrones sat ready to manipulate and control our fates, girls had to stick together. And it is time for some divine feminine intervention.

May and I had been secretly meeting in the library at The Crystal Palace since my arrival—collecting unlikely allies and scheming terrific and terrible schemes. She has become more than an ally, she has become my closest friend. And though Amira is Raven's spymaster, and I was endlessly worried she would uncover our plans, it worked to our advantage. Amira trusts May implicitly. As much as I dislike deceiving our friends, the future of entire kingdoms rests on our shoulders.

Raven will hate me. I am certain of it. But I need this change of fate more than I fear his hate. And while I appreciate all he did to help me, he, too, had stakes in the direction of my life. He, too, was steering the ship of my fate. And I am so tired of Faerie Princes herding me in the direction that benefits them most.

So, it is time for a game change. I need to disappear—to become a ghost, a phantom, a wraith. One who haunts The Ember Palace unseen—lying traps and setting down fuses I will later ignite. A ghost who bides her time, causing small problems until she can cause big ones. Catastrophic ones.

Kingdom come undone, ones.

As I watch the wedding progress, something incredible happens. Even as my soul folds in on itself and blackens. Even as I lose the last remaining member of my family to the enemy. I feel a bizarre sense of freedom.

I have nothing left to lose. I have shed the shackles of being the protector and provider of my family. I have lost the last thing I well and surely loved. And yet, I am free. By taking everything from me and stripping me of all I've known, they have unknowingly taken with them the expectations, the rules, and the worries.

I can do anything. Be anything. Burn anything. And I will.

So when Prince Archer is shot through the chest with a crossbow in the middle of my sister's wedding, I feign shock, truly putting on my best performance.

As an indie author, my readers are *everything*. You determine the success of my stories, and I am grateful to each and every one of you who has made it to this page. Thank you. Thank you. Thank *you!*

If you enjoyed this book, please take a few moments to write a review or share your thoughts on social media.

Your hype ensures I can continue doing what I love and bringing you more delicious and devious stories. Plus, who doesn't want to be the one who gets to say, "I read it first!" "I read it before she was big!" ;)

The adventure continues in *The Princess of Secrets & Shadows...*

And this time, Willa is ready to watch *everything* burn.

For more details, check out oliviamgeib.com

Acknowledgements

Wow. Um. Hello. I wrote a book, you're reading my book. How wonderfully strange. I can't believe this is real.

There are so many people I want to thank for helping The Daughter of Fire & Fury become the epic tale it now is. So many people I *need* to thank for me becoming the woman I grew into to be able to write this story.

To Auntie Serena: Thank you for being the very first set of eyes to read this story and offer your thoughts and edits. Thank you for believing in these characters and in me. Thank you for all the hours of hard work you put into helping shape this story and smooth out the rough edges.

To Sierra Campbell: Thank you so much for everything you did to help shape this novel. Editors are truly the backbone of all we do as authors. The Daughter of Fire & Fury wouldn't be here without you. Sometimes, you just know, and when I met you, I knew you understood not only my vision but myself. Thank you for becoming one of my closest friends. And cheers to future stories we craft together.

To Brent Heck and Grayson Silver, who believed in me as a writer before I ever fully believed in myself.

To Nya: Thank you for helping me name The Spring Court Palace when I was stuck. Thank you for all you did to help behind the scenes.

To Nati: Thank you for being the mother I needed. Thank you for taking me in as if I was your own. Thank you for all the months you let me sleep, rent-free, in your house when I had nowhere else to go.

To my Opa, Al Geib, my hero, my foundation. Thank you is not a big enough word for you and all you've done. Thank you for taking care of me. Thank you for letting me fail. Thank you for putting up with all my trouble and never asking me to be anyone but myself. Thank you for giving me a home when I believed I'd never have one.

To my brother, Griffin, who, when I told him I was writing this series, said to me with zero hesitation that he thought I could do it. And that I'd always been talented and able to do anything I put my mind to. You never doubted me. Thank you for drawing the first-ever map of this world for me and helping bring Elphyne to life. You will always be my partner in crime. And I will always put myself between you and trouble.

To Tima: Thank you for all the hours you spent proofreading this story. Sierra and I will forever be thankful.

To so many more friends and family (blood and found) who were my cheerleaders and sounding boards. To the *TSL*, you know who you are. Thank you for being my sisterhood.

To my dog, Loa: You didn't do much to help me as a writer, but you helped me stay sane as a person, and for that, I am grateful.

To my biblical rage: I'm sorry for believing you weren't a necessary emotion. I'm sorry for spending so long shoving you down. Denying you the oxygen you needed to ignite. I'm sorry for being afraid to feel you. You were the flame that shaped this story. I'm not scared to feel you anymore. Thank you for always being the catalyst that drove me forward, even when I didn't think I could go on.

To my **readers:** Thank you for taking a chance on me when you picked up this book. You had so many options to read, and you chose to read this story that is not only my first novel but one that is so very dear to me. So very personal to me. Thank you for going on an adventure with Willa and me. Thank you for being here, sharing this moment with me.

And honestly, to everyone who laughed when I said I wanted to be an author. To everyone who looked at me as if I had lost my mind and duct-taped myself to a silly, foolish goal. Spite is one hell of a motivator, and without you, this story, the emotions I needed to write it, wouldn't have existed.

So, thank you. Thank you for not believing in me so I could believe in myself enough for all of us.

www.ingramcontent.com/pod-product-compliance
Lightning Source LLC
Chambersburg PA
CBHW072051190726
48294CB00005B/1469